A TIMELESS Romance ANTHOLOGY

Spring Vacation
COLLECTION

A TIMELESS Romance ANTHOLOGY

Spring Vacation

COLLECTION

SIX CONTEMPORARY SHORT STORIES

Josi S. Kilpack
Annette Lyon
Heather Justesen
Sarah M. Eden
Heather B. Moore
Aubrey Mace

Mirror Press, LLC

Original Cover Design by Christina Marcano
Paperback Cover Design by Rachael Anderson
Interior Design by Rachael Anderson
Edited by Annette Lyon

Published by Mirror Press, LLC

E-book edition released February 2013
Paperback edition released March 2014

ISBN-10: 1941145067
ISBN-13: 978-1-941145-06-7

TABLE OF CONTENTS

OTHER TIMELESS ROMANCE ANTHOLOGIES

Winter Collection

Summer Wedding Collection

Autumn Collection

European Collection

Love Letter Collection

Old West Collection

Summer in New York Collection

Moonlight Kiss

Josi S. Kilpack

Other Works by Josi S. Kilpack

The Sadie Hoffmiller Culinary Mystery Series

The Newport Ladies Book Club series

Her Good Name

Unsung Lullaby

Sheep's Clothing

One

Clint: *So, you got your room extended?*
Sarah: *I did, 2 extra nights.*
Clint: *Can't wait to meet you in person.*
Sarah: *Me too!*

They shared a few more exchanges before Sarah shut down the instant messaging program and promptly dropped her head on the desk with a thud.

"Don't be so dramatic," Brylee said with a laugh from the other side of the cubicle also known as the billing department for the Omaha office of Bowman and Skagg, Attorneys at Law. "We're going to have a great time. Seriously, when was the last time you went on vacation? And I don't mean using a vacation day so you can go to Rose's school orientation?"

"I'm going to throw up," Sarah said from her head-against-the-desk position. Having Brylee mention Rose made it all so much worse. "Probably throw up all over Clint. Why am I doing this?" The last part was said with a slight wail. But it was an honest question. Why *was* she doing this? She'd never done anything remotely like this in her entire life.

"Everyone has to start somewhere."

"But a weekend with a guy who lives in Seattle? I'm not *that* girl."

"A guy you've been talking to for four months," Brylee added, rolling her eyes. "You seriously need to chill out and just let yourself have this experience. Maybe it will lead to something, and maybe it won't, but even if it goes nowhere, you'll have some awesome memories when life gets dull, or, in your case, when life is already dull." Brylee had turned to face Sarah's side of the cubicle but Sarah's head was still on her desk, her brown hair spread all over her workspace. When Brylee spoke again her voice was softer, with less teasing and a little more compassion. "There's more to life than single-mommyhood, Sarah, and you're thirty years old, not dead. You deserve to walk on the beach hand in hand with a hot guy who thinks you're awesome. You deserve to be kissed in the moonlight."

Sarah lifted her head and tucked some hair behind one ear so she could turn to look at her co-worker-slash-friend-slash-bad influence. "I haven't been on a date in nine years. I haven't been kissed in almost six. I live in my parents' basement apartment and eat macaroni and cheese at least five times a week—sometimes cold."

Brylee scowled at her and shook a finger in Sarah's direction. "Don't get all tragic on me. The goal of this weekend is to have a good time for a few days. You're perfectly capable of doing that."

"What if he doesn't like me in person, or I don't like him, or he thinks I'm looking for some kind of fling?"

"Has he hinted that he's looking for anything sexual?"

"Well, no, but I watch enough TV to wonder if there are any guys left who don't expect a first date to end in the bedroom, ya know?"

"But he didn't ask you to share his room. He's simply extending a vacation so you can get to know each other. Why is it so hard to look at it that way?"

"Because I don't *do* this kind of thing. I don't know how."

"Which is why it's so exciting!" Brylee threw her arms up in celebration and grinned widely. Sarah remained deadpan, unable to tap in to the excitement due to the looming dread that had been building since she'd extended her hotel stay. Brylee dropped her arms and her smile then stood and headed toward the copy machine down the hall, her narrow hips and slender legs moving like a Barbie doll in her pencil skirt. Brylee was twenty-three. She'd joined a sorority in college and spent her spring breaks in Fort Lauderdale. She was a natural blonde, and her own eyelashes looked like the ones Sarah had paid good money for last month. For the twelve *hundredth* time, Sarah asked herself why she was taking advice from this girl. And yet, something about Brylee's youthful optimism and YOLO—you only live once—attitude had rubbed off over the year they'd worked together.

At Brylee's encouragement, Sarah had stopped wearing her hair in a French braid every day and had started wearing contacts. She'd discovered that she looked fabulous in purple and bought her first pair of high heels. When she wore them, her legs didn't look like Brylee's, and she had only dared wear them around the house so far, but she *owned* them. Rose, her six-year-old daughter, had found them in Sarah's closet one day and clomped around the house for hours after which Sarah hid them so that they didn't end up in the toilet. Shoes tended to meet that fate more often than Sarah liked to admit. Toilet-seat locks were effective only if you remembered to lock them after every single use.

Sarah turned back to face her computer, and her eyes shifted to one of the photographs tacked to the cubicle wall.

In it, Rose was smiling so big that her eyes were slits above her pudgy cheeks. She held a participation medal from her first Special Olympics race. It was one photograph of many, all showing the same bright smile, all reminding Sarah of her purpose, her role, and what made her life different from most women's.

Brylee came back to grab the master copy she'd forgotten, then headed back out of the cubicle as a confession bubbled up in Sarah's throat. "I haven't told him about Rose."

The clicks of Brylee's heels stopped then slowly backtracked until she poked her head around the cubicle wall. "You haven't told him you have a daughter? Or you haven't told him about *Rose*?"

"I haven't told him I have a daughter."

Brylee was back in her chair in a flash, the document she needed to copy back on her desk as she rolled across the floor and forced Sarah's chair around so that they were facing each other, with their knees almost touching. She opened her mouth to say something but paused, furrowing her eyebrows. And then, to Sarah's surprise, Brylee smiled. "That's actually rather perfect."

"It's horrible," Sarah said. "This whole time that I've been emailing and IM-ing Clint, I've never said a word about my *daughter*. What kind of person am I? I've gone and created a fantasy world that doesn't include her. I'm a bad mother."

Brylee was shaking her head before Sarah finished, causing the light to reflect off her shiny hair. She should have gone into modeling, not accounting. "*Relationships* are built on trust and full disclosure but this isn't a relationship. Clint not knowing about your particular circumstances gives you the chance to get to know him, unencumbered. You can then decide if he's someone who deserves to know more about you."

"But I haven't been honest with him," Sarah said. "That's no way to start a relationship."

"It's not a relationship!" Brylee said, too loud for the office. She made a face and leaned in closer, lowering her voice. "The goal is to just have fun for a few days." Brylee patted Sarah's knee and stood again. She was beginning to sound frustrated. "It's been such a long time since you had any fun that you don't know how to do it anymore, so it's getting overcomplicated in your head. Chill out and relax. It's going to be a great time and if it feels right, you'll tell him about Rose. If he turns out to be Mr. Right, he'll be open to it."

Brylee left the cubicle again. It made sense when she said it, but by the time the words worked their way into Sarah's brain, everything felt jumbled. Sarah turned back to the computer but saw the picture of Rose again and felt another pinch of shame. Her eyes moved to her most recent family photo, which included Rose, Sarah, and Sarah's parents, who watched Rose during the day and made up for the fact that Rose's father couldn't handle the reality of their Down syndrome child.

Because of her parents help, Sarah had been able to go to college, and once she graduated with her degree she got a job that helped offset the expenses of their expanded family. She could afford to move into her own place, and from time to time thought about doing so, but she needed the emotional support more than she'd ever needed the financial help.

It was through an online company webinar four months ago that Sarah "met" Clint. He was also an accountant for Bowman and Skagg, but in the Seattle branch. He'd contacted her following the conference for some reason she couldn't remember anymore, and before she knew it, they were emailing or instant messaging almost every day. It had been a safe flirtation in the beginning—he lived four states away, after all—and she liked to think of it as a stepping-stone toward the day when she might date again, something that for many years had seemed impossible.

And then Clint had suggested that they extend their rooms after the annual accounting department conference being held in Cozumel, Mexico this year. In a panic, Sarah had turned to Brylee for help, and Brylee had taken advantage of Sarah's shock to convince her that this was something she was ready for. Since agreeing to it last week, however, reality had set in. Sarah didn't know what to do. She'd talked to her mother, certain that of all people, her mom would be the one to convince her against this folly. Instead, her mother had simply made her promise to remember her standards and to buy a new swimsuit before she left.

"Every journey begins with a single step," her mom had said. Sarah wished she had a better idea of what journey she was on. She wanted to see the situation like Brylee did—an extreme opportunity to break out of her shell and have a good time—but when she dared to be truly honest with herself, she knew that what she really wanted was a partner, a commitment, a life with someone who would love her and her daughter.

Her cheeks flushed at admitting, even to herself, how much she wanted that. She stared more intently at the computer screen. Debits and credits and transfers and checks—that's where her head needed to be right now. Yet just to the left of the family photo was a picture she'd downloaded of palm trees and white sand beaches. She would meet Clint at cocktail hour the night before the conference. After everyone else went home two days later, they would stay, along with Brylee—Sarah's roommate and safety net for the weekend, and the guy from Clint's office he was sharing a room with, Mark. The four of them would go snorkeling and parasailing and eat at nice restaurants together. Clint hadn't said anything to make Sarah think he had expectations beyond that.

"Two weeks from now, I'll be in Mexico," she said and felt the tingle of those words all the way to her toes. "I just want to have a little fun." And Brylee would be there to offset any awkwardness. Rose would be fine staying with Sarah's parents.

Sarah grabbed her mouse, expanded the expense report she was proofreading before this afternoon's meeting, and hoped that Brylee was right, that the memory of these extra days would remain bright and shiny even after returning to Nebraska. But in her heart of hearts, she hoped for more than that; she hoped that this trip would be a beginning of something far more than an extended weekend.

Two

"So what do you think about Sarah?" Mark asked as he and Clint left the introductory session of the conference. Their flight had been delayed in Denver yesterday, meaning they'd missed the cocktail hour last night, and then they'd slept through breakfast. But Clint had texted Sarah when they slid into their seats—late—and she'd turned around to wave and smile, albeit a little nervously. The opening session had gotten out late and Clint was now in a hurry to get to a collaboration he was scheduled to lead on the other side of the hotel. There hadn't been time for Clint and Sarah to shake hands or hug or whatever their greeting might have been. "Does the in-person view match her picture?"

Clint finished sending a text then shrugged before putting the phone into his shirt pocket. Though they were in a resort location, everyone was dressed in casual business attire. Men wore khakis and short-sleeved, button-down shirts, while the women wore slacks or skirts. Clint smirked.

"Does it matter? She's here, and we've got four days together before she goes back on home to Omaha. I've got high expectations."

Mark frowned. The bad feeling he'd had since first realizing who Clint was flirting with on the company IM system grew a little stronger. Mark had met Sarah two years earlier at orientation. Back then, he'd taken note more of her disposition than of her looks, but she'd also stood out because of her daughter, who she had said had Down syndrome. Her name was Daisy or Violet or some other kind of flower. Sarah had teared up, saying that the orientation was the longest she'd ever been apart from her daughter. It had been sweet, even though he knew she'd been embarrassed by her show of emotion at the time.

Mark had meant to talk to her after that opening session, but he let nerves get the better of him on the first day, and then she'd flown home before the closing reception the following afternoon. After returning to Seattle, he'd thought about contacting her, but an introduction via the Internet seemed awkward. When he reflected on his own situation, he'd wondered what he hoped would come of contacting her anyway.

Now and then, he'd seen her name on a report or shared correspondence, but he never reached out to her—never felt confident about what he'd be reaching out for. And then Clint showed him the picture of the woman he was flirting with in Omaha, the woman who had agreed to stay the weekend so she and Clint could "get to know each other better."

Mark didn't know Sarah, not really, but he hadn't thought she was *that* kind of girl. He knew exactly what kind of guy Clint was, as did at least three women in their office who had already fallen for his charm at one time or another. When Clint said that Sarah's friend was staying longer too,

Mark offered to stay as well to give them even numbers. He was still trying to make sense of why he'd made the offer.

The big windows along the south side framed flowering shrubs and lazy palm trees of the Cozumel beach, but there were still five hours left of day one of the conference—five hours until the employees of Bowman and Skagg were free to pursue the evening as they chose. Mark had never been to Cozumel, and though he looked forward to seeing more of the island, he had growing concern about how this weekend might unfold.

"So you're meeting Sarah at lunch, then?" Mark asked.

"James got me that spot at Bowman's table, so I told her we'd meet up at dinner instead."

"Right," Mark said, nodding while walking fast to keep up with Clint's long-legged strides. Mark wasn't quite six feet tall, while Clint was six three, leaner, tanner, and with whiter teeth. Not that Mark was some kind of pariah, but he didn't look like he'd stepped out of any type of magazine, other than maybe *Average Guy Weekly*.

As they passed a room with a workshop about to start, Mark did a double-take when he noticed Sarah standing just inside the door. She caught his eye but quickly turned her attention to Clint, who hadn't seen her as he continued down the hall. She looked great in a lavender blouse and slacks— curvy the way women should be, with big brown eyes and thick brown hair that fell just past her shoulders.

"I'll, uh, catch up with you after class," Mark said.

Clint nodded and immediately increased his pace. "Good deal."

Mark slowed his step and, once Clint rounded the corner, turned back to where he'd seen Sarah. The sign outside the conference room said that this workshop was training for the new software that would be implemented company-wide next month. The Seattle office had piloted the new program, which meant Mark had no need to attend training for it. But that wasn't why he decided to go.

"Hi," Mark whispered when he reached Sarah, who was still standing where she'd been a minute earlier. She was doing something with her phone and startled, dropping it into her purse and looking up at him with her pretty brown eyes. She had those fake eyelashes that were all the rage and though he'd seen worse sets, she probably should have saved her money. He liked what she'd done with her hair, though. At the orientation two years ago she'd kept it pulled back. It looked nice worn down like she had it today. He put his hand out. "Mark Leavittson. We were in orientation together a couple of years ago."

He didn't expect her to remember him, but was still disappointed when no recognition showed on her face. He'd come to terms with the fact that he wasn't the kind of guy who stood out, but that didn't mean it didn't sting a little. She took his hand and smiled politely. "I'm sorry, I'm not very good with names, or, well, faces, either, apparently."

They dropped hands, and he put his in his pockets as she glanced down the hall where he and Clint had parted company not long ago. "You're a friend of Clint Hunter?" she asked. Her eyes snapped back to his a moment later. "Wait, you're *Mark*? The guy staying for the weekend with us?"

Us.

Mark nodded. "Yeah. Should be a lot of fun."

"Oh, I think so too," she said eagerly, but with some nervousness mixed in. The same sweetness still radiated from her. All over again, he experienced the feeling that she was someone he could connect with. But he hadn't taken the opportunity when he'd had it. Two years later, Clint had.

"It's really nice to meet you, or, well, *see* you again, I guess," she went on. "It's kind of funny that I met you before Clint."

"I'll introduce the two of you at dinner, but from what he's said, you guys have really hit it off."

She blushed and looked away, tucking her hair behind her ear. He wanted to ask about her daughter. Then he could tell her about Dillon, too. The common ground could be something they could build on. But this was Clint's weekend, not his. There was no reason for him to build anything. Mark wasn't sure Clint even knew about Sarah's daughter. Then again, Clint insisted this was a weekend fling. Maybe all of Mark's impressions about this woman had been wrong. Maybe she was just as casual as Clint about these things. The problem was that Mark's impressions didn't *feel* wrong. Sheesh. *Feelings.* He forced a smile. He was Clint's wingman. That was all.

"Clint's got a lunch commitment he can't get out of," Mark said.

"Oh, that's fine," she said, but seemed relieved. "I'm glad he got in okay. Were you on the same flight?"

Mark nodded and put a hand over his stomach. "If I never eat another airport meal, it will be too soon."

She smiled again, more genuine this time, less nervous. He liked that. The voice of the instructor filtered back to them as he welcomed everyone to the class. "We'd better get our seats," Sarah said, adjusting her purse on her shoulder. "Do you want to sit together? It's always nice to sit by someone you know."

"That'd be great," Mark said, smiling again and holding her eyes long enough that she looked away first, perhaps a tiny bit confused at his interest. That made two of them.

Three

"Did Grammy put the bubbles in the tub?" Sarah asked into the phone.

"Yeth," Rose said, then went on to tell Sarah all about her bath. Rose was better at signing than with verbal articulation, but of course, over the phone, that wasn't an option. Sarah tried to pick out the words she could understand and gave lots of "Wow" and "How fun" commentary. She had to remind herself not to be sad that she wasn't missed. This was why she and Rose lived with Grammy and Pops—so Rose would have lots of love and nurturing. This call was proof of that success.

The conversation on the other end of the line suddenly stopped, as though the phone had been dropped. "Rose?" Sarah sat up a little on the bed. "Rosey?"

"She wants to show you her picture," Sarah's mom said into the phone a moment later, allowing Sarah to relax. "It's pink and green and brown. Okay, now she's back."

"Oh, and it's so pretty," Sarah said after the hand-off and hearing Rose's garbled explanation of the picture Sarah couldn't see. "I love the pink."

She lay back into the pillows and listened some more, ignoring the double ache in her chest—first, because she wasn't there to see the picture in person, and second because she was having a good time. She felt a little guilty about both. In less than an hour, she'd meet Clint for the first time. That thought awakened the butterflies in her stomach, but she pushed them away; Rose was in the spotlight right now and Sarah didn't want to miss a thing.

Rose dropped the phone twice more before Sarah's mom said in the background that it was time to go. "Love you, sweet girl," Sarah said into the phone.

"Luff, luff," Rose said.

Sarah's mom got back on the line and assured Sarah that everything was going well. "Don't call tomorrow; you're going to have a ridiculous phone bill next month, and she's fine, really."

"I won't make any promises," Sarah said. "But thank you for doing this, Mom. I really appreciate you guys."

"It's our pleasure; you know that. Are you having a good time?"

"It's just been the conference so far, but I meet up with Clint for dinner in an hour, with Brylee and Clint's friend too, of course."

"Good," Mom said. "You can tell us all about it when you get home. We'd better end this phone call before we have to get a payday loan to cover it."

Sarah laughed, they said their goodbyes, and then she hung up, took a deep breath and put her phone—and that part of her life—on the bedside table. A minute later, she pulled the dark purple faux-wrap dress she'd wear to dinner from the closet, and her nerves rushed in as though she'd turned on a faucet. Clint. Thirty minutes. Dinner. Beach. Moonlight.

"Holy crap, what am I doing?"

❦

Brylee showed up five minutes before they were supposed to leave the hotel—she'd gone out for drinks with the group that she'd collaborated reconciliation procedures with who were now her BFFs. The woman was a social genius. Sarah was putting the final details on her hair—for the sixth time—and wondered how on earth Brylee could get ready in five minutes. Brylee threw off her slacks and blouse, pulled a red sundress over her head, took her hair out of a bun and—bam—she was ready. Like Supergirl without a phone booth. Sarah was comfortable with her figure unless she spent much time with Brylee, who made size four women feel like fatties. Sarah was not a size four.

"Okay," Brylee said, grinning widely. "Are you excited?"

"Yes," Sarah said with a sharp nod and a smile she hoped matched Brylee's. "I am *so* excited."

Four

It started raining on the way to the restaurant, which was only half a block from the hotel. Brylee and Sarah kicked off their heels and carried them, making a run for it and finding safety in the foyer where a good laugh at the drama helped cover Sarah's disappointment over the weather. There would be no walk on the beach tonight, apparently, but that was okay. They still had the rest of the weekend, and having a little less pressure this first night was probably a good thing. They ducked into the bathroom and fixed their hair. Well, Sarah fixed hers; Brylee didn't need to, although she did apply a little more lip-gloss.

Clint and Mark stood when Sarah and Brylee got to the table a few minutes later. Clint gave Sarah a quick hug—no kiss. That was a good sign. But she'd hoped to feel some kind of tingle when they first touched, and she didn't. The anticipation of this meeting must have mitigated whatever electricity she might have felt. Brylee and Mark shook hands.

When the chips and salsa came to the table, Clint pushed his salsa toward Sarah so they could share. The four of them talked about Clint and Mark's delayed flight and how horrible it was spending eight hours in an airport. The conversation eventually moved on to the different break-out sessions they'd attended that day.

"You two were in the class on the new software together?" Clint asked after Sarah explained how she and Mark had met. Clint gave Mark a look Sarah didn't understand.

"It was really good," Sarah said while attempting to decipher the look. "I think it will make tabulating the reports so much smoother."

"Oh, it will," Clint said with a grin. "We've been using it since the first of the year—Seattle was the pilot office for the program."

Sarah and Brylee both looked at Mark, who was intently dunking his chip in the salsa. Why had he attended the class if he didn't need to learn the software?

"None of the other breakouts in that block interested me," Mark said with a shrug.

"They didn't *interest* you?" Brylee said, leaning forward slightly, her eyes wide with feigned surprise. "Proper accounting of insufficient fund transactions and collection procedure doesn't light your fire? Who are you?"

Mark leaned forward too, a teasing smile on his face. "Don't tell my boss or my mother. It would break their hearts."

They all laughed, and Sarah joined in half a beat after the others. *Relax. Have Fun.* She did not want to betray how out of her element she felt right now. Too bad she wasn't a drinker, though now might be the perfect time to start. Surely she could relax better with a few shots of vodka in her. Then again, they might make her sick, and she still worried about the whole throwing-up-on-Clint scenario. Not worth the risk.

"What about tomorrow's classes?" Clint asked. "Are there any that stand out to you guys? 'Cause if not, we could play hooky and hit the beach early."

Sarah tensed and dipped another chip. Her boss had emphasized how essential it was for every employee to attend each block. He'd be following up with them next week and Sarah wasn't sure she could lie about it.

"I thought tomorrow looked like a good lineup. Plus I'm moderating the partner panel after lunch," Mark said. Sarah glanced up at him, relieved that he was supporting her silent position, and smiled her thanks. She didn't know how, but she could tell he understood exactly what she meant with that smile. She was suddenly so glad that Brylee and Mark were here with her and Clint; she'd have never made this weekend work without them.

"Besides, our boss will be asking us for a detailed report," Brylee said with a nod. "I bet he'll have quizzes and everything."

"Okay, okay," Clint said, putting up his hands in surrender. "I withdraw the offer, but who's up for parasailing after the conference tomorrow? It gets out at, what, two o'clock?"

"I'm totally up for parasailing," Brylee said. "If the weather's good."

"Me, too," Mark agreed.

Sarah was chewing, but she nodded and smiled. Clint smiled back; she hoped it was because she was endearingly cute, even with her mouth full.

Dinner was fantastic—shrimp tacos with mango salsa—and by the time the waiter came around with coffee, Sarah was feeling much more comfortable.

"So what's on the agenda for the rest of the night?" Mark asked after the waiter took their checks—they'd each paid for their own meals tonight.

"Weren't we going to catch the game?" Clint asked, turning to Mark. "You're the guy who pointed out the sports bar at the hotel on our way over here."

"I don't know if the ladies wanted to listen to you swear all night, though."

Game? Sarah didn't know enough about sports to even know what type of sport was played this time of year. Baseball?

"The Trailblazers-Bulls game?" Brylee said, straightening up and leaning slightly forward. "They're showing it here somewhere?"

"We just call it the Trailblazer game," Clint said with a playful grin.

"Oh, the Bulls are going to wipe the floor with the Blazers tonight," Brylee said, throwing down her napkin as though it were a gauntlet. Sarah kept her mouth shut so as not to betray her ignorance.

"No way." Clint hit the table sharply with his palm. He took a final sip of his drink and stood, holding his hand out to Sarah once he was on his feet. "You up for it?"

"Sure," she said, far more interested in spending time with him than in watching the game. But this was the kind of thing normal women did, right? Hang out in sports bars with their men? The thought made her cheeks burn. Clint wasn't her *man.* Thank goodness no one could read her mind.

"Why are you blushing?" Brylee whispered a few seconds later as they headed toward the hotel.

"Nothing," Sarah said, but worried she was blushing all over again. "Let's go watch some basketball—it *is* basketball, right?"

Five

It was still raining when they left the restaurant for the sports bar, which was back at the hotel, and once again the girls took off their shoes and made a run for it. The bar was loud and smoky, and it got louder and smokier as the evening wore on. Sarah cheered when everyone else cheered and even ordered a fruity drink, though she only took tiny sips. Mark stayed in the booth with her for a while, explaining the game, while Brylee and Clint cheered with the crowd gathered in front of the large TV. Sarah told Mark several times that he could join the group—she felt bad dominating his time—but he said he didn't mind and she appreciated his efforts to both educate her and not leave her alone at the table.

By the last few minutes of the fourth quarter, Sarah felt like she actually understood what was happening—her dad would be so proud. "Thanks for your help," she said to Mark. They sat on opposite benches of the booth. "I hope it didn't take away from your enjoying the game."

"Made it even better," he said, smiling over the rim of his drink. He did that thing again where he held her eyes a second longer than it seemed like he should. She felt herself blushing as she looked away. He wasn't hitting on her, was he? She wasn't experienced enough to know.

"And that's the game," Clint said when the final point had been scored, winning the game for the Trailblazers 104 to 99. He came back to the booth and slid into the bench, automatically draping his arm around Sarah's shoulder. Like they were a couple. Like they watched games together at sports bars all the time. Sarah searched for that tingle again—the chemistry she'd been expecting to feel. But once again, her nerves seemed to take center stage.

Brylee slid into the booth next to Mark. "If the refs hadn't been obviously drunk, it would have turned out completely different," Brylee said, dunking a chip in the salsa.

"You are so full of it," Clint said, loudly enough to make Sarah wonder how many beers he'd had. Five? Six? He and Brylee went on to argue about the game. Mark joined in a time or two, but he was the least determined of the three. Sarah ate more chips, fully aware of Clint's arm still draped across her shoulders.

"What do you think?" Clint asked, turning to Sarah, his face only inches from hers. She could smell alcohol on his breath, so she faced forward, suddenly tense all over again. "Who do you think deserved to win that game?"

He started slowly trailing his fingers up and down her arm. How long had it been since a man had touched her like this? Tender. Flirty. "I think the Yankees deserved to win the pennant this year, no question," she said.

Everyone laughed—thank goodness—and then Mark and Brylee began discussing a particular play while Clint leaned back against the seat, pulling Sarah with him. His hand was still rubbing Sarah's shoulder, but as much as she wanted to enjoy it, she could only take note of her rising anxiety. With his other hand, he continued drinking his beer.

She tried to relax into him, and was halfway to convincing herself that she was enjoying the closeness, when she felt his fingers brush her hair away from her shoulder. A moment later she felt hot breath on her neck. Her entire body froze. Apparently he'd put down his beer.

She felt his lips on her skin a moment later. Rather than melting inside, she stiffened even more, and goose bumps broke out across her body. His lips felt hot. And wet. That should have turned her on, right? But it didn't. It completely freaked her out. She wasn't ready. This was their first evening together, and he wanted to make out in a bar? "I'm going to get some more salsa," Brylee said, but she flashed Sarah a smile on her way out of the booth. Sarah didn't return it.

Sarah glanced at Mark, but he was intently watching the TV, though she suspected he was ignoring them on purpose. She was on her own.

"Hey," she said to Clint, unwrapping herself from him as carefully as possible and looking toward the end of the bench. He was blocking her from being able to get out of the booth. "We've got an early morning, don't we?" His features were soft, his eyes glassy. He was so drunk. "Aren't you tired?"

He scooted closer. She pulled away, but that simply cornered her against the side of the booth. She felt her heart rate increasing for all the wrong reasons. She looked toward Mark again, needing help, and this time, she caught his eye.

"Hey, Clint," Mark said, moving toward the end of his bench. "It *is* getting late."

"The night's young," Clint said, smiling at Sarah, who pressed against the wall of the booth as much as she could.

"Clint," Mark said again, some sharpness in his voice. Clint turned to look at him, annoyed. "Let the lady out of the booth."

"She doesn't want to get out," Clint said, turning back to Sarah and putting his hand on her knee, smiling drunkenly.

"I really do," she said, forcing a smile that she knew showed her discomfort and moving his hand from her knee. She lowered her voice a little in hopes that only Clint would hear it. "This is a little fast for me."

"Fast?" Clint said. "We've been together all evening."

A moment later, Mark's hand appeared on Clint's shoulder. "Come on, buddy," he said. "You didn't sleep any better than I did last night. We need to rest up for tomorrow."

Clint protested a little, but Mark didn't let go, and eventually Clint got out of the booth, which allowed Sarah to scoot out as well.

Once she was on her feet, Mark stepped in front of her so that he stood between her and Clint, though he wasn't overt about it. "You okay?" he asked her quietly.

"I'm fine," Sarah said, feeling embarrassed now that she was free. She didn't like needing rescue. Yet, Mark *had* rescued her, or at least, he'd spared her from having to make a scene. "Thank you."

"I'll walk you to your room," Clint said, pushing in front of Mark.

Mark grabbed Clint's arm just above the elbow and pulled him back. "I think she'd rather find it on her own."

Sarah understood what Mark didn't say—*Go!*

"See you in the morning," she said, smiling at them both. "I had a really nice evening. Thanks."

Clint mumbled something she didn't hear, because she'd already gone to get Brylee, who said goodbye to a guy she'd met at the salsa refill station.

"So," Brylee said, nudging Sarah with her shoulder as they headed out of the bar. "I saw you getting all snuggly. How was that?"

"Weird," Sarah said, shaking her head at the memory. "He's wasted."

"And?"

Sarah turned to look at her friend. "And I'd prefer for him to be in his right mind when we . . ."

"What?" Brylee said, a teasing glint in her eye as they reached the elevators. "When you what, Sarah?"

"When we walk on the beach in the moonlight." Sarah waved toward the windows behind them as the elevator doors opened. "But it's raining anyway, so I guess I'm taking a *rain*-check."

Brylee laughed at the pun and hit the button inside the elevator. "You're happy with the way the evening went, though?"

"Yeah," Sarah said, but the parts that stood out to her were the meal, Mark helping her understand the game, and Mark getting her out of an awkward situation at the end. She felt guilty, and a little ungrateful, that it wasn't Clint taking center stage in her memories of their first date. "I think I built this up too much in my head."

"What do you mean?" Brylee asked as they stepped off the elevator and headed toward their room.

"I'm so nervous around Clint," Sarah said. "I had hoped for this spark between us, ya know? Some . . . chemistry, I guess, but I'm just so tense."

"It's the first day," Brylee said. They'd reached their room, and Brylee used her key card to open the door. Sarah followed her in and kicked off her shoes. "And you're probably right," Brylee continued. "Nerves can get in the way. I bet tomorrow will be better."

"I hope so," Sarah said, locking the door behind them. Her life was routine, very predictable and safe. She liked those things, which was why accounting worked so well for her as a career. This wasn't accounting though; it was personable and emotional and . . . new. "Tomorrow will be better," she said out loud as a kind of affirmation after Brylee disappeared into the bathroom. "Tomorrow will be great."

Six

Sarah and Clint sat next to each other at breakfast the next morning. The other conference attendees at their table helped ease Sarah's nerves and kept the conversation moving. Neither Sarah nor Clint said anything about how last night had ended.

The day's classes and events went as expected, and when they were over, the four of them hit the beach in search of a boat that could take them parasailing. The storm from last night had moved on, leaving sunny skies, soft sand, and a glittering ocean for them to enjoy.

Sarah didn't think she'd have the guts to parasail—she'd never done anything like that before—but she didn't back down when her turn came, and then she loved every second of it. Being alone up there, looking down on the ocean and the beach, was completely different than what she had expected—exhilarating, to say the least. When she came in for her landing, Clint, Mark, and Brylee were cheering for her, which felt equally fabulous. Once she was out of the harness, Clint gave her a big hug and kissed her on the cheek.

She happened to be looking at Mark and Brylee at that moment. Brylee had a big smile on her face and gave Sarah a thumbs-up. Mark looked away. There was no time to ponder on Mark's reaction, because Brylee announced that it was time for them to get ready for dinner—they had reservations in just over an hour.

On the way back to the hotel, the two women completely dissected the day, and by the time Sarah was showered and ready for dinner, she felt more confident than ever. She'd had a wonderful time today—unexpectedly good—which would, no doubt, help with her anxiety tonight. She thought about calling Rose but decided not to, wondering if part of her being so on edge last night was because calling her daughter had made Sarah miss her more. If her theory was wrong—and tonight she was as nervous as ever—she'd be sure to call tomorrow.

Dinner was wonderful—she had an enchilada salad, and Clint had only one glass of wine. The four of them conversed easily and about many topics. Though they had all just met, they felt like old friends, laughing and joking and enjoying the night. When the checks came, Clint paid for her meal, which was both exciting and a little nerve racking. Mark paid for Brylee's too, though, and there didn't seem to be anything romantic between them.

"Anyone up for a walk on the beach?" Clint said when the meal came to an end. The sun had set during their meal, leaving a few swaths of orange across the evening sky.

Sarah had been aware the entire time that it wasn't raining tonight. She'd known this would be coming. Yet nerves and butterflies seemed to combine within her chest, making her dizzy with anticipation. "I'd love to," she said, hoping she didn't sound too nervous or inexperienced.

"I wanted to check out the club next door," Brylee chimed in, taking the napkin from her lap and putting it on the table. Sarah knew that what her friend really wanted to do was leave Clint and Sarah. "Mark, would you like to join me?"

"Um, sure," he said, scooping the final bite of his dinner with his fork. He'd completely cleaned his plate. Rose got a star on her chart every time she ate her entire dinner. "I can't say I'm much of a club kid, but I'm happy to head over there with you."

"Maybe I'll make you into a club kid by the end of the night," Brylee said with a smile. A pang of jealousy took Sarah off guard, but she didn't know where it came from. She wasn't jealous of them going to a club—not by a long shot. Was she jealous that Brylee was spending the rest of the evening with Mark? Sarah mentally shook her head—it was probably nerves again, masking what she *really* felt.

The night was breezy but warm when Sarah and Clint left for the beach. The half-moon gave everything a shimmery look as the sun disappeared from the sky. Sarah felt like someone from a postcard as she reached down and took off her shoes so she could feel the sand beneath her feet. It felt different than sandbox-sand—softer and finer. Sarah had been to some of the lakes in Nebraska, and some of them had sand on their shorelines, but this was different than that, too.

"I've never been to a beach before," she said when they reached the wet sand. She looked behind her at the near perfect indentation of her footprints and smiled. Someday she needed to bring Rose to a beach like this. She would love playing in the sand and watching her footprints fill up with water. She looked over at Clint walking a few feet away. The wind had messed up his hair just enough to take him from handsome to devastatingly so. *Will he kiss me tonight? Will I let him this time?*

"You've never been to *any* beach, or a Mexican beach?"

"Any beach," Sarah said, facing forward again. She shook her head, letting the breeze catch her hair and lift it off her neck. "Well, if you don't count the lakes in Nebraska—I've been to a few of those, but they aren't anything like this."

"Seriously?"

His comment pulled her back from the moment she was getting lost in. Normal people with normal lives vacationed on beaches sometimes, didn't they? The reminder that she wasn't normal raised her insecurity, but she tried to push them away. "But I've been to Mount Rushmore about eighty times. That helps make up for it, right?"

Clint laughed, and she relaxed a little. "I love the ocean," he said, waving his hand at the water, which disappeared on the horizon. "I grew up in Santa Barbara and would love to move back one day—I miss early-morning surfing and taking a boat out to Catalina."

"No surfing in Washington?"

He looked at her in surprise. "You've never been to the Pacific Northwest either, have you?"

"Nope," she said, her insecurity knocking again. "I'd like to one day, though." *Maybe to see you,* she added in her mind.

Waves crashed several feet to her right before stretching within a few feet of where they walked, as though each wave were trying to reach her. She veered a little closer to the water so she could walk in the surf, glad her dress only went to her knees.

Clint moved a little closer to the water as well, but he hadn't taken his shoes off so he didn't go as close as she did. The next wave washed over Sarah's toes—the water was warmer than she'd expected. "So basically, you need a man to show you the world," he said, giving her a coy grin.

Her stomach flipped—this was the first time he'd ever said anything about a possible future between them. Did that mean he liked her? That he could envision them seeing each other after this weekend?

"The world?" she repeated. "I'd be happy to go to Des Moines."

Clint laughed at that. "You'll be easy to please."

She looked over and smiled; he smiled back and reached for her hand, the one that wasn't holding her shoes. Whatever she'd been thinking to say completely left her brain as she watched him move closer. *Oh my gosh, he's going to kiss me! What do I do? Let him? Slap him? Run?*

"I've really liked getting to know you better here in Cozumel. It's a perfect romantic getaway, don't you think?" He ran his thumb across the back of her hand.

Sarah was mesmerized, her head going further back so she could see him as he moved closer. The waves crashed in the background. Music from a restaurant farther up the beach filtered down to them. The breeze blew her hair across her face. He lifted his other hand to brush it away.

Sarah was speechless. *Is this happening? Am I ready?*

"I'm a big believer in chemistry," he said, only inches from her face now. "And you look amazing in that dress, the way it . . . *what the—*" He looked down, jumped back and dropped her hand.

She looked down too, but couldn't figure out what he was freaking out about until he said, "My shoes!" and took off running for the softer sand higher up the beach, shaking his shoes as though that could spare them from the salt-water bath they'd just had. The bottom two inches of his pants were soaked.

Sarah hurried up the beach after him.

"Why didn't you tell me the water was coming so far up the beach?" he snapped when she reached him. He sat on a low cement wall and was pulling off his shoes, scowling.

"I didn't notice," she said, tempted to add that she'd been too spellbound by him to keep track of the surf. "I'm so sorry."

He had both shoes off and lifted them up, dripping. "I can't believe this," he said. "They're ruined; I just bought them."

"You might be able to save them, at home I always—"

"You're from Omaha," he said, making her take a step back as he looked up at her. "I don't think you're an expert on how to save shoes from salt water." A moment later, he softened a little and looked back at his shoes. "I'm sorry. These are just really expensive."

Sarah swallowed her hurt feelings, justifying his reaction with the fact that he really *had* ruined a pair of brand new shoes. "I might be able to fix them."

He looked at her skeptically. "Really?"

"I've learned a few tricks over the years," she said, keeping to herself that she'd learned those tricks because Rose absolutely adored jumping in puddles after it rained and had a penchant for dunking stray shoes in toilets.

She put her free hand out. "I'll take them back to my room and see what I can do tonight." Sarah smiled in anticipation of him laughing about all of this—it was kind of funny, right? And they'd had such a nice day.

Instead of laughing, he cursed and shook his head before sitting back down and peeling off his wet socks as well. "Awesome," he said under his breath as he threw the wet socks into the bushes. He took a deep breath and pushed his fingers through his hair.

The briefest thought crossed her mind—what would he do if Rose dumped *his* shoes in the toilet?

"Hey," she said after a few more seconds. He looked up with an aggravated expression. She held up his shoes. "I'd better take care of these before the leather starts to warp. I'll call you in the morning and let you know if the shoes work out, okay?"

"Alright," he said, standing and scowling at his feet covered in sand. "But I doubt you'll be able to save them. They got completely soaked."

"I'll give it my best shot," she said, still smiling, even though she no longer felt it. He wasn't going to apologize for making such a big deal about wet shoes? Or thank her for trying to save them?

He did open the door for her when they got back to the hotel, and they hugged—somewhat awkwardly, since she had two pairs of shoes in hand—before parting ways in the lobby. After he disappeared in the direction of the elevators, she went to the front desk and asked for some old newspapers.

Brylee wasn't in the room when Sarah returned, which didn't surprise her since she and Clint hadn't been on the beach very long. Half an hour later, after thoroughly washing the salt from Clint's shoes, Sarah crumbled up the newspaper and shoved them inside the wet leather, then put the shoes on top of the air conditioning unit, which she turned to FAN ONLY. She hung her dress in the closet, put on her PJs in preparation for an early bedtime, and once in front of the mirror to take off her makeup, dared ask herself a question that had been tapping at her consciousness. Were the interactions she'd had with Clint so far strengthening her feelings toward him?

She closed her eyes against whatever answer might come. She was invested in this weekend. She *wanted* so much for it to work. She opened her eyes and found herself staring at the window. She went to it and looked out over the beach in search of distraction from thoughts she didn't want to ponder. It had only been two days; she needed to keep an open mind.

The waves crashing onto the beach seemed to be calling to her, calming her, taking away her growing doubts. She was in Cozumel, Mexico, a place she might never see again. What on earth was she doing in her hotel room?

Seven

"You're sure you don't want to stay?" Brylee shouted at Mark, trying to be heard above the thumping music and other screaming patrons at the club.

"I'm sure!" Mark screamed back. "Thanks for inviting me, though. It's been fun. I'll see you tomorrow!"

"Okay!" Brylee gave him a thumbs-up sign.

She melted back onto the dance floor, and Mark headed toward the exit, glad to have stayed long enough to be able to leave without being rude. He'd danced a little at the beginning then hung back by the bar and talked to a few people he knew from the conference. Though he could handle pretty much any kind of setting, he was happy to escape this one.

When he exited the club, the silence was jarring, and he let out a breath of relief amid the ringing in his ears. He headed toward the hotel, but in the space between the buildings caught sight of the moonlit waves. Without any need to contemplate other options, he turned onto the walkway that would take him to the beach. When he reached the sand, he left his shoes on an empty beach chair and rolled up the legs of his pants. A minute later, the warm Caribbean waters washed over his feet, and he smiled as he started walking along the waterline. His feet sank into the sand with every step. He watched the wet sand in front of him while thinking about the evening.

Dinner hadn't gone as bad as he'd feared it would—Clint hadn't been all over Sarah this time—but part of him had hoped she'd distance herself after his embarrassing behavior at the bar. Instead, she'd agreed to walk the beach with him, alone. The memory of last night, seeing Clint slobber all over her, was almost more than Mark could bear. The only reason he hadn't left the table was because he could *feel* her panic rising. He didn't think he'd ever felt someone *else's* anxiety in his life. It was a relief when she'd looked to him for help, and it had been all Mark could do to stay calm and reasonable as he helped her get out of there.

Where were Sarah and Clint now? What were they were doing? Mark wasn't there to help this time if she needed him, and he hoped she wouldn't get herself into a compromising situation. His impressions of her and Clint's continued expectations were at such odds with each other, that he couldn't decide for sure what hers were for this weekend.

After she'd left the bar last night, Clint had told him not to interfere again. "If I don't get lucky by the end of this trip, I'm blaming you."

Another wave washed over Mark's feet. Again, he wondered what could have been if he'd followed up on his interest in Sarah two years ago. "Probably nothing," he said aloud. Yet what if that had been his opportunity? What if he'd missed his chance? She was attractive, and kind, and she would understand what it meant for him to have Dillon in his life. But she was here with Clint. And Clint planned to get lucky. The thought made Mark take a deep breath and consciously unclench his jaw.

"You are insane," he said and kicked at the surf, sending foam and water into the air a split second before he heard a startled scream a few feet away. He looked up "Oh my gosh, I'm so sorry!"

The woman he'd kicked water at was wiping at her eyes as she hurried up the beach. He ran after her. "I didn't see you there, I'm so sorry. Wait, Sarah? Is that you?"

"Yeah." She was still blinking quickly and dabbing at her eyes. "I thought that was you. I was coming to say hi."

"I'm so sorry," he said for a third time. There was a deck chair a few yards away, set under a light. "You can sit down up there."

"I, uh, can't see."

Mark hesitated a moment before stepping forward and putting one hand around her back and guiding her toward the chair, apologizing for a fourth time. She fit within the length of his arm perfectly, and though he told himself again that he was nuts, he could swear he felt something when he touched her, a whisper of energy he wished he understood.

"It's okay," Sarah said.

He relaxed when she didn't sound mad.

"You were watching the waves." She was still blinking a hundred miles an hour. "Dang, that salt water really burns. I think it got under my contacts. I should have taken them out before I came down to the beach."

"What can I do to help? Do you have glasses in your hotel room?"

"I do." She stood and started walking toward the hotel, covering one eye and reaching her other hand in front of her like a blind person. "I'll see you in the morning, okay?"

"Let me make sure you get to your room."

"You don't have to," Sarah said, still feeling around with her hand. "I think it's getting better."

"I insist," he said and put his arm around her waist this time, guiding her toward the sidewalk. The cool night breeze was suddenly not cool at all. Being this close to her made his heart rate speed up. He hoped she couldn't tell and that her room was on the far side of the hotel so she'd stay close for as long as possible.

It wasn't until he opened the side door to the hotel that he realized she was wearing a t-shirt and rolled-up flannel pajama bottoms. And that Clint wasn't with her. Once inside the building, having his arm around her didn't feel appropriate anymore—there weren't any hazards to steer her clear of. He kept pace beside her, with a light hand on her back, mostly because he thought he could get away with it. He was a glutton for punishment. "Where's Clint?"

"He went back to his room."

Mark tried to read something into the surprising comment, but she didn't betray anything in her tone. "Is everything okay?"

Sarah looked at him, still holding her hand over one eye, but blinking the other one. "Oh, yeah, everything's fine. His shoes just got wet."

"Oh, well, good. I'm glad things are okay between the two of you."

She nodded and faced forward again. "Where's Brylee?"

"Back at the club."

"Guess she didn't make a club kid out of you after all," Sarah said with a smirk.

"It was a valiant attempt, but I think she had other motivations when she invited me along."

Sarah didn't respond. A quick glance at her showed that she was uncomfortable with his comment. He kicked himself mentally and tried to change the subject. "So, after Clint's shoe issues, you went back to the beach alone?"

Sarah nodded, but then looked down at her clothes and dismay registered on her face. "Oh my gosh, no one was supposed to see me like this." She wrapped the arm not covering her eye across her stomach as though she could hide her t-shirt from view. The shirt had a tire store logo on the back.

Mark couldn't help but laugh. "You look great."

She turned to look at him. "I must not be the only one who's blind at the moment."

"Seriously, you look cute."

He heard her say "cute" under her breath, as though she couldn't even entertain such an idea.

He smiled and attempted to change the subject. "How was the beach? Before I blinded you with my mad skills, that is."

"It was nice," she said, but he could hear insecurity in her tone. He hated that. The last thing he wanted to do was make her uncomfortable. They reached the elevator, and he pushed the up button. The doors opened immediately, and she told him that her room was on the third floor. He and Clint were on the second.

"I love the beach," Mark said, hoping to distract her from her discomfort and continue the conversation. "But especially at night."

"Have you been to beaches before?"

"Some," he said, finding her question interesting. "Mostly on the Washington coast. How about you? Are you a beach dweller?"

"I live in Omaha," Sarah said as the elevator opened. He waved for her to exit before him and she dipped her head in thanks.

"Right, but do you like beach vacations?" Mark said as he hurried to catch up with her.

"This is my first one."

"Really? What do you think so far? Try not to let the partial blindness influence your answer too much."

She slowed down in front of a door and pulled her room key out of her pocket. "I like it," she said simply. "A lot."

She let herself in, and he expected her to dismiss him with a "thank you." When she didn't, he stepped forward and held the door open while she headed to the bathroom. He could still see her from where he stood.

"This is why I didn't wear contacts for so long," she said as she dug through a bright pink bag. She pulled out a glasses case, then fumbled some more. "I never know when I should and shouldn't wear them."

She removed her contact case from the bag and leaned over the sink, holding one eye open with the other hand so that she could take out the first contact. "So, did you grow up in Seattle?" she asked after removing the contact, putting it in her hand, and then squeezing contact solution into her palm. "You don't talk much about yourself."

"Portland," he said, not sure he was comfortable with the direction this conversation was going and noting that no one had asked much about her at their dinners either. Clint and Brylee had dominated the conversation.

"Is your family still there?" She took out the second contact and blinked several times.

Mark paused for half a beat then spoke—there was no point in hiding anything. "My dad passed away a few years ago. After that, my mom and brother moved in with me in Seattle."

"They live with you?" Sarah said, screwing the caps onto her contact case while turning to look at him. He felt himself bracing for her reaction—women didn't typically find a man living with his mother to be a positive trait. But he saw no judgment in her expression and heard no censure in her tone.

"Dillon—my brother—has cerebral palsy and is confined to a wheelchair most of the time. Mom can't take care of him on her own."

"They live with you so you can help with your brother?" Sarah asked. Was that sympathy he saw in her eyes? Understanding? Pity? *Please don't let it be pity.*

He shoved his hands into his pockets. "It works well for all of us. A home nurse comes in every morning during the week to help my mom get Dillon up and I'm usually home by 4:00 to help with the evening stuff."

"What do they do when you're not there, like this weekend?"

"A care center nearby does respite care. Mom's in Portland for a few days to see some old friends while I'm gone. She doesn't get to do that very often."

Sarah was still watching him. He was growing increasingly uncomfortable with the idea that she might think he was a pathetic Mama's boy. "What about you?" he asked. "Who's taking care of your daughter while you're on this trip?"

Eight

Sarah stared at Mark. *He knows about Rose? How?* But then she remembered how he'd recognized her from their orientation two years ago. An orientation where she'd completely embarrassed herself by breaking down when she'd talked about Rose during her introduction.

The silence stretched a few seconds past awkward before she opened her mouth to say something, only to find no words. Mark had a disabled brother who he helped care for, and he didn't keep it from people. What if he'd told Clint about Rose? She wasn't completely sure why the idea horrified her so much, but it did.

"Are you okay?" Mark asked, looking concerned.

"I'm fine." But her voice cracked, and she clenched her eyes shut in frustration.

"Did I say something wrong?"

She let out a breath. *No, I did. Or rather, I didn't say something I should have.*

"No." Her stomach started to burn. "I'm just . . . well, Clint doesn't know about Rose."

"I'd wondered about that," Mark said, his voice even, steady, and calm. "He didn't say anything about her."

"You didn't tell him did you?" She asked, pleaded, really, then realized how bad that sounded. "It's not cause I'm embarrassed by her or anything," Sarah said, wincing at her choice of words. "Gosh, that sounds bad, it's just that . . . I just . . ." How could she explain this? She hadn't told Clint about her daughter because she thought it would change his feelings toward her?

"We're just supposed to have a good time together, ya know? And Rose is . . . complicated." She closed her eyes, sickened by what she'd said and horrified that it was true. She really had come on a weekend with a man she didn't trust enough to tell about her daughter. Since meeting Clint in person, she'd never once considered telling him about Rose.

Yet she harbored some hope that there might be a future here?

She raised both hands in front of her face, wishing she could disappear completely.

"I get it," Mark said.

She was still covering her eyes like a child; like Rose did whenever she did something wrong. Mark *didn't* get it; he *didn't* understand. "I'm not explaining this well," she said, lowering her hands. "I just . . ."

"Don't worry about it," he said, and though he smiled on his way back into the hallway, it was too polite to be genuine. "I won't tell Clint. I hope your eyes will be okay. Have a good night, Sarah."

Nine

Brylee didn't come back to the room until almost two, but come morning, Sarah was willing to bet that she'd had the worse night's sleep. Clint texted with a time and place the four of them could meet for breakfast.

"You okay?" Brylee asked after she'd showered and gotten dressed. "You look . . . stressed."

"I'm fine." Sarah simply didn't know how to form the words to explain what had happened with Mark. "How was the club?"

"Fun," Brylee said. "Mark didn't stay too long, though, which was a bummer. He seems like a really nice guy." She was buckling a sandal as she turned her head to look at Sarah. "Don't you think?"

"He does seem like a nice guy," Sarah said while gathering the clothes she planned to wear today.

"So how did everything go with Clint last night?" She waggled her eyebrows. Sarah explained what had happened with Clint and his shoes.

Brylee nodded in understanding. "I have a couple pair of shoes that, if they got drenched like that, I would lose my mind over."

Sarah smiled in response and got into the shower, dreading the moment she'd have to face Mark again. When she attempted to put in her contacts, she realized that one of them had been scratched. She would have to wear her glasses today, a thought that did nothing to boost her confidence.

Mark didn't meet them for breakfast. When Brylee asked about him, Clint said he'd be joining them later. "He had to call home or something—did you know he still lives with his mom?" He rolled his eyes. Brylee and Sarah both gave weak smiles in response.

Clint thanked her for rescuing his shoes, which she'd brought with her, but he made it sound as if he'd done Sarah a favor to let her fix them. "You ready to go snorkeling?"

"Sounds fun," Sarah said with as much enthusiasm as she could muster as she picked at her fruit plate. "I've never snorkeled before."

"You know you can't snorkel in glasses, right?" Brylee asked.

Sarah looked up. "But I ruined my contacts last night."

"How?" Brylee asked.

"Um, I went for a walk on the beach, and got ocean water in my eyes."

"You didn't bring an extra pair?" Clint asked.

"I didn't think I'd need any. Maybe you guys should just go." Hiding in her room today sounded like a really good idea.

Brylee and Clint wouldn't have it though, and they convinced her to go with them, saying that maybe the company would have some prescription goggles. Mark joined them at the last minute, and although he was as polite as ever, he didn't make eye contact with her like he used to. She hoped his call home was typical, and that nothing was wrong with Dillon.

The company they rented the snorkeling gear from did not have prescription goggles, and although Sarah tried to snorkel without her glasses, watching colored blobs float back and forth beneath her didn't hold her interest for long. She got out of the water a full forty minutes before the others did, then sat back through lunch at an open-air café on the beach where they talked about the things they'd seen. Both Clint and Mark had scuba-dived in the past, and Brylee wanted to learn how, so the conversation eventually drifted to that topic—another one Sarah couldn't participate in.

Maybe in an attempt to draw her into the conversation, Clint asked if she'd ever wanted to scuba dive.

"Can't say that it's ever crossed my mind," she said. "I swam in high school, though."

The table was quiet. Apparently high-school swim team wasn't close enough to the topic at hand.

"I love swimming," Mark said, glancing at her ever so quickly before busying himself with his hamburger. "What was your stroke?"

"Butterfly mostly," Sarah said, unsure how to feel about him talking to her. Did it mean he'd forgiven her? Or was he such a nice guy that he wanted to make sure she was included, even if he thought she was a putz?

"Tough stroke," Mark said. "What was your fastest time?"

Clint signaled the waiter for a beer; Sarah could tell he was bored by the conversation. She sent a grateful smile to Mark, who looked away without returning it, before shifting the conversation back to Clint again, who seemed to be his favorite subject. She didn't like being the center of attention. "Is there much surfing here on Cozumel?"

Talk of surfing took them through the rest of lunch— there was no great surfing in Cozumel, she learned. They took a cab back to the hotel. Brylee wanted to sunbathe, and

Clint and Mark were both up to a little sun as well, but Sarah begged off with the excuse of a non-existent headache.

Once alone in her hotel room, she flopped on the bed and tried not to cry. She had so wanted this weekend to fit the fantasy she'd structured around it. Instead of magic, she'd felt nothing but nervous around Clint, and their time together had showcased the kind of qualities she couldn't admire for a weekend, let alone for any period of time beyond it. It was discouraging, and yet she felt surprisingly calm about admitting those things to herself. The goal of this weekend was to test the waters, and she didn't want to go in any further than she already had.

Without warning, Mark came to mind, and she felt her face burn. He had been so nice to her all weekend; even today, when he had every reason not to, he'd tried to involve her in the conversation. He'd helped her with Clint that night in the bar, and he'd remembered her from a brief encounter two years ago. What he would do if Rose dumped his shoes in the toilet? She finally let her tears fall as she accepted the fact that she'd pinned her hopes on the wrong man, and in the process, had pushed away the better one.

Ten

Sarah felt a little better when she woke up from the nap that had followed her pity party. She still had a full day left of this vacation, and she really did want to have a good time. She took another shower and determined that while she wouldn't make a big deal about her shifting feelings for Clint, she would try not to be alone with him again either.

She also hoped for a chance to explain herself to Mark. She didn't want to revisit the subject, but she wanted to leave it unspoken even less. After this weekend, there was little chance of her seeing him again, other than at the conference next year. Even so, she wanted to try to redeem herself in his eyes, if she could.

Brylee came in around five o'clock and told Sarah about all the fun she'd missed. They'd played beach volleyball, and apparently, became the team to beat. "We're meeting at The Carlos in an hour. You feeling better?"

"I am," Sarah said, glad to be able to say so without feeling like a liar. "Um, can you do me a favor and help me not end up one-on-one with Clint tonight?"

Brylee stopped re-ponytailing her hair and looked at Sarah in the mirror. "What? Why?"

To her credit, Brylee didn't argue after Sarah explained what had happened with Mark last night and what she'd realized about her feelings toward Clint today. "I just want to enjoy the rest of the weekend, *without* ruining it for everyone else."

When they arrived at the restaurant, Clint tried to give Sarah a kiss on the cheek, but she turned it into an awkward hug and quickly took her seat. She had hoped to change his expectations without having to say so, but prepared herself for a conversation about it if that's what it took. For now, she tried to ignore the frustrated look he gave her, hoping to at least postpone the conversation until after the meal. Clint threw back two beers before their entrees arrived.

There was a different feel around the table tonight, and though conversation continued, as it always had, the difference was palpable, but not unexpected. Clint was frustrated with Sarah's lack of response, Brylee was disappointed that Sarah had backed off in her interest toward Clint, Mark thought Sarah was a jerk, and Sarah *felt* like a jerk. Not rocket science to figure out the reasons for the shift of mood.

Mark suggested they go see some Mayan ruins tomorrow—their last day in Cozumel.

"I was hoping we could charter a boat," Clint said. "There's some really good fishing off the coast."

"I'm not much into fishing," Brylee said.

Sarah took her example and decided to be honest about her preference too. "I'd love to see the ruins. I didn't realize they had any here."

"I didn't realize it either until I talked to a guy in the lobby earlier—he'd just come back; said it was pretty cool."

"I'm game," Brylee said.

"Me, too," Sarah agreed. Maybe a trip to the ruins would give her a chance to talk to Mark.

Clint's mood changed after the girls poo-pooed his suggestion, which made Sarah realize that up until now, they'd done everything he'd wanted to do. He ordered another beer and asked for a side of guacamole for his enchiladas. The waiter delivered the beer a few minutes later, but forgot the guac. "Very sorry, sir. I will get it right away."

"You can use some of mine," Brylee said, scooting her bowl toward him. "I've got plenty."

Clint shook his head. "I guarantee they'll put it on my bill, and I've asked for it twice already."

Everyone went back to their meals. Now that Sarah wasn't hoping for something to blossom between them, she could see that Clint was charming when he got his way, and bratty when he didn't.

Another minute passed, if that, and Clint waved their waiter to the table again. "I ordered a side of guacamole. I've now asked for it three times."

"Did Beto not bring it out?" the waiter said, searching the table. He pointed to Brylee's bowl.

"That's *her* guac, not mine. The service here is complete crap."

"Clint," Sarah couldn't help but say, embarrassed by the scene he was making. "Don't be rude."

"What?" Clint said, turning his glare on her. "He thinks I have my guacamole, but I don't." He turned to face the waiter, who looked both embarrassed and confused. "Do you think I'm some kind of retard who doesn't know what you're trying to pull here?"

Sarah, Mark, and Brylee all froze—Mark with his fork halfway to his mouth.

The waiter apologized and promised to get it immediately. He hurried from the table while the other three began to unthaw.

Clint looked around the table. "What?"

"You used the R word," Sarah said automatically, as though she were talking to a child—which didn't feel far off. "It's offensive."

"'The R word'?" Clint replied, a teasing lilt in his voice. "What, are we in the fourth grade?"

"Clint," Mark warned.

Clint turned on him. "Oh, right, I forgot about your *R-word* brother." Clint shook his head. "I didn't mean anything by it. Chill out. It's just a word, and if someone acts like a retard, they deserve to be called one."

"My daughter's retarded," Sarah said quickly, a rush of heat running through her. "And when you use that word to describe someone who simply hasn't met your demands, you say a whole lot more about yourself than you say about them."

Clint blinked at her. "You have a daughter?"

Sarah took a breath. "Her name is Rose. She's six."

The silence that descended on the table was out of place in the noisy restaurant. The waiter showed up with the guacamole, apologizing again for not getting it out sooner.

"It's okay," Clint said, subdued and not looking at Sarah. He scooped a spoonful of the guacamole and put it on top of his enchilada. The rest of them exchanged looks and went back to their food.

After a few seconds, Clint looked up at her, his expression accusing. "You didn't you tell me you had a daughter."

Sarah took a breath and looked at him. "No, but I should have. I'm sorry." Brylee and Mark were watching them, but stayed out of the conversation. "And *that* says a lot more about me than it does about you."

"Damn straight it does," he said, under his breath.

"Clint," Brylee said in reprimand. "What's your problem tonight?"

Sarah took a breath, but when she looked up, it was Mark's eyes she caught.

"What's my *problem*?" Clint said, looking at Brylee and then at Mark as though hungry for an argument. "I was completely snowed into this trip, wasn't I? Here I was thinking I was gunna have a hot hook-up, and—"

"Whoa," Sarah said a split second before Mark or Brylee could. "I never said that's what this weekend was about. I thought we were going to hang out and get to know each other." She almost added that she'd planned to tell him about Rose—but had she?

"Yeah, right." Clint took another drink of his beer. "'Cause *getting to know each other* is totally what people go to beach resort vacations for. Finding out you've got a kid puts everything into perspective. If I'd known that you were a . . . a *mom*, I'd have never invited you. If I'd know your daughter was—"

"Clint," Mark said this time, cutting him off. Clint shrugged and went back to his meal.

Sarah stared at her plate, but only for a few seconds before her hurt and anger changed to pity. No wonder there'd been no chemistry—they were polar opposites. She forced a smile that seemed to confuse him. "I accepted your invitation because I took you at your word about this being a fun weekend together. I'm sure you can hit the clubs and find a hot hook-up, but I *never* had any intention of filling that role. Not for an instant. As for why I didn't tell you about Rose, well, I guess I have to figure that out for myself but I guess I'm glad I didn't. Then I'd have never extended this trip and had such a great time." She turned to Mark and Brylee, using all her ability to remain calm. "Thanks for making this a wonderful weekend, you two."

She turned and took her purse off of the back of the chair. Without looking back, she headed for the exit, her heart thundering in her chest. Brylee caught up with her a few steps later. "Oh. My. Gosh. Can you believe he said that?"

"Actually," Sarah said, feeling more . . . *herself* than she had all weekend. "I can. You don't need to come with me."

"I'm not staying here. Are you going back to the room? Are you all right?"

"I think I'd like a little time to myself, if you don't mind, but really, I'm okay."

Brylee tilted her head. "You're sure?"

Sarah smiled and gave Brylee a quick hug. "I'll see you back at the room in a little bit. Do you mind taking my purse with you? I'd hate to get it wet."

Eleven

Sarah adjusted her glasses and looked out across the Caribbean Sea, knowing that the hem of her dress was getting wet but not caring. It was a beautiful night, just like last night had been, yet different. Her anger towards Clint had gone out with the tide. Good or bad, he'd facilitated her learning some important things about herself, which helped keep this weekend in perspective. It hadn't been a waste, just a very different experience than she'd expected and it was a relief to know that Clint wouldn't invite her to his room or slobber all over her after too many beers. As embarrassing as the final moments had been, at least she was done trying to protect parts of her life, or pretend to be someone she wasn't—or whatever it was she'd been doing. They could all move on with their lives now. Clint wasn't the kind of guy a girl like her could pin her hopes and dreams on.

Mark was the one who was harder to walk away from. As long as she was connected to Clint, there was a chance she could have found a chance to explain herself to Mark. Of everything that had happened, he was her biggest regret. How different could things have been if it had been Mark, not Clint, she'd come to spend time with this weekend? She couldn't begin to imagine.

She looked at the foam swirling around her ankles as her feet sank a little lower into the sand. The what-ifs would doubtlessly haunt her for a very long time.

"Hey."

Sarah looked over her shoulder then dropped her arms to her sides as she turned to see Mark standing farther up the beach, wearing the shorts he'd had on at dinner. No shoes to spark a tantrum should they get wet, but then Mark didn't strike her as the tantrum-throwing type. A wave hit the backs of her ankles, splashing up her legs and soaking her dress almost to the knees.

"H-hey," she said back after she got over the surprise of seeing him there and found her voice again.

"You okay?"

He'd followed her out of the restaurant even though he had every reason to dismiss her. She crossed her arms over her chest, rubbing her upper arms, which had broken out with goose bumps. Was this was her chance to try and redeem herself? "About my daughter—"

"You don't need to explain yourself to me."

"I feel like I do." Sarah talked fast, hoping he would let her at least try. "My life orbits around Rose, and I love that and everything about her, but . . ." Words abandoned her.

"But you wanted to feel like a normal person for once?" Mark filled in, smiling just enough for her not to feel judged by his assumption, which was spot on. "You wanted to see if Clint was someone who could accept *you* before you had to tell him everything about your reality?" He held her eyes for a moment as hers filled with tears; he spoke the very words she'd been unable to find. "You think I've never feared rejection or loneliness so much that I held back with someone? I live the same life, Sarah. I have a lot of the same limitations you do, and I feel the same devotion." He took a step toward her, bringing the distance between them to just a few feet. She couldn't take her eyes off of him, though she tried to blink back tears. "I really didn't come out here to talk about that, though. After what happened in there, I wanted to be sure you were okay."

Her heart fairly melted as she nodded in response. "I'm fine. Better, even. Thank you for checking on me, though." Did she dare say more? If she didn't say it now, she might never have the chance. "My biggest regret from this whole week is not realizing what a great guy you are sooner—and not being who I really am. I'm sorry."

He watched her for several seconds, as though puzzling out what she'd said. Or maybe, like her, he was trying to decide how much he should say. "I owe you an apology too."

"We both know that's not true," Sarah said, shaking her head slightly. "You've been kind and generous, and now you're being forgiving, too. What could you possibly have to apologize for?"

"Because two years ago, I listened to you introduce yourself and talk about your little girl, and I thought 'this is a woman I would like to know better,' but then I didn't do anything about it." He'd wanted to know her better way back then? Before the hair and the contacts and the fake eyelashes? He smiled, a little sad, but a perhaps a little hopeful too. Sarah felt the hope bubbling up in her own heart as well. "If I'd at least tried to get to know you then, just talked to you at all, maybe things would have been different."

It was so easy to discount what he said, but why should she? He was right here, and he had been all weekend. He had nothing to gain from being insincere. Suddenly the what ifs shifted. What if there was something here? What if Mark was who she'd hoped Clint could be, but never could? The thought gave her boldness she seldom felt, drawing a smile from her lips.

"When you put it that way, maybe you do owe me an apology." The breeze blew her hair across her face, and she tucked it behind her ears again. "Consider yourself forgiven." She took a step toward him, closing the gap a little bit more.

His expression relaxed, and he cocked his head slightly to the side. "Perhaps I'm not too late after all?"

Sarah smiled a little wider as the words washed over her. "Maybe you're just in time. Two years ago, I wasn't ready to think past tomorrow."

"And now?"

"I have a different perspective, and that's something I can thank Clint for. He made me think differently about my future, even if he was the completely wrong person for it."

Mark reached out his hand, holding it there in the moonlight, inviting her to take it. "Have you ever walked on a beach hand-in-hand with someone who thinks you're pretty amazing?"

"No." Sarah slowly shook her head while taking his hand, and feeling electricity travel throughout her entire body. He pulled her toward him, and the closer she got, the more the air around them shimmered with expectation. She hadn't felt this energy with Clint, let alone this . . . rightness.

"I live in Omaha," she said, grasping the last shred of reality she could think of. She was close enough to see the tiny ring of green on the outer edge of his blue eyes, to smell the cologne he must have put on before dinner. "I live with my parents. They help me raise Rose."

"I live in Seattle with my disabled brother and my mom, who can't take care of him without me."

Saying those things out loud should have felt like stop sign for both of them. Instead, she found it comfortable and familiar. "It would be complicated," she said.

"What about our lives *isn't* complicated?" Mark replied. She could feel his breath on her face as her gaze moved to watch his mouth as he spoke. "If it's right, we could make it work."

The calm she felt at his words was surprising. Mark knew her world, and it didn't frighten him. Being separated by a few states felt like a paltry obstacle. "Know what else I've never done?"

He lifted his eyebrows.

"I've never been kissed on the beach in the moonlight."

He smiled bigger, revealing a dimple on the right side of his mouth that she hadn't noticed before. He dipped his head and she went up on her toes to meet him halfway. Their lips met beneath the Cozumel sky, melting away the challenges and complications that defined their lives and leaving in their wake, promise, hope, and possibility.

This was the kind of man she could pin her hopes and dreams on. *This* was the kind of beginning that could grow into something beautiful.

Josi S. Kilpack is the author of eighteen novels, which include women's fiction, romance, mystery, and suspense. Her suspense novel *Sheep's Clothing* won the Whitney Award for Best Mystery in 2009, and she was the Best in State Award recipient for Literary Arts in Fiction in Utah in 2012. Josi is one of the co-authors of The Newport Ladies Book Club series (*Daisy*, 2012 and *Shannon's Hope*, 2013). *Fortune Cookie*, the eleventh book in Josi's Sadie Hoffmiller culinary mystery series, has a release date of March 2014.

Josi and her husband, Lee, are the parents of four children and live in Northern Utah. In addition to writing, Josi loves to read, bake, and travel. She's completed six half marathons to date, but may never run another one, because right now she hates running.

Author website: www.josiskilpack.com
Blog: www.josikilpack.blogspot.com
Twitter: @JosiSKilpack
Facebook: Author Josi S. Kilpack

Chasing Tess

Annette Lyon

Other Works by Annette Lyon

Band of Sisters

Coming Home

A Portrait for Toni

At the Water's Edge

Chocolate Never Faileth

The Golden Cup of Kardak

The Newport Ladies Book Club Series

There, Their, They're:
A No-Tears Grammar Guide from the Word Nerd

One

Tess spritzed the curls cascading from her up-do one last time then checked her bun using the mirror in her compact. Almost there. She bit her lower lip as she turned to face her image in the full-length mirror. *Yes,* she decided, smiling with pleasure. The coral pink chiffon was the right choice for tonight. Feminine and light, perfect for a warm spring evening.

One last thing, and her ensemble would be complete. She took the jeweler's case from the dresser top and opened it with a creak. Inside lay a thin gold chain with a heart pendant, a diamond glittering at the center point. Gently, she lifted the necklace from its box, unlatched it, and moved toward the mirror so she could put it on easier. With the clasp done up, she smoothed the necklace with her fingers and tilted her head.

"Perfect," she whispered, although she felt silly talking to herself.

The necklace was pretty, no question. She hadn't worn it since Valentine's Day, when James gave it to her. For the last two months, the box had sat in her underwear drawer, covered by a pair of fuzzy pink socks so that when she got dressed each morning, she didn't have to look at it. James had created the ideal romantic evening—dinner at a French restaurant and a stroll through a park, during which he slipped his jacket over her shoulders in true gentlemanly fashion. A full moon. It was all so ideal, she'd assumed that when he sat beside her on a park bench and pulled out a jewelry box that it would contain not a necklace, but a ring.

They'd been dating for nearly three years, since he began law school. *I can't even think about a future—about marriage yet,* he'd said more than once. *But after I graduate . . .* And then his eyes always got that dreamy quality, and she couldn't help but imagine their life together *then.*

She'd understood that law school would be a hard time, what with all the long hours of studying and tests and writing. He'd even edited the law review, a high honor, and something that would look fantastic on a résumé.

But after I graduate, everything will change, he'd assured her. *I'll be able to focus on other things. Like us.*

Even now as she stood before the mirror, she remembered the goose bumps that had broken over her arms and down her back the first time he'd made that promise. *Us.* Everything would change now; graduation was two days ago.

I suppose it was silly of me to think he'd propose on Valentine's, she thought wryly as she took a step back to look at her reflection one more time. *I shouldn't have gotten upset over this necklace. He's always said* after *graduation.*

Tess was rather pleased with herself for getting over the disappointment of that night, of no longer hating the sight of the box, and, most importantly, for wearing the necklace tonight. It was the first time she'd worn it since he'd given it to her.

Tonight, everything would change. The law school graduation ceremony was over. James's parents had planned a party to celebrate his achievement and "something else," as he'd put it over the phone yesterday. He wouldn't say what the "something else" was, but when she'd prodded and asked specific questions, he'd admitted that it had something to do with the future.

Which could only mean one thing: tonight was the night. He would pop the question. She would look perfect in her coral-pink dress, with his pendant resting on her breastbone, her hair curled and stacked just right, her lipstick matching her dress.

My heart will pound as he kneels and asks for my hand in front of his friends and parents.

The thought caused a flutter in her chest.

Her phone's alarm went off, making her start, but then she smiled. She'd gotten ready exactly on time. Even if she hit traffic, she'd reach the old art museum with plenty of time to walk around the building, find the room where the party was being held—where she would finally, *finally* get that ring on her finger and be promised to the one man she planned to be with for the rest of her life. As she tucked her phone into the little cream-colored purse she'd bought just for tonight, and went out to her car, she tried not to dream too much into the future. She'd done a lot of that anyway over the years. Five months into dating James, she'd known what colors she wanted for her wedding. Granted those colors had changed three times since with the fashions. And she'd picked out the perfect cake almost two years ago. Her dress last fall.

She refused to let herself think too far past the wedding day itself, or she'd be liable to start planning how many children they would have and even name them before James had gotten the question out. She wouldn't plan their *whole* lives, tempting as that might be. She couldn't wait to experience life with him, the ups, the downs, all of it. Together.

The drive to the museum felt twice as long as it should have, even though she hadn't hit more than two red lights. After parking, she flipped down the vanity mirror to check her face one last time. She looked flushed from the excitement.

Didn't need to use blush, she thought with a laugh.

She headed inside and found James in the entryway, wearing a brand new charcoal gray suit with a silver tie. He was talking to a member of the staff and didn't see her right away, so she stood by the door and admired the view. His hair was newly cut and styled with just the right amount of gel. He must have spent some time outdoors lately, because he seemed more tanned than usual.

The worker nodded and headed back into a large room—her cue to step forward. Her sandaled heels clicked on the marble floor, echoing slightly and making James turn his head. His face lit up in the smile Tess had come to know and love.

And call mine. No one else got that exact smile. *He loves me. He really does.*

James extended both arms and reached for her hands, pulling her close and kissing her, then nuzzling her ear with his lips and whispering, "You look fantastic."

"I could say the same about you," she whispered back, loving how close he was, smelling his cologne mixed with the faintest hint of spearmint on his breath.

He took her hand and led Tess into the main room, which had a flagstone floor, a raised stand on one end, a live band setting up on it, and caterers moving about smoothly at their tasks as they set up the buffet table. A good twenty tables were interspersed throughout the room, leaving a space between them and the platform. James pointed to that spot.

"For dancing after we eat." He nodded at the band. "I've already requested our song."

Perfect. Beyond perfect. Until that moment, Tess hadn't been sure if he thought of "Unforgettable" as their song the way she did—the duet version Natalie Cole did with her late father, the legendary Nat King Cole. To her, it had been their song ever since they'd danced to it by moonlight behind a willow tree during a friend's wedding reception. The branches hid them from view of the wedding guests, making James the only person Tess could see.

James had sung along to Nat's deep voice. James twirled her into a circle then brought her back and held her close. They gazed into each other's eyes—so long it had felt like a lifetime, so short, it passed before she knew it. "I'll never forget you, Tess," he'd said as he pulled her close and pressed his cheek to hers and they kept swaying. After that night, any time they heard the song—and there had been a surprising number of times—James had taken her into his arms, danced, and sung in her ear. Even if they were in the middle of a crowd, a street, a mall.

"It's gorgeous," Tess said, taking in the room. She could picture their reception in this room, her cake on a table against that wall . . .

His parents must have put a lot of money into the evening. They arrived shortly after she did.

"Well, hello," Mrs. Kennington said, sandwiching Tess's hand between her own; Tess wanted to pull it free. His mother had never liked her, never thought her good enough for her beloved son.

"Hello," Tess said with a smile.

She repeated James's words in her mind. *She'll learn to love you. It'll take time. She doesn't know how amazingly wonderful you are . . . yet.*

Tess and James ate dinner at the same table as his

parents and a few of his law school buddies. She said little, hoping not to give any kind of fodder for Mrs. Kennington's negativity. James had a spot beside Tess, and had he stayed there, Tess would have been happy to sit beside James as they ate, even in silence. In the past, he'd taken her hand under the table to squeeze it in their code: three squeezes meant "I love you," to which she replied with four squeezes, "I love you too." He'd been known to sneak her the occasional wink and make sure to keep her glass filled, her roll buttered, and her salad drizzled with dressing.

But tonight, he hadn't sat more than five seconds before guests greeted him, and he stood to say hello—then vanished into the crowd again. The same thing happened over and over, leaving Tess with an empty seat beside her and James's parents pointedly ignoring her across the table.

Surely the stream of well-wishers had to end. James would eventually return to his meal beside her, wouldn't he? But too many people and too many things pulled him in different directions. Every time he sat down and began cutting into his steak, a friend came over to talk, or he needed to meet so-and-so's new fiancée, or something else, leaving Tess at the table, awkward and as silent as ever, giving Mrs. Kennington the occasional smile before plunging her fork back into her salad. She'd added the dressing herself. Whenever James returned, he whispered an apology as he sat and smoothed his napkin on his lap. But he never took more than a bite before he was interrupted and called elsewhere again.

Tess wouldn't ruin his big night by complaining or nagging over being "neglected." This party was about him. She could sit in the background and bask in the glow of her husband-to-be, who only had to pass the bar before being a bona fide lawyer. As the noise in the room increased, Tess found herself zoning off into her imagination, planning more of her upcoming nuptials. The evening would end with the spotlight on them both; she could wait.

How long of an engagement would his mother insist they have? Tess could plan a decent wedding in three months, if she hurried a few things. July or August would be perfect.

The band finished a song but didn't start another. The conversation around the room gradually quieted as everyone turned to see the singer, who had given the microphone to Garrett Pack; she recognized him from several law-school parties. James considered him his best friend; they'd studied and crammed together, and they were both on the law review staff. Garrett made a quieting motion with one arm and waited for the remaining chatter to die down.

"Thank you for coming, everyone. This is quite an exciting night, as we all know, celebrating the accomplishment of one James D. Kennington, Esquire!" He clapped against the mic, sending a heavy noise through the speakers. The crowd clapped and whooped their approval.

As the roar died down, Mrs. Kennington leaned in to her husband and said, "I would have thought that with us footing the bill for the evening, that that Pack boy would have let *us* address the crowd first." She sniffed and straightened.

Tess pretended she hadn't heard anything.

Garrett nodded at the applause. "It's great, isn't it? Three years of hard work, finally completed. I happen to know that James is ready for the next stage of his life, and he would like to come up now to tell you all about it."

More clapping. Tess joined in as her heart went wild in her chest. *Here it comes. This is the "something else" he hinted at.* She prayed she still looked nice—that her curls hadn't drooped, that her dress wasn't wrinkled from sitting, that she hadn't eaten off all her lipstick. All of these thoughts passed through her mind in a flash as she watched James, in his slick gray suit, move from a spot near the left side the room to the front. He hopped onto the platform and took the mic from Garrett, the two of them slapping each other's backs in a manly variation of a hug.

Garrett stepped into the background beside the band, grinning ear to ear. He had to know what James had planned. Tess never expected to have such a public proposal—had always envisioned something more intimate, private—but so long into this relationship, she would be thrilled just to hear the question any time, any place.

Grinning broadly, James faced the audience. When he caught her eye, his face brightened a little more, which warmed her head to toe.

Oh, how I love this man.

"My man Garrett is right," James began. "I'm now a law school grad, which means you can all officially crack evil lawyer jokes about me."

Laughter rippled throughout the room, including a polite chuckle from the Kenningtons.

James rubbed his chin and shifted from foot to foot. "I've been in this same place for three years now. It's been a hard climb at times, but it's been worth it. I'm sure my parents will be doubly glad when I've passed the bar and am practicing law, because then I can start paying off all those school loans, and they'll know I'm not coming back to live in their basement."

More rumbles of laughter.

"So the time has come for the next step in my journey, to leave this part behind and move forward to a new phase of my life."

Tess's heart threatened to hammer right out of her ribcage. She sat at the edge of her seat so that when he called her forward, she'd be ready, and so she'd stand gracefully in her heels.

"I have been given the once in a lifetime opportunity . . ." He let his voice trail off, building the suspense in the room. "To be an intern at Preston, Carson, and McNeil in New York City, with the possibility of taking on a full-time job after I pass the bar." He raised his glass and bit his lip, something he always did when excited.

This was it. Tess could feel her heart pounding in her chest with anticipation.

"I'm moving to the Big Apple!"

Smiling broadly, Tess stood and took three steps toward the platform, when his words registered.

Wait, what? She stopped in her tracks, catching the toe of her shoe on a chair and nearly pitching forward. She caught herself on the back of the chair, saving herself from sprawling across the floor. James scanned the room. As Tess stood there, frozen, she couldn't help but wonder if she'd imagined the slight hesitation when his gaze reached her—and moved on.

How many miles is it from Tempe to New York? Hundreds? Thousands?

She felt a sudden urge to check a map. Or to run up to the platform and shake James by the lapels. This didn't make sense. An internship *couldn't* be the big "something" he wanted to say tonight. He'd promised that after law school, they would get engaged. Wasn't that *now*? What did he expect her to do, get married tomorrow by a justice of the peace? Not have a nice wedding?

Or worse . . . the other option came over her in a wave cold as ice. What if he didn't plan to marry her at all? What if he planned to settle in New York . . . without her?

That's exactly what he's decided. Her hand covered her mouth as she heard a cry. Not until all heads turned to look at her did she realize that *she* had made the sound. Her face went hot. Her knees felt ready to buckle, and she couldn't breathe. Tess shook her head and backed up.

James's eyes widened, and he called out to her. "Tess!

Please, let me explain!"

But there was nothing *to* explain. He was taking the internship. Moving to New York. He'd strung her along for three years, and what did she have to show for it? Drooping curls and a coral-pink dress she'd never wear again.

Tess whirled around, unable to stand the pitying eyes on her. She scooped her purse from her chair so she could drive home—right now—and saw, with another stab of dismay, that Mrs. Kennington wore a pleased, smug expression.

Hearing James call her name again, she fled, running out the door before anyone said more. When she reached her car, she fumbled with the keys, but despite her haste, she kept an eye on the door of the museum, wishing James would come out to stop her, to beg forgiveness, to offer the ring she'd waited for so, so long.

She sat in her car, worrying her keys between her fingers and fighting tears, hoping to see James push through the glass door. But five minutes later—she watched each one tick past on the car's clock—he still hadn't come out. She turned the key, backed out, and drove away. Tears blurred her vision. She swiped at her eyes with the back of one hand.

It wasn't the ring she wanted after all, although that would have been nice. It was James. Dear, sweet James. But he was lost to her now.

Two

Tess drove straight to her condo, where her sister Hope waited. *Fitting,* she thought. *I could use some hope about now.*

She could feel tears streaking down her cheeks; her makeup had to be a total mess. She didn't care. Nothing about her appearance mattered any more. James was leaving her. He didn't care like she'd thought he did.

The jerk!

By the time she got home, Tess had burning fury in her chest as much as horrid sadness washing through her. The mixture of emotions was upsetting and tiring all at once. And energizing. And so, so confusing. Right then, she both hated and loved James. Although how such a thing was possible, she didn't know. She opened the door and slammed it behind her.

Hope looked up from a magazine she was reading. "What's the matter?"

"James dumped me." Tess walked to the couch and collapsed on it.

"He *what*?" In a flash, Hope tossed the magazine to the couch scooted to Tess's side.

"Okay, I guess he didn't *technically* dump me—he didn't say the words. But what he *did* do was practically the same thing—and in front of his friends and family! You should have seen his mother's face. So smug. She never did like me. She must be thrilled I'm out of her son's life." She told Hope about the evening, finishing with, "Now everyone there—at least a hundred people—know it's over. I couldn't stay in that room another minute."

"I don't blame you." Hope's face was a mask of worry and confusion. "But I'm confused. Didn't he say he was going to propose tonight?"

Tess shrugged. "I thought so. He never said it exactly, but he was hinting about something big, about something he had to say to me tonight." She sighed. "So I assumed . . ."

"You assumed the same thing any woman would have three years into a relationship, having been promised an engagement 'after school.'"

"Maybe I missed some red flags. Maybe I was just kidding myself."

Hope scooted closer, and Tess leaned her head on her big sister's shoulder, like she used to when they were kids. "I should have known he wasn't really committed after the lame Valentine's gift."

"I don't think I heard about that one," Hope said.

Tess played with her fingernails in her lap. "That's because I didn't tell you. He put together this huge romantic night—everything was perfect. At the end, we were sitting on a park bench by moonlight, when he pulled out a jewelry box. What was I supposed to think?"

"That he was proposing," Hope said.

"Exactly! But it was a stupid necklace." She took it off and chucked it across the room.

Hope watched it smack the wall and scoffed in disgust. "The pig . . ."

"He was only a couple of months from graduating. I figured that if we got engaged in February, we'd have plenty of time to plan a wedding before fall. I figured he'd be able to pass the bar and get a job by then." She sighed, verbalizing her fantasies, the ones she'd let herself think about—just a little—regarding their future.

They would have gotten married in June or July. As he studied for the bar, she'd be his wife, the support he never had at home during law school. He wouldn't have to rely on Coke and Doritos to stay awake as he crammed for tests with Garrett. She would take care of him, be the nurturing wife she'd thought he deserved.

Hope's voice was flat as she spoke. "What a turd. And I'm only saying that word because, as your big sister, I won't swear in front of you. But I'm totally cursing him out in my head."

"He *is* a turd." Tess wiped at her eyes. Her fingers came away black from smeared mascara. "I better wipe some of this mess off my face before I stain the couch. I must look like the undead."

"You look great. You always do," Hope countered as Tess headed for the half bath.

Behind her, Tess's phone went off in her purse by the couch. She cringed, hearing James's ring—the Law & Order sound effect: "dun-kung." He'd put it on her phone as his ring tone because to him that sound meant "lawyer." It rang a second time. Tess spun around, marched back, and, before it could ring again, declined the call then set it to vibrate so she wouldn't hear that noise again. She stood there by the couch, Hope watching, Tess staring at the phone.

As much as she wanted to hate James, she desperately wanted him to be the man she'd thought he was. "Leave a message," she ordered, staring at the screen of her phone, hoping a notice of a message would pop up. "Leave one." But after a few minutes, the phone still didn't show anything but a missed call. No message of any kind. Not even a text. Tess tossed the phone back into her purse with disgust. As she headed to the bathroom, she wondered whether to block his number. Pro: blocking him would feel good. Con: she'd never know if he was really sorry and trying to contact her.

Why do I care? He's a jerk.

Tess closed the bathroom door, looked at herself in the mirror, and replayed Hope's words about how she looked great no matter what. Her sister was trying to make her feel good. It didn't work. She took stock of her reflection, noting every flaw. If her nose had been straighter, her complexion clearer, her eyes not so wide set—if she had been *prettier*, then would James have wanted to marry her? Why had he pretended he'd wanted to marry her for so long, when he obviously didn't?

He was the top of his law school class. He was smart. No way was he stupid enough to think that she'd stick around like a pathetic puppy, waiting around forever for any scrap of attention or affection he was willing to throw her when it occurred to him.

Except for the fact that she'd basically proved that she'd always be a puppy, always waiting, always there.

After wiping her mascara off with a tissue, Tess leaned against the bathroom counter and gazed at her reflection, studying it—really studying it, but this time not for flaws. She tried to be as objective as possible.

"I'm not ugly," she whispered, after taking a full inventory. Even with red, puffy eyes and no makeup, she really wasn't ugly. She was actually quite pretty. Not model gorgeous. Not even beautiful. But pretty. Maybe James was holding out for beauty bombshell.

Turd.

What now? *Mom,* she thought. *I have to go see Mom. She'll know what to do. She'll let me stay with her while I figure this out.* Her mother would make her famous brownies then hold Tess and let her cry it out over cups of Mexican hot chocolate. She could hide from James there at her mother's place in California. She'd screen her calls and never—ever—answer a call or text from him again.

Yes. The more she thought about the plan, the better it sounded. She wouldn't check her e-mail—or better yet, she'd just block his email address from her account. She'd unfriend him on Facebook. Change her relationship status back to single.

She'd take control of her life. She'd surrendered that control entirely to James for far too long.

Three years I'll never get back.

With the energy of anger and purpose, she pushed away from the counter top and headed back to the living room, where her sister still sat on the couch, now watching a dating reality TV show. The couple was making out in a Jacuzzi. Tess wanted to throw up at the sight—it created new questions for her. Had James fallen for someone else? Had he *cheated* on her? She'd never have thought so, but before tonight, she'd never thought James was capable of being a jerk, either.

Hope looked over her shoulder and noticed the look on Tess's face. She grimaced and punched a button on the remote and changed the show to some mystery series. "Sorry," she said. "I wasn't thinking."

"It's okay," Tess said, collapsing on the couch and pulling a pillow onto her lap. "Do you think Mom's home right now?"

Hope's eyebrows rose slightly. "Probably. Why?" She looked at her watch and added, "I doubt she's in bed yet. What are you thinking?"

"Just an idea." She smiled for the first time since leaving the party, feeling a strange rush, a sense of power.

I have no intention of letting James ever see me again.

⚮

Two hours later, Tess was in her red Mustang convertible, driving west on Interstate 10, headed for Newport Beach. After Tess's father suddenly died five years ago, her mother had moved there, leasing a house a few blocks from the ocean. It was a place Tess loved to visit. Going to the beach and strolling the pier always cleared her head. There was nothing in the world like the calm, cooling waves and the salty tang of the ocean. Only a six-hour drive from Tempe, yet a world away. Tess had called from her apartment before packing up her car with three suitcases. Her mother had happily agreed to let Tess stay in the guest room.

"See you tomorrow!" her mother had said before hanging up.

Tomorrow, yes, but earlier than her mother expected. Tess would drive straight through the night. She'd show up on her mother's doorstep for breakfast. Tess would collapse in her mother's arms, cry, then take a long nap, and they'd have those brownies and hot chocolate as she talked about stupid James.

Tess would be safe from him there. He knew her mother lived out in California, and near a beach, but she was pretty sure he didn't know exactly where, and California had hundreds of miles of beach. He also didn't know her mother's first name, so there wasn't much chance he could Google her to figure out where Tess was headed—assuming he wanted to find her, which she didn't dare hope.

Her gaze sketched over to her phone sitting in a cup holder—he had sent a few texts, none of which told her anything besides the fact that James probably felt guilty. *Which he should.*

She'd pulled her hair back into a ponytail so it wouldn't fly in her eyes then put the convertible top down, letting the warm desert air blow across her face. It was early enough in the year that the sweltering heat of the Arizona summer hadn't come yet. Instead the night was warm enough for her to enjoy the spring wind whipping her hair. Newport would be cooler; it was a bit early for lying out in sun or taking a dip at the beach. Good thing, too—she'd be able to have her time on the pier in solitude instead of sharing it with the packed beaches of summer. She couldn't wait to look out at the endless expanse of ocean, listen to the even rolling of the waves as they came in and broke on the shore, always the same yet new, and always reliable. She could fall asleep to the sound, it was so relaxing—and she'd definitely need something powerful to calm her down for the next while, until she decided what to do. Maybe she could move to Newport. Telecommute permanently, and pick up some freelance work. She knew plenty of graphic designers who worked freelance full time.

Even though Tess wanted to get away from everything, she'd brought along her computer. Only an hour away from Tempe, she was already glad her laptop was on the passenger seat. She hoped her boss, Gary, would be understanding about her sudden absence from the office.

Yet how would she explain the situation: "Sorry, but I'm having a crisis in my love life; I need some time away"?

She'd figure something out. And if Gary decided to be a turd like James, she'd find another job or find a way to freelance full time. She was good at graphic design; as long as she had her computer and an Internet connection, she could work. Assuming she could think of something besides James.

The signs along the freeway said that the exit to Buckeye was coming in up a few miles. She'd fill up her tank to get her over the next several hundred miles of almost nothingness, and while there, send Hope a text so she knew Tess was safe. As the car hummed along the asphalt, its headlights cutting through the darkness, she smiled, cranked up the radio, and sang at the top of her lungs to Journey's "Don't Stop Believing."

She would survive this. She'd get rid of James. Cut him from her life like the cancer he was. He'd already taken three years. He wouldn't take one more day. Sometime in the future, she would look back on this spring as the time she escaped that James guy.

She was free. Yet, until tonight, she'd never *wanted* to be free of James. Never thought of herself as being imprisoned to him. She'd loved him. Still did. And that's why it hurt. Tonight was so out of character for him.

Tonight was out of character for her, too. *But it's his fault. I can't wait for him. No more stringing me along. It's over.*

She punched the accelerator and cruised faster through the darkness.

Three

James stood on the platform, confused as he watched Tess run out. Was she sick?

He had been excited to tell everyone—including Tess—about the internship. Sure, he'd known she'd be disappointed a tad at first, knowing they'd have to put off planning their wedding a little longer. But she'd come around. She always did. She'd understand that this was the chance of a lifetime. She'd been supportive every time he'd taken time away from her, whether it was a law review deadline or a special dinner for his class with a professor.

I understand, she'd say. *It's temporary, right?*

And each time, he'd assured her that of course it— whatever *it* was that time—was temporary.

She'd looked into his eyes with her amber brown ones. *I'll always be here waiting for you when you're done chasing the law school dream. And when you're done, we'll begin our dream life together.*

Had he ignored a sad tone in her voice when she'd said those words? He racked his brain but couldn't remember. He hadn't paid attention to her reaction, because he's been so wrapped up in his ambitions, his goals, his life. The thought made his stomach go sour. Those thoughts were broken up by law-school buddies crowding the platform, cheering and thumping him on the back with congratulations. Through the chaos, he glanced at the door again, hoping to see Tess reappear. She never did.

The party didn't go late; an hour later, guests were already saying their good-byes. But James had an uneasy feeling the entire time. Whenever he thought no one was looking, he checked his phone to see if Tess had called or texted or emailed. Nothing. He'd have to call as soon as he could to smooth things over. She'd understand when he explained that he couldn't turn down an opportunity like this. He hadn't expected to have something amazing dropped in his lap, and she'd always been supportive of anything that would put him ahead. And after the internship, he'd be back. They'd have a bigger, better life because he'd be able to get a job at any firm he applied at, even if nothing opened up at Preston, Carson, and McNeil.

He checked his phone again. Nothing. He'd called once, but she hadn't answered—and he couldn't get himself to leave a message about something this important. He had to talk to her. Half an hour after trying to call her, he'd sent the first of four texts. His first, *You okay?* was followed by *I need to talk to you,* then *Please reply,* and finally, a simple, *Please.*

He'd slip out as soon as he could, which wasn't yet. His mother was a stickler for etiquette and wouldn't take kindly to the guest of honor leaving early from the party she'd paid for. Rather, that his *father* had paid for. But it was the same thing. Dad earned the money; Mom spent it. Finally, as the party died down and James felt like he could make an exit without ruffling too many feathers, he gave his mother a hug and a kiss on the cheek then shook his father's hand.

"I'm proud of you, son."

"Thank you," James said, suddenly realizing how formal he sounded with his parents. Tess was never like that with her family. When he heard her and her mother talking on the phone, they were casual and thoughtful. They laughed. He couldn't ever remember laughing with either of his parents.

"I'd better get your mother home," his father said he put an arm around her waist. "She needs her rest, you know." James nodded in response as he removed his mother's cashmere cardigan from the chair back and draped it over her shoulders.

"Thank you, dear," she said, clasping the front of her sweater with one hand and patting his cheek with the other. Looking into his eyes she added, "I'm glad you finally decided that Tess was holding you back. You're far more worthy of the life New York holds for you than practicing law in a little town with no name."

As his parents walked out, James stood there, feet planted to the floor in shock, face immovable. His parents assumed that he was dropping Tess altogether? That he somehow deserved *better* than Tess?

Is that why Tess ran away—she thought I was breaking up with her? He raked fingers from both hands through his hair, totally mussing it up. At least his mother wasn't here to see him ruin his perfectly coiffed hair. Not that he cared anymore. *Tess. Oh, no.*

He had to escape, find her and explain that she meant the world to him. Because she did—only now did he realize how much. The thought of the internship turned to ashes in his mind. A fancy life as a high-powered attorney would mean nothing if he didn't share it with Tess. He'd taken for granted that he'd have both. Maybe he still could.

He hurried out to his Mercedes and peeled out of the parking lot, speed dialing Tess. After two rings, it went to voice mail. Either her phone was off, or she was screening calls and not answering when she saw his number. Because she hadn't replied to any of his texts, he guessed the latter. After the beep, he opened his mouth to leave a message, but didn't know what to say. Too much for a voice message. He had to see her, talk to her face to face.

He hung up and tossed his phone into a cup holder in the console. What could he say so Tess would understand? He wasn't breaking up with her. He wanted to be with her.

But I can't pass up the internship, can I? It was the opportunity of a lifetime.

How to make Tess see that? Then it came to him—Tess always listened to her sister. If he could get Hope on his side, he might be able to convince Tess to come back to him.

Just before you leave her, a voice whispered in his head.

Yes, but I'm doing it for us, he countered.

Are you?

The thoughts were making him crazy. He turned on the radio and cranked it high, not caring what the music was, so long as it was loud enough to drown out his thoughts as he drove straight to Tess's condo. He'd assumed that she would be home but unwilling to see him, so he'd talk to Hope. But when he got there, her car wasn't in her spot. Not a good sign. Lights were on in the front room—someone was still awake—so he went up the steps and knocked on the door, hard and loud. Something inside—the television or some music, maybe—stopped suddenly, and feet padded to the door. When it opened, he saw Hope.

"Is Tess home?" He knew she wasn't, but he wasn't thinking clearly.

Hope, wearing red pajamas with Christmas trees—even though it was April—folded her arms and leaned against the door frame. James shook his head. Why was he noticing something as stupid as Hope's pajamas?

"Why should I tell you?" she asked.

"Where is she?" he demanded, looking over her shoulder in case Tess was inside after all. "Her car's not here. I'm worried." Images flashed through his mind of what could have happened. Did she drive around the city until she ran out of gas? Had she been in an accident? He wanted to yell, but he reined in his emotions and spoke calmly. "Just tell me where I can find Tess. I have to talk to her. Please."

Hope shrugged as if he didn't matter. He probably deserved that. "She left. Packed up a couple of bags and drove away." Her hand waved as if showing how the car had gone off into the distance.

The blood drained from James's face. "Drove away? Where?"

When Hope didn't answer—just stared him down with one raised eyebrow, as if he was about as pleasant to be around as a slug—he tried again.

"Look, she won't answer her phone. I've tried texting her too, a lot, but I get no answer."

Hope shook her head, lips pursed. "You know, if I'd been treated like crap by my boyfriend on the night he was supposed to propose but then instead, *humiliated* me in public, I probably wouldn't answer either."

He felt as if he'd been punched in the gut. *My big news. She thought . . . Oh, no.* "At least tell me when she'll be back."

"I honestly don't know. Not that I'd tell you if I did."

James ran his fingers through is hair again. At this rate, he'd look like Einstein soon. He tried another tack. "Did she say she was breaking up with me? What did she tell you— exactly?"

Hope laughed with a snort. "Men really are dense, aren't they?"

"Just tell me." James grabbed his tie and loosened it then undid the top two buttons. His expensive gray suit was already rumpled. He was far more rumpled in spirit.

She wore a smirk. "And I quote: 'He's been straddling the fence for too long. I'm done.' That clear enough for you? Good night, James. Although I don't think you deserve even that much. I really don't hope you have a good night at all."

With that, she slammed the door. It banged, followed by the thunk of the deadbolt sliding into place. The sound made the headache behind James's eyes throb. Instead of leaving, he turned and sat on the step. He gazed at the full moon, thinking about tonight, Hope's words combined with Tess's horrified look before she ran out of the room.

For three years, Tess's supportive mantra had always been *I'll wait*. He'd appreciated it—every day. Yet a niggling thought in the back of his head had sometimes tried to warn him that one of these days, he'd have to be the one who supported *her* dreams. Come to think of it, he wasn't entirely sure what those dreams were. Tess liked to take pictures. Did she want to be a photographer? How sad that after three years, he didn't know what drove her, besides being with him.

Am I worth that kind of devotion? He scrubbed a hand across his chin, newly shaved for the evening. His mother wouldn't have stood a son with a five o'clock shadow at his own soiree. Mother also didn't think Tess deserved him. Truth was, *he* didn't deserve *her*.

He looked over his shoulder at the door. He and Tess had stood by it countless times when he picked her up and dropped her off after nights out together. He'd first kissed her here at midnight under the moonlight, her soft lips with their ever-present peach lipstick, were tender and warm beneath his. He remembered her mouth responding eagerly to his.

He's been straddling the fence for too long. I'm done.

Recalling the words Hope quoted suddenly shattered the memory. Maybe he *had* been straddling the fence, not committing to anything, but not freeing Tess to find happiness either. He'd enjoyed having a devoted girlfriend. She was beautiful and kind—and *convenient.* He hated admitting the last one, but it was true. He'd enjoyed being single and having fun, no strings attached, when it wasn't convenient. He'd blown her off many times because of a paper due or a test to study for. He'd never lied to her about his obligations, but maybe he'd let them become a priority when he could have found room for Tess to be in his life along with the other things.

Suddenly he remembered one of many visiting guest lecturers. Something extra he'd attended. It wasn't required, but he'd gone anyway, at the expense of dinner with Tess's mother. He cringed at the memory, knowing he'd gone to the lecture and rubbed shoulders with the speaker afterward, not because he had to, but to impress everyone in the lecture hall. Law school was so much about impressions, about who you kissed up to. He'd done a great job of that. But at what price?

That particular lecturer had talked about life after law school—the realities of being employed by a firm, working your way up to partner, tracking billable hours. Working seventy or eighty hour weeks.

"In some respects," he'd said, "your firm will become your wife, your lover, your family. But that's the sacrifice every successful lawyer must make."

James had accepted the statement without question, because he'd always wanted to be a lawyer, and if that meant pulling long hours to contribute to his firm, then that's what he'd do, much like he'd done to get this law degree in the first place. In the process, he'd be able to buy a big house for his wife and children, and they'd never want for anything.

Except for me.

The thought dragged him down; he couldn't see an answer to the problem—being a high-powered lawyer meant working marathon hours. Graduating from law school wouldn't end his time away, his hard work. Or putting off Tess. Even *he* had believed the lie that things would get better some day.

What now? After some time, he stood and dragged himself to his car then drove back to his place, which he shared with three other new law-school grads. All of them would be moving out soon, making room for the next crop of students. And he'd be in New York, living the life he'd always dreamed of.

Hadn't he? Or had his parents invented the dream for their only son, making him believe it had always been his idea, his dream?

I do want to be a lawyer, he thought as he drove. *But I don't need to work in some boutique firm that brings in millions and insists I wear Armani.* His parents would be ticked if he became one of the lower-class lawyers, maybe someone who did nothing but research and read contracts for businesses, or worse—if he became a public defender.

He parked and went into the apartment, intent on avoiding his friends, who were back from the party, now dressed in sweats and t-shirts, eating popcorn and streaming some movie with lots of booms and blasts.

As he walked past, Garrett called out, "Hey where'd you go? We missed you—Andrew was going to give a toast, but you'd ditched us." He grinned. "I've never known you to pass up an excuse for some bubbly."

"Had to go somewhere." Had they not seen his girlfriend—his fiancée in all but name—run out?

He walked to his bedroom and took off his suit, which seemed to restrain him so much he could hardly breathe. He pulled on his favorite pair of jeans and a t-shirt—tattered, with the silk-screened text so faded it couldn't be read if you didn't know what it used to say. Truth be told, he *didn't* remember. He'd gotten it in high school as part of the honors society. The maroon text was probably some Greek symbols.

As he tugged it on, he suddenly remembered that Tess loved him in that shirt. He stepped over to the full-length mirror on the back of the bedroom door and tried to figure it out. *Why* did she like this shirt? It was old and faded and ugly. *But* it was tighter around his chest than most of his others. That was the best he could come up with.

Does the reason matter? He'd known she liked this shirt, but he rarely wore it—it wasn't exactly the image of a law student. Shouldn't he have worn it anyway, knowing it made her smile? Breathing out a huff of frustrated air, he grabbed his phone and tried calling Tess again. No luck. He hung up, still unable to find the right words for a message. He sent two more texts saying, Please call me. Then he waited, staring at his phone for fifteen minutes, hoping for a reply. What if she'd been in an accident? He thought of calling local hospitals to find her—hoping for and dreading the possibility at the same time.

I love Tess. He knew that now—fiercely, stronger than ever.

Before, he'd thought he loved her, but he'd taken her for granted. He'd figured Tess would always be at his side, whenever he needed her. Until now. He needed her, and she was nowhere to be found. He could no longer picture his life—not even in New York for a few months—without her. He wanted to be *with* her. To fall asleep by her side every night and wake up with their feet entangled, knowing that his ring was on her finger. That they belonged to each other.

That dream—what could have been—was slipping away, like sand through his fingers.

Tess wasn't at her apartment. But Hope seemed to know where she was, or at least she wasn't worried about Tess. That had to mean something. He went to his favorites list on his phone and called their apartment.

After three rings, Hope picked up. "Hello?" Her voice dripped with disgust. She'd obviously seen the caller ID.

"Hi, um . . ." Man, he should have planned this out better before jumping into the call. He rubbed his forehead. "Hope, this is James again—" A grunt, followed by background sounds. James spoke louder. "No, really—please don't hang up! Hear me out."

A few seconds later, he wasn't sure the line was still connected. He waited a bit longer, and when he was about to say something, Hope spoke. "After the way you treated my sister, I shouldn't be talking to you at all. You have thirty seconds to give me one good reason I shouldn't hang up and get a restraining order."

For a split second, he was about to argue the legality of getting a restraining order over something so small, but sense overrode his legal training. He sighed and simply said, "Because I love her." His voice cracked as he said it.

Silence for two seconds, then, "Oh." Her sister clearly hadn't expected that. "Really?"

"Really. I've done some stupid things over the years, and I've taken her for granted, but I'm done with that."

"Uh-huh. So what makes now any different? What makes tonight any different from Valentine's day, when she thought you were going to propose, and instead you gave her a lame necklace?"

"She thought—oh, man. I am so *stupid*." She'd worn that necklace tonight—something he hadn't seen since he'd given it to her two months ago. He'd wondered why she never wore it, but assumed it hadn't been her style. "And tonight was the second time she thought . . ." James let his voice trail off. He could *not* say the words.

"Of course she thought you'd propose. You hinted that you had something big to say at the party, and you'd promised, James—*promised*—to marry her after graduation."

James lay on his bed, eyes closed with one hand over his face. What a mess he'd made. Of course Tess would think all of those things; he'd all but told her to believe every one of them. And then he'd dashed her hopes. The quiet ride home the night of Valentine's Day finally made sense, as did her sweet but brief kiss at the door, when he was used to something longer.

"I don't know what I'd ever do without her," he said, as much to himself as to Hope.

"Really?" she said again. Her voice was guarded, but no longer rude.

It gave him a glimmer of light. Maybe she'd help him. The glimmer grew. Maybe Tess's sister would help. He waited for her to go on, almost unable to breathe. When she didn't say more, he finally squeezed one word through his tight throat.

"Hope?"

"I'm thinking. Okay, here's the deal. But before I say anything, I have to say that I still think you're a total turd."

"I deserve that."

"Glad you agree. You deserve worse."

"Is she back?" James sat up eagerly, ready to slide on a pair of sneakers and race to their place.

"No, but I know where she is. Or, at least, where she's headed."

His heart leapt in his chest. "Where?"

"Don't try calling her anymore; she won't answer."

"Hope, I *need* to make this right. I didn't realize what a jerk I'd been for so long, but I'll die without her."

Hope snorted. "Don't be melodramatic."

"Fine. I'll live, but I'll be miserable. I feel like someone scooped my heart out of my chest. I *need* Tess. I love her. I really, really do, and I'm going to make this right." As he said the words, he knew he'd never spoken anything more true. His voice lowered to a whisper. "I'll do anything to get her back."

"Such as?"

James's gaze sketched over to his desk, where he'd studied so hard for so long. On one corner sat a letter, the one officially inviting him to be an intern in New York. He picked it up and scanned the text, hesitating for only half a second. "I'll give up the internship. I'll work for a smaller firm with better hours, and maybe someday I can start my own law firm on my own terms."

"Wait. You'd seriously give all that up?" Hope's voice went up sharply in disbelief.

"Of course." He deliberately folded the letter into fourths and shoved it into his pocket, not wanting to see it again. He should destroy the thing in the garbage disposal. Too bad he wasn't a redneck; he could have used it for target practice if he'd been the gun type.

"Wow," Hope said with awe in her voice. "You really do love her."

He did—but hadn't realized how much until tonight. James had to swallow against the knot of emotion in his throat before he could answer. "Yeah," he said, his voice raw. "I do."

He loved everything about Tess. Her compassion for others. The way she always noticed when someone else needed something—and was prepared to help with that very thing. The way she always wore lipstick, even if she didn't have time to do her hair or the rest of her makeup. The same shade of peach lipstick. The little mole on her chin—her beauty mark. Her laughter. The way her hand fit perfectly in his. The way she could use the camera to capture the most ethereal, dazzling images. And so much more. He'd need a lifetime to learn all the lovable things about Tess. He wanted to have decades together to learn it all.

"Fine. I'll give you some information. Not a lot, but something."

"Thank you!" James said, now pacing the room with the energy of anticipation. "Anything. I'll guard the information with my life, and I won't hurt your sister. I swear it."

"Good thing," Hope said. "Or I'll have your head on a platter."

Four

arlier that evening, Tess had assumed she'd be up all night, but for an entirely different reason—that she'd be kept awake by excitement, rather than anger and a few cans of Red Bull as she drove. As the car hummed into the night, she remembered an odd dream from about a week before. In it, she was running toward the ocean, but it receded, farther and farther away from her, no matter how hard and fast she worked to reach it. On the horizon, James sat in a boat. Somehow she knew he was smiling as he was carried away by the current, but he urged her—quite merrily—to keep on running. Reaching James was crucial. Why, she didn't know, but it made sense in dream logic.

Only now, as Tess glanced at the half moon in her rear-view mirror, did she realize that in the dream, even though she had to reach him, James had never tried to reach her. Not once. He hadn't jumped out to swim to her. He hadn't so much as used the oars in the boat—there *were* oars; she remembered that now. Instead, she waded through waist-deep water, then shoulder-deep, then she was swimming with all her might, arms burning from the strain, and all the while, James called, "Keep going, sweetheart!"

That dream was essentially a snapshot of their relationship. Tess gripped the steering wheel; she would *not* live that way another day. If James didn't want to be tied down by a wife, fine. She wouldn't be the eagerly waiting girlfriend—always the girlfriend, always waiting.

I deserve more than that.

With Buckeye behind her, she felt her anxiety melting away. She kept the top of her convertible down—somehow driving that way felt freeing. The late-night radio was boring, playing what felt like the same five songs over and over again. Inspired by the radio earlier, she pulled out her iPhone and blared Journey's Greatest Hits. Hey, if one of their songs had cheered her up before, the whole album could certainly do the trick. She sang along, bopping her head up and down, enjoying the warm night air blowing her pony tail in the wind. The album ended sooner than she expected—had she really been driving almost an hour already since starting it? She let the play list go to whatever came next.

Familiar piano chords began from another play list— definitely *not* Journey. Still classic rock, but something else. Tess's hands stiffened their grip as an electric guitar joined the piano. Tess's breath hitched right as Peter Cetera's iconic voice broke over her. This was the song that played when James first kissed her: "You're the Inspiration." Slow danced and kissed as the French horns rose in a crescendo.

She'd never kiss him again.

She fumbled with her iPhone, yanking the plug out and cutting off the music. Her breath shuddered with relief when the noise screeched and then stopped, replaced with the slight buzz of the car's auxiliary jack. When she had herself under control enough to drive, she punched the FM button so the radio would replace the emotions bubbling up inside her.

Like the song said, she'd *thought* their love was meant to be—that it would be forever. They'd never be apart, and they'd never be able to go a day without thinking of each other. *She* never went a day without thinking of James— sending him a text, helping him with an errand, or, on some days, watching old episodes of Law & Order on his apartment couch. Not because she particularly liked the plot lines, but because the show was so *James.* He got all excited watching the courtroom scenes.

He probably doesn't think of me every day, she realized with dismay. *That is, unless it's in the sense of, "Oh, good. I can get her to take care of something for me."*

She'd gone to the grocery store for him. Dropped off dry cleaning. Picked up a prescription. Run to the post office. She glared at the gray band of freeway ahead. She might as well have been a servant instead of a girlfriend. Sure, he always said thank you. But did he mean it?

And why did I always say yes? Her brow furrowed as she considered the question. She popped open a Monster drink—the gas station had been out of Red Bull—took a swig, and focused again on the ribbon of road ahead of her. Did she say yes because she truly wanted to be kind and loving to James?

Or was it because I worried he wouldn't love me if I said no?

Her anger at him eased a bit as she pondered the question. If he'd found an easy way to get things done, could she blame him for using it? She was the one who hadn't said no when running an errand really was inconvenient. She was the one who jumped at the chance—encouraged him—to give her things to do.

I'm an under-appreciated doormat! Why hadn't she felt strong enough to say no sometimes?

In a moment of random insanity, she plugged the phone back in and started up the Chicago play list again. She listened—really listened—to the lyrics of "You're the Inspiration." As the song moved through her, she swallowed back tears, telling herself that she couldn't cry now, not yet, or she wouldn't be able to drive safely. The truth was, she didn't want to think about how much she loved James. Had always loved him. Still loved him.

I want to be his inspiration. I want him to want me to be with him. But was I ever more than his errand girl?

In spite of her efforts, tears streaked down her cheeks. Their relationship hadn't been always been so one-sided. He used to call her for no other reason but to say he was thinking about her. She used to find sweet notes he'd slipped into her purse. Texts saying nothing but "Love you." They used to talk about their future, like seeing the Grand Canyon, or traveling to Rome. Over the course of several months, they'd read *The Count of Monte Cristo* together—the unabridged version. Now she was lucky if he agreed to watch a DVD or go on a ten-minute walk. He was always in a hurry, trying to finish one thing or another. Finally, last night, he'd shown what really mattered to him.

And it wasn't me.

With one hand, she swiped at her right cheek and then the other. She pushed harder on the gas pedal.

Five

James could hardly believe where he was and what he was doing—racing across the desert in the middle of the night in hopes of catching Tess, or finding her . . . somehow.

He also couldn't believe that he'd called Preston, Carson, and McNeil. He'd left a voice message turning down the internship. It was official. He wouldn't be moving to New York after all. Which meant he needed to find a place to live ASAP. Even if Tess hated his guts and never wanted to see him again, he wouldn't be spending his summer in the Big Apple. He felt remarkably calm about the decision—and realized that he'd wanted it more because it was something his parents would have wanted, and he was used to thinking that their wishes were his.

He glanced at the clock, wondering how much of a lead Tess had on him. Hope had said that her sister was driving to their mother's place in Newport—and even provided an address, which he'd promptly added to his GPS. He shook his head and sighed. Good thing Hope had opened up at least that much; he hadn't known where their mother lived exactly. California, sure. And a beach rang a bell. Had Tess ever told him where her mother lived? Had he been distracted, thinking of something else, when she did? Or had she not told him, because she knew he wouldn't remember? Why had he never asked about her family? Did she have siblings besides Hope? He didn't even know that. What kind of moron of a boyfriend didn't know things like that?

Yet *she* knew all about him. She asked about his childhood, his school years, his favorite movies from junior high, his first crush. He'd loved how she wanted to know everything about him. *But I don't know half as much about her.*

He pressed harder on the accelerator, determined to find her and change things. Tess always obeyed the speed limit. Using that fact, he did math in his head, figuring out how soon he could overtake her if she kept the law, while he went twenty-five over. It could happen, but he'd gotten a late start. There was a good chance she was halfway to Newport already. What if he came upon her in the dark? Would he recognize her car in the dead of night? And if he did, then what? Would he wave at her, telling her to pull over so they could talk? Would she pull over?

His fist hit the steering wheel, hard. Why had he gotten himself into this mess?

Because I've been an immature idiot.

Again thoughts of Tess's quiet probing questions returned. She always managed to talk about him, learn about him, whether it was on a walk under the stars or over dinner at their favorite Italian restaurant. Why hadn't he asked the same questions in return? He couldn't say. Maybe he'd been so flattered, so thrilled to be in her spotlight, that reciprocating hadn't mattered.

It matters now.

The seatbelt dug into his shoulder, and the seat felt hard beneath him. James shifted his position, uncomfortable for more reasons than that. He was suddenly grateful he'd changed clothes. He looked a sight—jeans and a t-shirt with sneakers, a far cry from the top-of-the-line suit he'd worn a few hours earlier. He glanced in the rear-view mirror and grunted at the sight of his hair standing every which way. His usual attention to grooming now seemed about as important as the internship, meaning not at all. Tess loved him no matter what he looked like; he was sure of that. She'd love him in old sweats with the two-day scruff he grew on weekends.

That's just the way she was.

He passed a sign announcing an upcoming exit for Buckeye. Hope had told him to be sure to fill his car there, as there weren't too many gas stations beyond that for miles. Good thing—he wouldn't have thought to stop if she hadn't told him to. Truth be told, he didn't want to exit now, either—any delay would mean increasing the distance between him and Tess. But running out of gas meant not finding her at all.

His Mercedes rolled to a stop at the only gas station he found still open after midnight. After filling up, he went inside to use the restroom—a precaution against needing to make a second stop—and bought a few snacks and drinks to keep his energy up for the drive.

The cashier rang up James's items and made small talk. "Don't see too many people in these parts at this hour."

"No, I suppose you wouldn't," James said, getting his debit card out. As he slipped the card from his wallet, his head came up. If Hope recommended that he stop here because she and Tess often did . . . "This may sound crazy," he began. "But by any chance, did a young woman come through here earlier tonight?" He held his hand shoulder high. "About this tall, light brown hair."

"Pretty as a peach?" the man said. "I seen a gal about like that not two hours ago. But then, that description could be a lot of women."

The cashier was right. James nodded, now searching the pictures on his phone until he found a good one of Tess, one taken at another friend's wedding. A new thought intruded on his mind: How many weddings had they attended together, and how many had been daggers to Tess's heart? Shaking off the thought, he showed the picture to the man.

"Yep. She's the one. Came through an hour and a half, two hours ago. Got some gas and food, just like you."

Tess was *two hours* ahead of him? James's stomach twisted a bit; what were the chances of him making up that kind of time? Assuming it was really Tess that the man had seen.

"Pretty Mustang she got," the man continued. "Powerful engine. But good luck catching up to her." The man chuckled, making his middle jiggle.

So it was Tess then. "Thanks," James said as he tucked his phone back into his pocket. He swiped his card, gathered his purchases, and pushed the convenience store door open, heading for his car with a determined stride.

Two hours ago, Tess had been here. Or less time than that, maybe.

I'll catch up to her yet.

Six

Tess pulled into her mother's driveway on Irvine Avenue as the velvety dark of night gave way to purple gray. The black sky was gradually surrendering to morning, but the sun had yet to make its appearance. Tess glanced at the car's clock, surprised she'd made the drive in just over five hours.

No way can I wake up Mom yet. Tess could only imagine the heart attack she'd give her mother if she tried ringing the doorbell at this hour; she'd answer the door in a frenzy, panicked that cops would be on the stoop, waiting to give her horrible news. Ever since Tess's father died, her mother had been on the overly protective side.

Tess had a key, but she didn't dare use that, either—her mother might think she was an intruder and come into the kitchen with the pepper spray from her purse. That would be quite the welcome. No, waiting for an hour—or two—would probably be wise. Tess put her car into reverse and back out of the driveway then headed for the nearby peninsula and the piers along it. This early, the businesses near the beach wouldn't be open. She'd be able to meander along the boardwalk and think. Ponder what came next in her life.

The drive took her only a few minutes, and she found a parking spot easily; the beach was deserted except for a middle-aged woman walking a dog. Tess snagged her old college sweatshirt from the back seat, locked the car, and headed for Newport Pier. As she crossed the sand, she suddenly hated how little she moved forward with each step—the sand seemed to suck up her energy and drag her back. The adrenaline that had carried her all night was gone, leaving exhaustion in its place. She'd never noticed or cared about that part of walking in sand before, but after last night, even the beach had become a hideous metaphor for her relationship with James: movement without progress.

She finally reached the pier, where she closed her eyes, hugging herself, as she breathed in the salty air. *A new day, a new life,* she told herself as she stepped onto the boardwalk. Soon she'd watch the sun come up behind her, making the sea sparkle like diamonds.

She made her way halfway down the boardwalk, about a hundred feet, then leaned against the rail and gazed out over the ocean as the light turned more gray than purple at morning's promised arrival. Usually the pier calmed her, focused her thoughts. It was her personal yoga whenever she visited her mother. Not today. Not when thoughts of James plagued her. She tried to get rid of them by closing her eyes and breathing deeply, but his face, his smile, his touch, were there.

Tess sighed, turned to rest her back against the railing, and pulled out her phone, something that was almost a reflex. She almost didn't turn it on. She'd kept it on Do Not Disturb mode—after removing James from her Favorites list—so only important calls would sound. But she'd see any missed calls and texts now. Her finger hovered over the button as she tried to get the courage to check. Had James called? Texted? And if not, should she care?

"Enough!" she said, chastising herself. No more of letting James's behavior—or lack thereof—influence her actions. She clicked the button, and the screen lit up. She swiped her finger and entered her passcode. With a gulp, she looked down. Ten missed calls. Two voice messages. Seven texts.

Her thumb hovered over the text message icon for just a second before tapping it—just to see if they were all from James. They were. She checked the phone log too. All the missed calls and both messages were from James's number. Good. Let him suffer.

Why am I still caring about what he does? Stop it! She clicked her phone off and tucked it into her back jeans pocket, gritting her teeth. Again she leaned against the rail, staring over the water, willing the sun to come up and start her new life. She'd freelance from Newport, living in her mother's guest room until she was on her feet and could afford her own place—one that, granted, wouldn't be in such an expensive neighborhood. But it would be away from James in Tempe.

Except that he'd be in New York.

Fine. Away from memories of James in Tempe.

In spite of herself, tears welled in her eyes and ran down her cheeks. At the sound of footsteps on the wooden boardwalk, Tess swiped her face dry with both hands, not wanting some stranger to see her crying. It was probably someone who worked at the restaurant at the end of the pier, heading over to get the place ready to open for the day.

"Tess?"

James? James!

Her heart beat furiously, and she whipped around in shock. With the first rays of dawn slipping over the horizon behind him, Tess couldn't make out his face at first. But when he saw her turn around, he began running toward her. Adrenaline shot through her. Did she want to see him? Should she send him away? Was her heart hammering with anger or hope?

An image of the party last night flashed into her mind again. That decided it. She folded her arms and glared at him. He was wearing the t-shirt that showed off his defined chest, the one she'd nearly drooled over the first time he'd worn it. Glaring at him suddenly became a challenge. *Focus, Tess!* She hardened her face.

James must have seen her face, because he slowed then stopped several feet from her. Her heart ached—for only a moment—that he hadn't scooped her into his arms and kissed her. That she hadn't been able to feel his chest beneath her hands, thread her fingers through his hair as she kissed him back . . .

Focus! she ordered herself. *First things first.* "Why are you . . . I mean, you're here. How did you find me?"

James took a step forward, but at her raised eyebrow, he halted and put up both hands as if to show he meant no harm. "I *had* to find you. When you weren't home—"

"You went to my apartment?" Why that surprised her, she didn't know.

"What else was I supposed to do when you wouldn't answer your phone or reply to my texts?"

Maybe he did care. The safe shell she'd constructed around her heart softened a tad. But only a tad. She wouldn't be sucked into his world of girlfriend limbo again.

"I was so worried that something had happened to you, that maybe you'd been in an accident or something."

"Wait. You came looking for me to be sure I was *safe*? Because if I wasn't, oh, *dead,* of *course* I'd answer your every beck and call?" The shell hardened. "What about—about—" She couldn't get the words out. *What about humiliating me?*

What about leading me on? What about discarding me after I gave you my heart?

"Hope told me you'd gone to visit your mother."

Tess's arms were still folded, but as much to hold herself together as to pretend she was strong. Because she wasn't strong, not even almost. James could crook his finger, and it would be all she could do not to melt into his arms. But she couldn't do that. Wouldn't.

He'd known she was safe—on her way to California. So why follow?

"How did you find me? I never gave you my mother's address." She sighed. "Hope, right?"

He nodded. "I sort of managed to get her to tell me."

"I can't believe her."

James continued, speaking over Tess. "And when your car wasn't at your mom's, I called Hope to ask where else to look. She told me to drive down here, and I found your car. Wasn't hard to recognize."

Emotions clashed inside Tess. Her thoughts were little more than a tangled jumble. She clung to one clear thought. "Hope helped you—twice? She *swore* she wouldn't say a word to you, because—because—"

He raised his gaze to hers again. "Because I'm a fence-sitting jerk." He said it so matter-of-factly that it sent a stab into Tess's heart.

"Yeah." The single word came out in a whisper of surprise. Her brow furrowed. Needle pricks at the corners of her eyes threatened more tears. None of this made sense. Why was James here? What was last night about? What should she do? "I-I don't understand."

"But *I* finally do." This time when he stepped closer, she didn't protest. He hesitantly reached for her left hand, and then her right. Tess let him hold the fingers of both hands— just her fingers. Her eyes were locked on their hands—they fit together like puzzle pieces.

She shook her head and swallowed, but as she opened her mouth to protest, James spoke first. "You were right to leave. I have been a total jerk. I've taken you for granted. I made promises I didn't keep. I haven't respected you for the smart, funny, hard-working . . . *hot* woman you are."

Tess couldn't help but smile a bit at that.

He squeezed her fingers. "And then, when you left last night, my world fell apart. I finally realized that if you aren't in my life, nothing else matters."

The shell around her heart was cracking, and a glimmer of light peeked through. She studied his eyes. He seemed to be studying hers. His were bloodshot, and—was she imagining those tears at the corners?

"I'd give up everything for you," he said. "My parents can go hang if they don't approve. I want to be with you, always." He closed the distance and pulled her close. "Oh, Tess. I wish I could show you how much I love you." He rested his head against hers.

She nestled into his embrace, inhaling his musky cologne, but she didn't quite dare to relax. Instead, she pressed her hands against his chest—oh, that chest—braced to push him away. For good, if she needed to.

"What's the point? You're going to New York, and you'll be too busy for me . . . again." She gazed at the faded maroon markings on his shirt, waiting for his answer.

James reached down and lifted her chin so their gazes met. At the expression in his eyes, goose bumps shot down her arms, and her middle erupted as if a cluster of butterflies were trying to escape. "I gave up the internship."

"But that was your dream . . ." How could he turn it down, especially after he'd told his family and friends all about it? Unless . . .

"I don't care about some snooty internship," James said with a shake of his head. "Not if it means losing you. I'll sell used cars if I have to. But I won't be apart from you for another day, not if I can help it." He stared at her for a long moment then slowly lowered to one knee. "Marry me, Tess," he whispered.

She couldn't answer for several seconds; her mind spun with everything he'd said—it was like everything had rewound. This was the moment she'd imagined for so long, but it was nothing like she'd pictured it.

When she didn't speak, color drained from James's face. He stood again, holding her hand to his chest, pain in his eyes. Tess could feel his heart speeding up.

"Please," he whispered. "Tell me I'm not too late."

Emotions coursed through Tess, making her tears finally fall. "No," she finally said.

His voice hitched as he said. "No? I—Tess, please."

Tess laughed, sending happy tears down her cheeks as her exhaustion and emotions got the better of her. "I meant *no*, you're not too late."

James's entire body shuddered with a sigh of relief. He pulled her close and held her as if he'd never let her go. When he finally pulled back, he leaned in and kissed her long and hard. She'd missed his kiss all night, but this was no ordinary kiss. It was enough to make her toes curl in her shoes. She came away lightheaded.

"So what time do you think we can find a jeweler open?" James asked, stroking the bare finger her left hand. "We need to put ring on that *today*."

"After we tell my mom, and she feeds us breakfast," Tess said, slipping her arm around his waist as he rested his arm on her shoulders. They walked back toward the beach together, Tess resting her head on his shoulder.

"I don't suppose that when we tell your mom, we could leave out the part about me driving after you all night because I was a total idiot?"

"I think we could manage that," Tess said. She stopped at the edge of the boardwalk, and James took her cue and paused in his step too.

"Something wrong?" he asked hesitantly.

"No," Tess said. She nodded forward, where dawn was breaking. "It's a new day." She went on tiptoe and kissed his cheek—deliciously rough with a hint of stubble. "A new day for us."

About Annette Lyon

   Annette Lyon is a Whitney Award winner, a two-time recipient of Utah's Best in State medal for fiction, plus the author of ten novels, a cookbook, and a grammar guide as well as over a hundred magazine articles. She's a senior editor at Precision Editing Group and a cum laude graduate from BYU with a degree in English. When she's not writing, editing, knitting, or eating chocolate, she can be found mothering and avoiding the spots on the kitchen floor. Find her online:

   Website: http://annettelyon.com
   Blog: http://blog.annettelyon.com
   Twitter: @AnnetteLyon

Dancing at the Flea Market

Heather Justesen

Other Works by Heather Justesen

The Ball's in Her Court

Rebound

Family by Design

Shear Luck

Blank Slate

The Switch

Brownies & Betrayal

Homecoming

Homecoming: Second Chances

One

It had already been an insanely long day when Mara's plane finally touched down in Corpus Christi, Texas. She threaded through the crowd and found the luggage conveyor for her flight, where she waited for her suitcase, exhaustion pulling at her as much as her heavy carry-on did. Her meager sleep the previous night and short nap on the flight from North Dakota hadn't been nearly enough.

She shifted her carry-on farther up her shoulder, holding her heavy winter parka on the other arm then pushed her long brown hair out of the way. Bags kept flowing from the machine and whirling past her. They stopped coming, but hers hadn't appeared, and all of the other passengers had cleared off. Mara was alone. She checked the sign again. Yes, this was the right spot. Her heart beat a little too fast; a sinking feeling said her bag hadn't made one of the transfers during her two layovers.

She was still standing there with the vague hope that a miracle would happen, and her suitcase would magically appear, when she heard a shrill voice calling her name.

"Mara!"

She turned and saw Anna, her old college roommate, running toward her, wearing too-high heels, a short skirt, and a sleeveless top, her blonde curls bouncing as she ran. Mara wondered how Anna could be so energized after her long flight from Vegas.

Mara met her partway and moved her coat to her other arm. They hugged tightly. "It's so good to see you!"

"I know. I can't believe I finally convinced you to leave the snow for a few days for some sun." Anna adjusted her carry-on over her own shoulder; it was only big enough to hold her makeup, and maybe a swimming suit. "Where is your other suitcase? Didn't your plane arrive like half an hour before mine? I haven't picked up my bag yet."

Mara glanced back in time to see a whole new load of luggage start to shoot onto the conveyor. "Looks like mine got lost somewhere en route."

Anna's pink-lip-sticked mouth fell open. "Oh, no. Please tell me you packed a swimsuit and change of clothes in your carry-on. I mean, your bag will probably come in tonight or tomorrow, but you have to have something to wear to dinner and at the beach. We're on vacation, and it's spring break, baby."

"We're way too old for the spring-break crowd," Mara said, thinking that at twenty-six, she would feel like a cougar even looking at college guys. "But I did pack a change of clothes in my carry-on."

"Oh, good." Anna snagged Mara's arm. "Come on. Let's grab my stuff, and then we can go talk to someone about your luggage."

By the time they made arrangements for her lost suitcase and picked up their rental car, it was after three.

Anna turned the car west, heading for the mainland and the condo complex where they would be staying, talking almost as fast as she drove. "We have to do some shopping tomorrow; I hear there are great boutiques nearby. Oh, and I can't wait to show you the great swimming suit I bought for the trip." She stopped to suck in a breath. "Look at all of these gorgeous beaches."

"Beautiful," Mara agreed.

"Remind me again why we're staying at an inland lake instead of at a hotel out here?" Anna adjusted her sunglasses.

"Noisy, obnoxious college students with spring-break fever."

"And they're a bad thing because . . ."

Mara poked her friend, knowing she was only half joking; Anna would be eternally twenty-two. Mara sat back, getting into the vacation mindset—it had been too long since she put real life aside and let herself go with the flow. That was one of the reasons she'd agreed when Anna bullied her about this trip—Anna was totally fun and spontaneous and would insist Mara get involved instead of allowing life to pass her by while they vacationed.

They arrived and checked in at the condo complex a little before dinner. The building was tan stucco, and looked like it had recently had a facelift.

"This is what I'm talking about." Anna lowered her sunglasses to peer over the top at some half-clad college men who were striding up the boardwalk from the shore.

"Come on." Mara grabbed the enormous suitcase Anna had shoved into the trunk and staggered under the weight before setting it on the ground beside her. "What do you have in this thing, rocks?" She didn't bother to wait for an answer as she rolled the suitcase away from the car. "Let's go get changed and grab some dinner. After being on the go all day, I need decent food and a relaxing evening to recuperate for the lake tomorrow."

"Agreed."

They reached the stairs to the second floor, where Mara pulled the bag up behind her. The stairwell was narrow and steeper than she'd expected. "I wonder how many people have nearly killed themselves on this thing."

"Well, hello there." Anna's voice was soft and teasing—and definitely not directed at Mara.

Mara looked up to see a man standing at the top, waiting for her to finish making the trek to the second floor. The downward curve of his lips indicated impatience, marring what would otherwise have been a nearly perfect face. His hair was dark, almost black, and cut short. Startlingly pale blue eyes were highlighted by thick brows and a face that was all planes and angles. She had to catch her breath just looking at him.

"Do you need some help with that?" he asked, looking a little annoyed. "I'd rather not stand here all day."

"What?" Mara realized she'd been staring, so she turned her attention back to the suitcase.

"Sorry." Heat flooded her face as she began pulling the suitcase again. Way to make an idiot of herself.

There was a grunt, and the man appeared at her side and placed his hand over hers on the strap. "Let me get that." His voice was more than a little grudging. "I really do have somewhere to be. Second floor or third?"

"Second." Mara knew she must sound like the biggest moron ever.

He lifted the bag easily, his arm muscles bulging beneath the short sleeves of his shirt while he carried it to the top.

Though Mara had been the one towing it, Anna was the one who responded. "Thanks for your help." She fluttered her eyelashes a little, and her voice went breathy.

"No problem. Have a good day." His tone didn't match the words. He took off for the parking lot without giving

Anna's flirting so much as a second glance—an amazing accomplishment.

Mara watched him for a moment as he walked away—all graceful ease as he strode off. She pulled herself out of her trance when Anna started to titter. "He's hot, isn't he? And definitely *not* a college man."

She agreed, putting his age around thirty. "Annoying that he was so abrupt. But at least he was nice enough to help with your enormous suitcase. How much extra did you have to pay to get this on the plane, anyway?"

"Don't ask." Anna minced her way to the door and slid the keycard in the slot, letting them into the condo. It was small: a kitchen/living room area, a medium-sized bedroom with two double beds, and a bathroom. They had a tiny walk-out balcony on the far side, facing the lake.

Mara walked through to the sliding glass door and stepped out to check the view. "Come take a look; it's gorgeous." She sometimes joked that the winters in North Dakota were the best nine months of the year, but she could have sworn it had been longer than that since she last saw anything green that wasn't a house plant.

The grasses and trees around the lake filled her soul with joy. This trip would be everything she'd hoped for—when she finally got her luggage.

"Nice," Anna said flatly, apparently unimpressed. "Come on, let's get cleaned up and grab something to eat. I looked up some restaurants before we came."

Mara took one last glance at the water then went back inside. She was starting to get her second wind. Her stomach growled, making her agree that dinner took first priority. Plenty of time to soak in the beautiful weather tomorrow.

⸙

Carter checked his watch, wondering if Paolo, his former father-in-law, was already waiting for him at the restaurant. It had been two years since Rosa's death, but Carter still tried to keep in touch with her family, if only to help keep her memory alive. He'd lost track of time while swimming in the lake earlier, and he'd been waylaid by his boss's executive secretary, who was having trouble with her computer and didn't trust anyone else to fix it. The fact that he'd been on vacation hadn't mattered to her. Then those slow-poke women had put him even further behind schedule. He hated being late for anything.

He pulled up to the restaurant and nearly groaned when he saw the sign that read "Karaoke Every Night." Just what he needed—people singing off-key while he ate. It was bad enough that he had to face the emotional meeting with Paolo without having his ears assaulted. He wondered if his father-in-law had eaten here, or if he'd chosen it from the local chamber of commerce site.

Paolo and his wife lived in Florida, but when he'd mentioned that he was making a business trip to one of Carter's favorite places, Carter decided a vacation was overdue and arranged to be here at the same time.

Carter found Paolo at a table near the stage. "How are you doing?"

He stood and gave Carter a hug. "I'm well. You're looking well. That college job must be agreeing with you."

Carter was head of IT at University of North Texas, and it kept him busy, but he enjoyed the work. "Can't complain," he said with a smile. "How are things for you? What are you doing now?"

Paolo started talking about his new business selling nutritional supplements and the magical, life-altering powers they had. He always seemed to be looking for the next best thing to support him and his wife. Somehow he'd managed to keep food on the table when he was raising Rosa and her two brothers.

They ordered dinner, and more people filled the tables around them. By the time the waiter brought out their food and the emcee announced the beginning of the karaoke for the night, the place was packed.

Carter focused on his roast beef sandwich and his companion, trying to ignore the screeching, off-key singers behind him.

"Are you dating yet?" Paolo asked after he'd had a few bites. They'd been putting off that topic since they sat down.

"Not much." That was an understatement. He'd had a few dates here and there, but Carter always felt guilty about spending time on a woman, as if he were cheating on his wife. Besides, no woman he'd ever met could hold a candle to Rosa.

"You need to start dating again," Paolo said. "It's been too long. Rosa wouldn't want you to be alone forever."

Carter dragged a French fry through his ketchup. "I haven't met anyone who could hold my interest."

"You mean you won't get to know anyone, because you're afraid of getting hurt again."

Carter opened his mouth to protest, but Paolo held up a hand. "Don't make excuses. I can only imagine how hard it must be to lose someone you love, but you're still young. I want you to promise me that next time you see someone who intrigues you, even a little, you'll take a chance and get to know her."

Carter wanted to argue, but Paolo was right—he did need to get out and start dating for real. He was lonely, and a little companionship—even if he wasn't ready yet for anything serious—would be a welcome change. "Okay. I promise."

Two

ara felt the familiar rush of excitement when they pulled into the restaurant parking lot after she saw the sign announcing karaoke. "Did you pick this place because of that?" she asked Anna, pointing to the sign.

"Yes. You need to use that talent, girl. You're languishing working on payroll for a furniture factory. I keep telling you to move to Vegas where you can get a job singing, but do you listen? No."

Mara had no desire to live in Vegas, but she felt an enticing tingle at the thought of being on stage again—even if it was at a second-rate karaoke bar. "I could sing a song, I guess."

They were ushered to one of the last open tables and quickly placed their orders. Anna asked the server when the karaoke was supposed to start and grinned when they were told that signups would begin in a few minutes.

Mara felt her cell phone buzzing in her pocket and pulled it out to see she'd missed a call earlier and now had a text message from her younger sister, Jo.

Where is the heating pad for Dad's back? Did you make it safe? Haven't heard from you.

Mara wrote back, mentioning that they were out to eat and couldn't hear the phone ring over the music.

"Your dad?" Anna guessed.

Mara snorted. "Are you kidding? Dad doesn't know how to text. It was Jo, She's taking care of him while I'm out of town." Though she lived with her father to help him recuperate after his stroke, her sister took Dad duty whenever Mara needed time away.

"How's he doing now?"

"A lot better, actually. Not independent, but he doesn't need someone to watch him every minute anymore." She didn't know if she'd ever be able to move out, though. What if he had another stroke, and no one was there to find him in time? Mara's mother had passed away years earlier; she didn't think she could stand to lose her father, too.

"Then you can start living your own life again," Anna said. "Go back to school and get a job you like better."

"I'll think about it," Mara said, though she didn't know if she would. A couple of years earlier, she'd had an interview set up for another job, but her father had his stroke a few days before. That had been the end of her grand plans to make a life of her own choosing.

The announcement came for karaoke signups. Anna nudged Mara's shoulder. "Go. You know you want to."

Trepidation trickled into Mara as she stood, but she wasn't about to back down from a chance to perform.

❦

Carter was nearly finished eating and was thinking about returning to his condo to sack out for the evening. It was great to see Paolo again, but hard, too. A warbling teenager finished singing the latest Taylor Swift song. He barely glanced up when a woman took the stage and the emcee announced that the next singer was named Mara and would be singing "Someone like You."

A mature voice with the richness of Swiss chocolate filled the room. He looked up at the singer, his hand paused in midair, holding his last French fry, and recognized the brunette he'd met on the stairs at the condos, though in his irritation, he'd barely looked at her before.

He stared at her, totally taken in by her voice. What was she doing singing karaoke when she could be singing for pay on a stage anywhere? The noisy restaurant quieted as everyone turned to listen. He nearly forgot where he was. She mesmerized him with her long, brown hair, oval face, and thick eyelashes. Every emotion in the song showed on her face, and came out through her voice.

The final notes floated over the almost-silent audience, and two beats passed in near reverence before the room exploded with applause and whistles.

A smile of exultation covered her face as she waved to the crowd, passing the mic to the next person in line.

When the whistling went on for a long moment, the emcee stood and addressed the crowd. "Do you all want to hear Mara sing again?"

The noise level rose in confirmation, so the emcee looked at Mara, who had stopped at the edge of the stage. "Would you do one more in a while?"

She paused for just a second then nodded.

"All right, everyone stay tuned. Get another round of drinks and order dessert. She'll be back." He announced the next singer and started the music.

Carter sat back in his chair, stunned.

"She was terrific, wasn't she?" Paolo said.

"Yes, she was." Carter glanced at her table, where she sat with the blonde. Their heads were bent together. He really hoped to get another chance to talk with her.

Several songs later, when she stood and headed back to the emcee, Carter decided not to leave yet. He'd wait until she'd sung a second time before he returned to the condos.

Three

Carter was up early the next morning. He went for a run before breakfast then headed for the lake for a swim. It was a couple of hours before he saw Mara and her friend running through the shallows, splashing each other and having fun. He didn't approach right away, not wanting to come across stalkerish, but waited until she headed back to the beach to stretch out on her towel for some sun.

He walked over and asked, "Are you having a good time? Didn't I see you singing last night at that karaoke place?"

Mara lifted a hand to shield her eyes from the sun and squinted up at him. A look of recognition came over her face. She sat up. "You were there?"

"I was really impressed. You have an amazing voice." He glanced at the empty sand beside her. "Mind if I join you?"

"Go ahead."

The blonde friend tipped her sunglasses down her nose and peered at him. "Aren't you the one who helped us with my suitcase yesterday?"

"Was that your suitcase?" He looked back at Mara. "So where was yours?"

"Lost somewhere by the airline. I have to go pick them up later today unless I want to wait for delivery tomorrow."

"That's a pain. I've had that happen before," he said. "By the way, I'm Carter. I don't think we exchanged names yesterday. I was in a bit of a hurry, and inexcusably rude. I wanted to apologize about that." He was embarrassed when he looked back on the conversation.

"I'm Mara, and this is Anna." She gestured to the blonde.

"Where are you two from?" Carter leaned back on his hands.

"I'm from North Dakota," Mara said. "She's from Vegas. We roomed together in college."

"Sounds like fun. I bet this is a nice change of scene for you." He looked at Mara, admiring the light sprinkle of freckles across her nose.

"It's nice to see something besides mounds of snow for a change."

"How about you?" Anna asked, a smile teasing her lips. "Where are you from?"

"Fort Worth." They spoke for several minutes—long enough that the water droplets had evaporated from Mara's pale shoulders. Anna caught the eye of a guy who looked young enough to still be in college and started chatting him up.

Paolo's words rang through Carter's head again. Mara wasn't from Texas, and he wasn't about to move to North Dakota, so there was no reason they couldn't get to know each other. He needed to start somewhere with this dating thing. "Would you like to grab some lunch? The burger stand isn't exactly high class, but . . ." He was so bad at this. Had dating changed much in the past five years?

"Yeah," Mara said. "I'd like that."

❦

Mara was surprised when Carter came over to join them, and even more surprised when he asked her out. Contrary to her first impression of him, he'd been nothing but pleasant. Lunch might be a good chance to find out what he was really like. She grabbed a t-shirt to slide over her swimsuit and put on her flip flops.

"I bet those haven't been worn much," he said, indicating her footwear. "Not a lot of sunny beaches in North Dakota at this time of year."

"No, they aren't very practical in snow. Does it get cold where you live?"

"A bit in the winter and at night. But not by your standards, I'm sure. Have you ever thought of living somewhere with a warmer climate?" A Frisbee landed at his feet and he picked it up, winging it back to a group of kids farther up the beach. "Or did you choose North Dakota for its lovely weather?"

"I never *chose* Bismark. I grew up there and moved back after college while I put in applications for jobs. Somehow I ended up staying." She shrugged, not regretting being around for her father, but longing for the opportunities she had given up.

"Where do you work?" Carter asked.

"I do payroll for a furniture manufacturer. It's pure excitement all the time." She half-heartedly twirled one finger in the air. How about you?"

"I'm the IT manager at a community college. It keeps me busy."

"Who keeps you hopping: students who like to do things they shouldn't, or inept professors?"

His smile totally transformed his face, adding a dimple in his chin. That was far sexier than it should have been. "A bit of both. Mostly it's routine issues and lots of software updates."

"My whole job is routine." She looked around at the lake and trees and took in a deep breath of appreciation. "This is a nice change of pace."

They arrived at the window and ordered. A couple of minutes later, they took their drinks to a nearby table while they waited for their food.

"So did you always want to work in payroll?" he teased.

"I have an accounting degree, but I didn't go back for my master's like I'd planned, so I took what I could get. I can't complain—it's a nice, regular paycheck with benefits."

"But you don't love it." He studied her for a few seconds. "What would you do if you could have any career you want? Sing?"

She felt her face flush. "No, I love music, but it's my second love, after accounting."

"That's a shame. You're really good." He leaned forward on the table, bumping his drink. They both jumped to grab it. It knocked against her hand, splashing a little on her before his fingers wrapped around the cup, overlapping her fingers. Mara sucked in a breath of surprise, and their eyes met. He pulled back, looking away. "Sorry."

"No problem." She set the cup flat again, then dabbed at her hand with the napkins he passed to her. Her heart pounded, and she found she was a little out of breath. *It is just the adrenaline from the surprise,* she told herself, but she knew it was his touch.

"Math, huh?" His voice was a little desperate as he returned to the previous subject. "I'm good enough at it, but I don't see the appeal."

She shivered a little with awareness but followed his lead and focused back on the conversation. "I like puzzles. Math and accounting are puzzles. You have to figure out how to put it all together, and when the pieces fit, it makes a nice picture. If you're lucky. I always meant to go back to school for my master's."

"Maybe it's time to give that some more thought."

Mara nodded. "I will."

The conversation moved on to talk about movies and their mutual love of football. Though he didn't touch her again, the imprint of his fingers lingered on her skin. When the food was long gone, Mara noticed the time. "I probably ought to head to the airport for my things."

"Right." He stood, collected their garbage, and threw it out. When he returned and faced her, he hesitated for a moment. "Come on."

She returned to where Anna sat with the college guy. Anna grinned at them. "I'm going out with Tom on his boat. The keys to the car are on the kitchen counter."

Mara froze. She hadn't been paying attention when they had driven from the airport. "I have no idea how to get back to the airport."

Anna sent Carter a knowing look. "I bet you could find someone to go along with you as your navigator."

"I'd be happy to go with you," he said almost before Anna finished speaking.

"But that would take a couple of hours of your day. I don't want to keep you away from your plans."

Except she didn't want to say goodbye, and she really hoped to spend more time with him.

"I'd like to go with you, if you don't mind the company." His hand brushed against her arm.

Mara felt her breath back up in her chest. Her tongue tripped over itself, but she managed to nod then make her mouth work again. "I'd like that."

They picked up their things and headed to their condos to clean up and change. While Mara took a quick shower, she considered his offer, her feelings, and what they might mean. It had been a very long time since she'd been involved with someone who set her off-balance like this.

When she came out of the condo, Carter waited on the walkway by her door, wearing blue jeans and another muscle-defining t-shirt. "You were pretty quick," he said. "I expected you to take longer."

She glanced at her watch. "I thought we said twenty minutes."

"We did, but most women don't watch the clock that closely when they're getting ready. At least, in my experience."

"I guess I'm not your average woman." She hooked her purse over her shoulder and wrapped her hand tighter around the keys to the rental car then turned toward the parking lot. "I wish we'd rented a convertible. It's too beautiful to be cooped up in a car."

"Yeah. It's just about perfect. Maybe later today we could rent a paddleboat and go to the east end of the lake."

He was already making plans for later that day? She didn't respond for several seconds. "I . . . look, I'm having a really great time with you. Really great." She stopped and turned to face him, waiting until he met her gaze before continuing. "I'd like to see more of you, but I'm not really sure what to do about this. It's just a weekend, and then we both go back to our real lives, right?" She wasn't sure which answer she wanted to hear.

Carter picked up her hand, turning it over and running his finger down her palm, making goose bumps rise on her arm. "I know. Maybe that's why this seems so easy. No expectations. I admit I'm a little rusty at this dating thing, and maybe I needed to meet you to break out of whatever it is that's been holding me back. All I know is that I'm having a lot of fun, and if you're having fun too, I'd like to spend more time with you."

"Same here." *Lots of time*, she thought. Reassured that they were at least on the same page, she smiled. "I guess we should get going."

Carter gave her fingers a little squeeze, and she led him over to the car.

He directed her to the main road before she dared bring up the question that had been lingering in the back of her mind. "Why are you rusty at dating?"

"What?" He seemed to be taken off guard by the question.

"You said you were 'a little rusty with the whole dating thing.'" She glanced at him quickly, then back at the road. "Why haven't you been dating?"

She kept her focus on the road, though she really wanted to watch his face as he responded. Her head had been filled with reasons why he had been out of the dating pool: a longtime girlfriend, a stop in a mental hospital, a major illness? Though that one seemed unlikely, considering the shape he was in.

It took him a moment to respond. "My wife died a couple of years ago."

"Oh." She didn't know what else to say. He was a widower. That brought up a whole new set of concerns she'd never considered. Was he over his late wife? "I'm sorry for your loss." The words felt hollow.

"Thanks. It's been a rough couple of years, but it's getting easier." There was another long moment of silence. "How about you? Seeing anyone back home?"

"No." She tried to process what he'd said and come up with a response at the same time. "I've been busy with work and my family. Haven't had a lot of time to meet new people."

"Tell me about your family."

How much detail should she go into? Was there a reason to hold back if she wasn't going to see him again? "My mom died a few weeks before I finished college. I came home for the summer to help Dad adjust, but then I got this job, and I've been there ever since . . ." She told him about her father's stroke and how it had changed her life. Then again, while things seemed to be easy for Anna in the romance department, Mara always had a harder time.

"How's your dad doing now? Does he still need a lot of care?" Carter asked.

"He's doing better. My sister Jo is taking care of him while I'm gone."

"That's good. Family is important." He stared out the windshield. "I was at the karaoke bar with my father-in-law last night."

"You keep in touch?" Mara was impressed by that, and maybe a little intimidated. Maybe that was a sign that he was still grieving his wife. Or was it just sweet?

"I keep in touch. Not like I ought to, maybe, but we catch dinner when we have the chance and, and we email." He fidgeted in his seat. "I can't imagine losing touch with him."

"Tell me how you met your wife," Mara said, wanting to see inside his personality.

He complied, talking about how he and Rosa met in college and fell for each other instantly. They dated for six months before he popped the question and were married a few months later.

In return, Mara told him about some of the terrible dates she'd been on—having nothing comparable to discuss.

Before she knew it, they were pulling into the airport. Time had never flown by so fast, nor had it been so enjoyable. When Carter mentioned a restaurant he'd like to take her to that evening, she felt a tingle of warmth in her chest, knowing that he wasn't in a hurry to part ways either.

Four

The next night, Carter took Mara out for Mexican food and salsa dancing. He taught her the steps at the edge of the floor so they wouldn't get trampled.

"I can't get it," she said with a laugh when she lost the rhythm for the third time.

"You can do it. It takes a little time to get the steps right." He loved that she was willing to try something new and was having fun, even if she was messing up.

"Step forward with the left, then lift your right foot and put it back. Good. Now return to center." He showed her, taking her hands in his to walk her through it.

They went slow at first, and then he sped up when she caught on, going through the motions. "Great, now try to act like you're having fun. Put your hips into it a little."

She did and a smile slid onto her face as she grew more confident. "This is fun!"

"I told you it would be."

They danced for nearly an hour then ordered fried ice cream for dessert. He enjoyed listening to her talk about her family and home. She had the kind of love that showed through her soul. He respected the way she'd put her dreams on hold to take care of her father.

The weather was perfect when he walked her back to the condo. The moon was nearly full, making it easy to see the ripples on the lake even in the darkness.

"I had fun today," she said when they were only a couple of doors away from hers.

"I haven't had that much fun in a long time." He gave her hand a squeeze, happy they had spent the day together, and surprised that he could feel so at ease with someone who wasn't Rosa. "I think this is my best vacation ever."

"It ranks pretty high for me, too," she said.

"Glad to hear it." He came to a stop in front of her door. "Thanks for joining me." Her hair shone in the lamplight. Her lashes fluttered against her cheeks when she closed them for a moment then opened them with an expression of pleased embarrassment. His gaze drifted to her lips.

She rubbed them together, as if she felt his gaze. "I never knew salsa dancing could be so much fun."

"Now you know." He stepped closer, unable to draw his attention from her face. They'd spent two full days together. It couldn't possibly be too soon to kiss her, could it? The light scent of gardenias drifted on the breeze as she lifted her face to his.

Then the image of Rosa came into his head. Rosa had always worn gardenia perfume.

Guilt shot through him. How could he even be *thinking* about kissing someone else? He pulled back abruptly. "Yeah, well, it's getting late. Meet you for breakfast tomorrow?"

Disappointment flickered in her eyes. Mara nodded. "Say about nine?"

"Perfect. I'll pick you up." He stepped back even more, his heart racing, his palms sweating, and guilt zipping through his system. "Goodnight."

"Goodnight, Carter."

He nodded and turned away, confusion twisting through him. This was supposed to be a chance for him to get used to dating again, but it was starting to feel like much more.

He hoped sleep would help sort it all out by morning.

❧

"Will we be able to move the boat without hitting a duck?" Mara asked as she stepped into a paddle boat the next day. She'd seen the way the birds clustered around people feeding them.

"I guess we'll have to see." Carter waited until she was seated, then passed over a bag of treats for the ducks.

Mara grinned. It was Saturday evening, and they'd been together nearly every waking minute since he'd joined her and Anna on the sand two days earlier. She'd never laughed so hard or so often. Carter was fun, and they had the most interesting conversations, discussing everything from their favorite shows to their biggest worries. She didn't think they'd run out of topics anytime soon.

They paddled around the lake, a determined crowd of ducks following. When the treats were gone and the ducks had scattered, Carter took Mara's hand. "I was thinking about what we should do tomorrow before we have to head to the airport for your flight home. Then I realized that you came to vacation with *Anna,* and the two of you have hardly seen each other."

Mara felt a sense of satisfaction in that. Though she'd looked forward to oodles of girl time, Carter had been a more than adequate replacement, and Anna had a different guy on her arm every day. "We had dinner that first night. And hey, we caught lunch with her yesterday."

"Yeah, and what else?"

She and Anna had talked long into the night about their respective activities, but Mara didn't want to admit she'd been discussing him. "We caught each other for chats."

"So you don't mind spending your final hours on vacation with me instead?" He reached out and touched her face, moving a lock of hair away from her cheek, and tucking it behind her ear. His thumb brushed her cheek as he pulled his hand back, and it made her shiver.

"No, I don't mind." She looked up at him and caught her breath when their eyes met. The look in his was so intense. This wasn't the first time she thought he'd kiss her, but he never had. She didn't know why—and didn't know what to think about it. Was he holding back because it would all end soon, or was there something else bothering him?

"Good." His finger trailed along her jaw, making her skin tingle. "Have I mentioned that I think you're beautiful? And sweet? And that I love spending time with you?" His voice had dropped a little lower as he spoke, turning it husky.

"I don't think you ever mentioned the first one." Her own voice seemed a little breathless. He was close enough that she could smell his cologne, a light, musky scent. She swallowed as he drew closer. "Feel free to tell me again if you like."

His lips curved, and then they covered hers. The kiss was careful, soft and uncertain. She leaned into it a little, and he grew bolder, sliding a hand onto her shoulder and pulling her closer. His fingers cradled the back of her neck, and a thrill shot through her. This man made her feel precious and loved. Her head spun as he pulled away.

She realized with a start that she'd gotten way too deep in the relationship.

How had that happened? And how was she going to

deal with it when she returned home to her predictable but lonely life?

Five

Mara tucked her makeup case into her carry-on. "Are you sure you don't mind that I've barely been around this weekend?" she asked Anna. "I can cancel with Carter or do something else with him. I really was looking forward to spending time with you this weekend." While she'd told Carter it was fine, after she and Anna had a long talk the previous night, she felt bad to have been away from her friend so much—even if Anna had been having fun without her.

"Are you kidding? I'm glad you're having such a good time with an actual man who isn't your father. You need to get out." Anna finished combing her hair and picked up the hairspray. "Besides, we've had a lot of fun together, even if it hasn't been quite as much as we expected. I had some terrific dates with several guys, and you're going all gooey and cute with Carter. The two of you are adorable together."

"You're sure you don't mind?" Mara wasn't entirely convinced.

Anna turned to face her, a hand on one hip. "You like him, don't you?"

"So much." She sat on the bed and looked at her friend. "I can't tell you how great it's been."

"Then why do I get the feeling that something's wrong?"

Mara frowned. "Because—he's just a vacation guy—we don't live anywhere near each other, and I'm going to miss him so much. But I don't want to be one of those stupid girls who think they're in love after only a few days and then pines for the guy they couldn't have had anyway."

"Who says you can't?" Anna put both hands on her hips.

"Hello, I live halfway across the country." *Not to mention the fact that he's still in love with his wife.*

Anna covered her mouth dramatically. "Oh, right. And phones and web video chats and email don't exist, so you're *totally* going to have to lose touch."

"Don't be stupid, Anna."

"No, *you* don't be stupid. The only thing keeping you from continuing this relationship is yourself." She ratted her hair to make it fluffier. Apparently satisfied, she smiled and tucked the comb into her makeup case. "Regardless, you've had a terrific few days, yes? Savor the time you have left together. And get his phone number."

There was a knock at the door.

"That would be lover boy," Anna said, tossing Mara the lipstick she'd left on the counter. "This isn't mine."

"Right." Mara tucked it into her pocket and answered the door.

Carter stood outside, a little tanner than he'd been the day they arrived and wearing a much bigger smile. "You ready?"

"Yeah, just a second." She took one last survey of the condo, grabbing the phone charger next to her bed, and stashed it in her suitcase, then zipped it up. "Let's go."

He grabbed her suitcase, and Mara shouldered her bag. She gave Anna a tight hug. "It was great to see you again. I'll call you next week."

"You'd better." Anna gave her a wink.

They got outside the door, where Carter took Mara's hand. "Are you sure I'm not monopolizing your time?"

She grinned. "You *are*, but that's okay. I don't mind one bit." She threaded their fingers together, loving the way his strong, big hand wrapped around hers. "Where are you taking me today?"

"Have you been to a flea market? They have a great one nearby that runs most weekends."

"You like to shop?" She didn't think she'd ever met a guy who did.

"It's *browsing*. And sometimes I find cool things."

They started down the stairs. "You seem really familiar with this area," she said.

"Yeah." His tone was flat, not giving anything away.

His reticence confused her. "When have you been here before?"

He didn't say anything for a while. "I came here once as a teen, and brought Rosa back several times. It's kind of a special place for me."

"Because it reminds you of her."

"Yeah."

Mara felt a sinking feeling in her chest and wanted to cry. He was still in love with his wife. How could she ever hope to compete with a dead woman?

"Is that why you only kissed me once? Because you still love her?" As soon as the words escaped, she wished them back. Did she sound like she was complaining? Did she want him to say that no, the real reason was because he wasn't attracted to her? It wasn't like she was the most practiced flirt. And she hadn't kissed many guys. But he obviously knew exactly what he was doing. The paddle boat had proven that.

"Is there a right way to answer that question?" he asked. "I could say that it had nothing to do with her, and then you'd think the reason I haven't kissed you much is because there's something wrong with you—which isn't at all true. Or, I could agree, but then you'll think I can't let the past rest." He glanced away. "Which is partly true, I guess."

She felt something inside—a sprig of hope that had started to blossom, crumble and blow away. "I'm sorry, I don't have any right—"

"Yes, you do." He stopped next to his car and set the suitcase down, then took her carry-on and set it on top. When her other hand was free, he took it so their bodies formed a circle. "Her memory does haunt me; I won't lie. I planned to spend decades with her, and that didn't happen. But my feelings for you are so different—hey, in a good way," he said as Mara was bracing for him to blow her off.

"You're the first woman I've dated more than a couple of times since Rosa died. Instead of getting bored with you, or having you wig me out by something you do, I just want to spend more time with you. I know what we promised each other a few days ago, and I don't want to overstep my bounds, but you're special, Mara." A smile slid onto his face. "And I definitely like kissing you."

She felt herself melting. "I've had a great time with you too." She leaned back against his car and lifted her face for the kiss he offered. A thrill of excitement and longing swept through her as he leaned closer. She pulled his hands behind her and released them so she could wrap her arms around his waist and slide forward for more. He took his time with her, shifting his head for a better angle, then kissing along her jaw to the soft skin just below her ear. She sucked in a breath of surprise as goose bumps raced along her spine. He returned to kiss her mouth for another moment before releasing her.

As she caught her breath, she knew walking away from him was going to break her heart. Still, she had four hours until she needed to check in at the airport. "You ready to go to the flea market?"

"Yes." He kissed her quickly again, then released her to load her luggage in the trunk with his own.

The ride was beautiful. They recounted childhood memories and made up stories about the people they passed, inventing errands and ridiculous backgrounds that had them both laughing.

The market was much bigger than Mara had expected. Carter pulled her through the tables, where they picked out furniture for their hypothetical beach house, discussed the relative merits of yard ornaments, and chose their favorite dinner plate patterns at a vendor whose table was piled with old dishes. It was remarkable how closely their tastes aligned.

They came to a vendor who had Christmas tree ornaments for sale, despite the off season.

"This is perfect," Carter said, holding up a silver duck.

"Cute. It looks almost like the ones in the lake."

He handed it to the vendor to wrap up. "I want that one for sure."

They poked around the ornaments a little longer, and she pulled out one that looked like a jalapeno. "Doesn't this remind you of salsa dancing?" she asked.

"Yeah. Let's get that one too."

"You always plan your Christmas décor this far in advance?" she asked after he paid.

He took her hand and led her farther down the aisle. "No, but I want something to remember you by, and I want you to have something to remember me by." He looked over, and a sweet ache filled her chest.

"I think that's a great idea." Her throat felt tight with emotion, but she forced on a smile. "What next?"

He tugged her toward the far end, with food vendors, and a group of musicians with their bucket on the ground, soliciting donations.

They ate juicy tacos from one truck then split a funnel cake piled high with strawberries and whipped cream. When the food was gone, Carter asked her to tuck the ornaments into her purse and then offered his hand. "May I have this dance?"

"Are you serious? Here?" She looked around them. No one else was dancing.

He leaned in and said in a low voice, "Are you afraid people will want to join us, and we'll start a whole new trend?"

She stared at him for a moment then accepted his offer, looping her purse strap up over her head so it couldn't fall off. The music changed to a country swing, and Carter twisted and twirled her around on a bare section of dirt. Mara laughed, loving his bright eyes and easy grin, and the fact that his gaze rarely left her face. The wind blew through her hair, cooling her neck.

When the song came to an end, the music group transitioned into a slow song. Carter pulled her close amid the babble of voices. The smells of frying food, spicy Mexican meat, and the fresh scent of outdoors lingered, surrounding them. She couldn't take her eyes off of him. It was time to head back to the airport, but she didn't want to go.

Not wanting to end a vacation wasn't new—she often wished that she could stay longer—but until now it had always been from reluctance to return to real life, not a desperate longing for what she would leave behind.

Today, what made her want to stay was all him.

The music came to an end, and he dipped her then lifted her back up against him. They stared in each other's eyes for a long moment, breathing heavy. He leaned in and kissed her, lingering over it.

When he pulled away, it was only a fraction of an inch. "I don't want to leave you." His voice was low and husky.

"Me, neither. Can we forget about real life and stay here forever, in this moment?" she asked in a whisper.

"I wish we could." He tucked his face against her cheek for a long moment. "We ought to go now."

"I know." Still, they stood there. It was nearly a minute before he stepped back. He kept hold of her hand as they walked to his car in silence.

She didn't know what to say anyway.

When they were belted in, he began a conversation on a general topic that wouldn't make things any harder for them. At least, it shouldn't have, but suddenly a discussion about favorite Christmas music became so much more than it would have been before.

He pulled up to one of the drop-off spots at the airport—he'd driven to the area rather than taking a plane. He unloaded her bags and set them on the sidewalk beside her. "I'd like to keep in touch."

"Me, too." She suddenly remembered the ornaments and pulled the sack out of her purse. "I don't want to walk off with these, or at least, not with both of them."

He pulled them out of the package. "Which do you want?" He held them in front of her, gleaming in the sunlight.

She stared at them both for a long moment then took the duck. "It'll remind me of the lake." And of their first kiss, but she didn't say that.

"Good." He glanced at his watch. "You really ought to go."

"I know." Her heart raced as she pulled out her cell. "Will you put in your number? I'd like to talk to you sometimes, if that's okay with you." What would he say?

He smiled. "Sure. And you?" They traded phones and entered their own contact information. She added a street address for her house, though she didn't know if he'd ever use it. She passed back the phone and accepted her own, sliding it back into her pocket. She was probably a fool; he was still messed up over his dead wife, and she was asking for heartache.

Carter pulled her close and kissed her again, his fingers delving into her hair. Mara touched his face, trying to memorize the feel of his skin, the rasp of whiskers on his chin against her fingertips, the scent of his cologne, and the way his lips molded hers. If there was a chance she would never experience this with him again, she wanted to remember every detail.

"I'll call you," he said when he finally pulled away.

I love you. But she couldn't say the words. It was supposed to be a fun weekend, no more. How had she let herself fall for him so hard? "I hope so."

"Goodbye."

Before her plane even took off, her phone dinged, announcing that she had a text message.

She opened it up. It was from Carter.

Miss you already.

Me, too, she responded. She slid the phone back in her pocket and smiled.

Six

When she touched down in North Dakota, snow was falling again. At home, after unloading her luggage from the car, grateful the roads hadn't been bad, she took a picture with her phone and sent it to Carter.

Home Sweet Home. I already miss the sun.

Jo greeted her at the door as Mara sent the message. "Writing to Anna again already?"

"Not exactly." Mara hadn't mentioned her holiday romance, but knew she would have to soon if she and Carter kept in touch. Her phone chimed again, and she pulled it out to check. There was a picture of grass and trees in the moonlight.

Not so cold here, but still awfully quiet.

Mara smiled and put the phone away.

"Okay," Jo said. "Who did you meet on your trip? Anna didn't put that smile on your face."

Mara tried to make light of it. "His name's Carter, and we'll see if it goes anywhere. He lives in Texas."

"Oh, man, that sucks." Jo took the extra suitcase from Mara and headed inside. "But it's terrific that you connected with someone. You'll have to tell me all about him."

"Maybe tomorrow." She wanted to keep the memories to herself for just a little longer. "Tell me about Dad."

❧

Three weeks passed while Mara and Carter continued to send regular text messages and talk on the phone each day. As she carried a load of groceries into the kitchen, she smiled at a funny comment he made about an overheard conversation on campus.

"Carter again?" her father asked.

"What makes you say that?" She pocketed the phone and began unloading groceries.

"That grin. You always get it when you've been talking to him." He set down the newspaper he'd been reading and stood. "What are you doing, Mara?"

"I'm unloading the groceries," she said, though she knew what he really meant.

"No." He took her hand and looked her in the eye. "I know you gave up a job opportunity after I had my stroke. I'm doing better, honey. Don't you think it's time you stopped putting your own dreams on hold for me?"

She looked up at him. "But I like living with you."

He smiled. "And I love having you here, but I'm doing much better, and you don't belong with an old fogey like me. You should be somewhere where you can reach for your dreams. Somewhere with opportunities. With a man who can put that kind of smile on your face." He tapped a finger against her chin.

She swallowed hard when he referred to Carter. Her father was right, but Carter still loved his wife. "It's complicated."

"It always is." He touched her shoulder. "But you deserve more than what you have here. Just think about it."

"I will." She grabbed his hand and gave it a tight squeeze. "But first I need to get these groceries taken care of. Since you're so strong and healthy, could you bring in the rest of them?"

He sighed dramatically. "I knew I was going to regret saying that even before the words were out."

She changed the subject to the impending spring thaw and the places she wanted to visit as soon as the ground was visible, but in the back of her head, she started thinking about master's of accounting courses. Maybe at a school in Texas.

❧

I miss you.

The text came through while Carter was eating a quiet dinner alone—as usual. The message was accompanied by a picture of a duck waddling in the snow. He wondered if Mara had taken the photo or if it had come off the internet.

He picked up the phone and wrote her back.

I'm enjoying a delicious TV dinner in front of the television tonight. Could use your company.

The television was off, but he left out that detail. His eyes drifted to the set and then upward, inexorably to the picture on top—a wedding picture Rosa had framed after their honeymoon. Guilt flooded him again. What was he doing? How could he keep up this long-distance flirtation? The closer he got to Mara, the more he felt like he was cheating on Rosa.

His phone rang, and he looked at Mara's name on the display. He answered the call with his happiest voice. "Hey, Mara. How are you doing?"

"Great. We got all the way up to *fifty-four degrees* today. Spring is just around the corner."

He chuckled. "You have a wacked-out idea of spring. Have I ever mentioned that?"

"Maybe. Once or twice. So what are you watching?"

"Nothing, really. I was thinking about settling down with a book. It's been years since I read *Salem's Lot*."

"Oh, Stephen King. I love his books. Read that one a few years ago and didn't sleep for a week. I started telling Anna about it, but she made me stop, said if I kept going, she'd never be able to walk alone on campus again."

He laughed. "That is one drawback. What's new in your neck of the woods?"

A long moment of silence followed, and he was about to check to make sure the call hadn't been dropped, when she answered. "I was thinking about going back to school for a master's degree."

"Really? That's terrific. Are you looking to head to Denver again?" How much farther away would she be if she moved there? Or would it come out to nearly the same distance?

"I was thinking maybe a little farther south." Her voice sounded hesitant, nervous. "I understand that University of North Texas has a great master's of accounting program."

His eyes flicked over to the picture of Rosa; he felt a little overwhelmed. Mara was talking about picking up and moving across the country to live closer to him. "I . . . wow, that is a long way from home."

"Not so far, compared to other universities. I could go to California or Hawaii . . ." She sucked in a breath. "Look, my feelings for you—I've never felt this way for anyone else.

I'd like to give things a chance, see what could happen if we lived closer."

He didn't say anything at first, his gaze riveted on the photo as both hope and fear shot through him. "You would move all the way down here just for me? What if things don't work out?" He wanted to date her for real, to have dinners and movies and long chats like they'd enjoyed on vacation, but there would also be pressure in knowing she'd moved halfway across the country to be with him. He didn't want her to regret it.

"The school really does have an excellent accounting program." There was distance in her voice now. "Don't feel obligated just because I move closer. I already put in my application. It's too late for fall semester, but we don't have to date if you're not interested . . ." Her voice broke, piling on the guilt.

"No, I mean, of course I want to see you again, and often. So much. It's just . . ." He stood and walked away from his half-eaten meal, no longer hungry.

"This is about Rosa, isn't it?"

More guilt. She must think he was leading her on—which he wasn't. At least, he didn't think so. He liked her a lot. Maybe more than liked her. He couldn't answer, clueless as to the right words to use.

At the silence, she said, "I see. Well, I guess that answers that question. I ought to go. I'll talk to you later." She hung up before he could even say goodbye.

Carter tossed the phone onto the couch, harder than he should have. Things between him and Mara were only supposed to have been temporary—a chance to ease back into dating, not have a real relationship right away—but he felt a stronger pull to her as the weeks passed. What was he doing going out with someone long distance, anyway? He didn't actually think that a woman as wonderful as Mara would be willing to be friends forever, did he?

He turned to the wedding picture. "What do I do now, honey? How do I put you away and give someone else a real chance?"

Rosa didn't respond—not that he'd expected her to. He rubbed his forehead. Had he blown things with the only woman he'd connected with in over two years, one he thought he might love, because he was afraid to try again?

Seven

The school year was winding down, and Carter was already getting requests from different parts of campus as staff asked for updated equipment for the following semester. The rush seemed to start earlier every spring.

A virus had rampaged through the south computer lab, so he'd spent the better part of the weekend getting it cleared up so students could work on their term papers. His eyes were gritty, his temper frayed, and he hadn't heard from Mara in nearly a week. When he called, she found excuses not to talk long—when she answered at all. He'd hurt her, though he hadn't intended to. And he missed her more every day.

His phone rang, and he answered it eagerly, hoping it would be her this time, but instead it was Paolo.

"How are you tonight?" Paolo asked.

"Staying busy, problems with the school computers. How about you?" Carter didn't want to talk about his own life right now, or his love life. He had told Paolo about the time he spent with Mara, and that they were still in contact, but he didn't want to discuss it now.

"Can't complain." Paolo went on to talk about the great experience he'd had the previous day while selling his miracle supplements. At the end he slipped in a question. "And how are things with Mara?" As if it had been part of the discussion and not an unrelated subject at all.

Carter stood from the computer where he was working—he needed a break before he got to the point where he couldn't see straight anymore. "Fine, I guess. We haven't been in touch much this week. You know how these vacation flirtations go." His voice was flat.

Paolo apparently picked up on it, because he made a tsking sound. "Why are you playing games with your heart, Carter? Have you told her how you feel?"

"How can I when I'm not sure?" He strode past rows of computers, desperately wishing he could get away from the conversation.

"I thought you were crazy about her," Paolo said.

"I was. I am." He sighed. "It's not that simple."

"Yes, it is." Paolo paused. "You loved my Rosa, and you always will, but it's past time to let her go. Move on. Making a new life with someone else doesn't mean you never loved Rosa She would want you to be happy. I think Mara might be just the woman for you."

"You've never even met her."

"No, but the woman's soul shines brightly when she sings. I saw your face and awe. I've heard the smile in your voice when you speak of her. If you love her, go for it. Love is not so plentiful that you can choose to ignore it."

Carter's heart confirmed what Paolo was saying. He had fallen in love with Mara, hard. Taking that leap, though, was terrifying. He missed her, and the part of himself that loved her warred with the part that was afraid to take the risk.

He turned and headed back down the row of computers. She was special to him, more important than she'd realized, but how was she supposed to know that if he didn't tell her? With a sense of peace, he realized it was time he put away the things of the past and focused on what could be instead of what was. "Thank you, Paolo. I always appreciate your advice."

"I'm glad one of my children does."

❧

A storm was coming on as Carter pulled through the cemetery gates. It wouldn't hit for another hour at least, so he wouldn't be lingering, which was fine with him. He took the familiar route around the east side, past mausoleums and cracking tombstones, to the familiar area of the cemetery with newer graves.

Flowers dotted the cemetery grounds, along with teddy bears, balloons and even a plastic violin joining them, decorating the graves. He pulled off to the side and parked under a tree, then picked up the mixed flowers he'd bought a few minutes before.

He hadn't visited Rosa's grave since his vacation, though not a day went by that he didn't think about her. The wind ruffled his hair, and he could smell rain on the air. It reminded him of the day she died. The rain had lashed against the windshield as he'd driven to the hospital. The phone call from the police had sent adrenalin rushing through his veins and worry filling his head.

Today's storm wasn't supposed to be as big, but the dark clouds overhead still made him nervous. Carter set his bundle of flowers in front of the grave marker, creating a slash of multi-colored brightness Rosa would have loved. He sat on the grass beside the grave to talk, as he often did.

"Hey, honey. I know it's been a while, but I've been trying to move on. I hate it, though. I miss you so much. Work is going well, I guess. I stay busy running around fixing computers for all of the professors. The other day a kid hacked into the system just to see if he could then left me a message where I would be sure to find it. He was pretty ingenious, but thankfully didn't mess up anything."

He shifted the conversation to his brother. "Carson is getting married in three weeks. He's so happy; he's like a totally different person when he's with Trista. They remind me of us when we got married, all bright eyes and hope for the future. She's already talking about kids." He choked up when he thought of his unborn son—they'd only learned the baby's gender the week before the accident. "How can I feel so lost when everything looks like it ought to be fine?"

He moved and crossed his legs. "I met someone last month. She has me all twisted up in knots." He told her about meeting Mara outside the condo when she arrived, of hearing her sing. He talked about all of the time they had spent together that weekend and how their friendship had grown since. "I know your father is right, that you would be fine with me moving on. Mara's important to me, so I'm going to take a chance and see what happens—if I haven't screwed everything up already. She makes me happier than I've been since you died."

Tears threatened, and he let them fall. "I love you, Rosa. Part of me always will. I hope you know that."

⁂

Mara got her acceptance to UNT quickly, even though she'd have to wait until January to start the program. She gave notice at work that she'd be moving to Texas during the summer to get established. Then she started sorting through all of her belongings. She had savings if she couldn't find a job right away, but hopefully she'd find something when she moved.

When the papers had first come, she'd still been smarting from the terrible phone call with Carter. She seriously considered declining and applying to another school, but her better judgment had taken over. The program was only a year, and surely it wouldn't be hard to stay out of Carter's way if he didn't want her in his life. It was time she took her future by the horns and charged forward.

Within a week of her acceptance, she had phone interviews for a couple of jobs in the Fort Worth area and was making arrangements for the move.

Sorting through her stuff was a bigger task than she'd expected. Her winter parka wouldn't see much use, but there was no point leaving it behind; she'd need it eventually.

The fate of other things were harder to decide. The little rosette her mother had tucked in her hair at her junior prom brought back memories. She found her photo album, planning to tuck the silk flower inside. Then she got caught up in the pictures of herself as a child, her parents laughing together at a family reunion, her mom helping her decorate cookies for a fundraiser.

Tears slid onto Mara's cheeks as she saw her mother's smiling face. What she wouldn't give to talk to her about what was going on now, to get the kind of advice her mother had been best at. Mara had tried to talk to Jo, but her sister said to walk away and find someone who didn't have a ton of hang-ups like a dead wife.

Mara wiped her face and spoke to the decade-old image. "I don't know what's going to happen with Carter. Maybe nothing, but I'm not ready to walk away yet." She touched the photo. The plastic curled a little at the corners of the album, but it was still protected for now. She needed to get it into an acid-free binder. Maybe this summer. She packed the album with the things she would take to Texas.

She tucked away her favorite girlhood treasures to be stored in her father's basement until she had somewhere of her own to keep them, then stopped when her hand came to the duck ornament.

She vividly remembered that first kiss, on the paddleboat, and all of the others they'd shared—there had been so few—but more than that, she remembered the sense of belonging, the rightness of being in his arms. Carter had been so easy to talk to, and they'd seen eye-to-eye on so many issues. She choked up again as she fought to stay in control of her emotions. The past couple of weeks had seemed lonely without their regular conversations.

He had sent a few half-hearted texts, called in the early days, and she'd replied with brief responses. She couldn't hold onto this uncertainty forever. Either they decided to be a couple, or they had to end things.

When she reached Texas, maybe she could find him and see if he felt any different standing in front of him than she did now. Hope rose inside her every time the thought of being near him crossed her mind. She wanted things to work out for them.

Eight

There was the sound of wheels on gravel, and since Mara wanted to talk to her sister about Dad's upcoming doctor appointment—preferably not within his hearing—she stepped outside.

A red four-door sedan had stopped in front her house. Not Jo.

Mara's heart skipped a few beats when she saw the driver; her eyes couldn't be working right. The door opened, and Carter got out, his gaze riveted on her.

She took a few steps across the green spring grass, still unable to believe what she was seeing. "Carter? How?"

He closed the door and stuck his hands in his pockets, sauntering in her direction. "I decided I could use another spring vacation, and Texas is well into summer, so I thought I'd go somewhere where it's still spring. Couldn't imagine spending my vacation without you."

She stared at him for a long moment. "But you haven't called me in almost a week." It was an inane thing to say, but her brain wasn't processing right.

"I didn't know what to say. I wanted to see you in person—see if you were as pretty as my memories said you were." He reached out and flicked a lock of her hair back over her shoulder. "Apparently my memory is faulty. You're far prettier."

She felt her face heat in the cool spring air. The sun would be going down soon, and she could already feel the chill starting. It didn't seem to bother him, even though he wasn't wearing a jacket.

"Maybe you should come in." She didn't know what else to say or how to respond. Did he think he could show up out of the blue and pick back up where they left off? Yet she had to hold herself back from leaping into his arms. He had come to see her. That meant something, didn't it?

She followed his gaze, glancing over her shoulder. Her father stood in the doorway to the house. She bit back a groan. She wasn't ready to make introductions. Not until she and Carter said what he'd come for.

Another car pulled into the drive—this time it was her sister's banana-yellow Toyota with its green hood.

Jo got out and walked over, taking her time as she studied the two of them. A smile crept onto her face as she offered her hand for a shake. "You must be Carter. I recognize you from your pictures. You're better looking in person." She gave his hand a squeeze and winked.

She turned to Mara with a disapproving, "You didn't mention how tall he is." She turned to Carter again. "We're having dinner soon—Mara's famous spaghetti and some cookies for dessert. She's a great cook. You should stay and join us." She took off for the house, calling over her shoulder. "Five minutes—that's all I can promise you before Dad charges out and demands an introduction."

"Nice to meet you," Carter said as it if were an afterthought.

"Don't worry," Mara said once her sister had closed the door behind her. "She runs roughshod over everyone. She's a school teacher, so she's been honing that skill."

He focused on Mara again. "I do feel a bit like I've been bulldozed."

"You should be able to bounce back. The effect is rarely permanent." Mara forced herself to stick her hands in her back pockets so she wouldn't reach out to touch Carter. "Why didn't you tell me you were coming?"

"I thought you might not see me. You've kind of been brushing me off lately."

"*I* wasn't the one who did the brush-off." She knew that wasn't entirely true, but it felt good to say. "When I called . . . well, you know how that went."

He touched her elbow. "I know. I didn't mean it like that. You caught me by surprise. I've been tied up inside ever since."

"Feeling better now?" she asked, though she tried to appear disinterested.

"Some. But there's one more thing I need before I'll feel right again." He took her shoulders, pulling her close and kissing her firmly, tipping his head to seal their mouths together.

Relief and joy rushed over her. She felt as if she had come home again as she melted into his kiss, shifting closer and putting her hands on his hard chest. His body heat radiated to her, and she moved into him in the evening chill, melding her body against his. She'd dreamed of kissing him again, but the real thing was definitely better.

"I missed you so much," he whispered against her lips. "I didn't mean to hurt you. Please say you'll give me another chance."

"You want another chance?" Her heart soared.

"More than anything. I was confused about moving on and taking risks with a relationship, but I've got it figured out now. Please tell me it's not too late for us."

She slid her hands around his neck. "It's not too late."

"Say you'll still move to Texas so we can give this a real shot."

Mara grinned. "I'm already packing."

"Say you love me as much as I love you," he said in a whisper. "I do love you, you know."

It seemed impossible that he'd said the words she'd been longing to hear. She let out a little laugh of joy. "I love you too. Being away from you has been terrible."

He held her tight, running one hand up her spine then running his fingers through her hair. "Then I have everything I need."

"Make me a promise?" she asked.

"What?"

"That you'll take me to feed the ducks often. And to dance at flea markets."

"You got it." He kissed her again, lingering over it until Jo came out.

"Hey, stop putting on a show for the whole neighborhood and bring him in to meet Dad."

Mara giggled and buried her face in his shirt, happier than ever that she let Anna talk her into that spring vacation.

Heather Justesen earned a BA in English Literature from Southern Utah University, where she met her husband, Bill. She worked in newspaper for several years, and they spent two years as foster parents. They now live in the little town where she grew up in Central Utah, work on their local ambulance as Advanced EMTs, and raise a cat, two dogs, and a whole slew of chickens, geese, ducks, guineas, and a tom turkey, which is very vain. When she can squeeze in the time, she gardens and bakes. She also writes serial stories for BigWorldNetwork.com, available in e-book and audio book formats.

You can learn more about Heather on her blog: http://heatherjustesen.blogspot.com/

Or her website: http://www.heatherjustesen.com/

Or via email at: Heather@HeatherJustesen.com

The Best Laid Plans

Sarah M. Eden

Other Works by Sarah M. Eden

Seeking Persephone

Courting Miss Lancaster

The Kiss of a Stranger

Friends and Foes

An Unlikely Match

Drops of Gold

Glimmer of Hope

As You Are

Longing For Home

Hope Springs

One

"It's Cancún, Madison. How can you say no to *Cancún*?"

Madison slid her smartphone across the desk to Beth. "From my mom." She indicated the chain of texts already open.

Beth gave her a curious look, but picked up the phone, reading out loud. "'I had a wonderful evening with Mr. Fabulous. He took me to the new Italian place on Vine. He likes lasagna. That is a good sign, don't you think—'" Beth looked up, eyes wide with amusement. "Her texts get longer all the time."

"I know. It's like she's writing a novel."

Beth dropped her gaze back to the phone. "I'm surprised she doesn't have arthritis in her thumbs." She took up the reading again. "'Mr. Fabulous is coming over tonight again. He is so wonderful. Also, the water heater broke and flooded the basement. Talk to you soon. Mom.' Wow. A flooded basement is an afterthought now?"

"Exactly." Madison took her phone back. "I think it's time I met 'Mr. Fabulous.'"

"You haven't yet?"

Madison dropped her phone in her purse, packing up for the end of the day. "I haven't been home since summer. Mr. Fabulous wasn't in the picture then."

"Is his name really 'Mr. Fabulous'?"

Madison hadn't thought of that. "Ugh, I hope not."

Beth slung her own bag over her shoulder. They'd had desks next to each other at the bank for a year. "What was the name of the last guy?"

They walked to the doors together. Madison waved to the afternoon tellers before pushing the door open.

"Mom called him 'Captain Dreamy.' The nicknames are a very reliable early warning system."

"What was he captain of?"

"Being a pig." Now in the parking lot, Madison unlocked her less-than-pristine Altima with the key-chain remote.

Beth's sportier compact sat next to it. She spoke across the roof. "Was Captain Pig the Vegas guy or the Aspen guy?"

"Vegas." Half the miles on Madison's car were from driving to various places to pick up her mother after one guy or another had ended a relationship hundreds of miles from home. Vegas. Aspen. Anaheim. Phoenix. Madison had seen America saving her mother from romantic disasters.

"How about this time you let your mom deal with the loser, and you come with the rest of us to Cancún?"

Beth's suggestion was tempting, but Madison needed to nip this latest star-crossed love story in the bud. "I don't have enough vacation days to go to Cancún right now, and in another month or two, I'll have to take more time off to chase my mother to San Francisco or Albuquerque or wherever she lands herself next."

"So you're picking Folsom Lake over Cancún. Are you insane?"

Madison tossed her purse into the car. "Sometimes I think I am."

Beth crossed her arms on the car top, apparently settling in for a conversation. "Will *he* be there?"

Nothing beyond the pronoun was necessary. When speaking of Madison's hometown, there was only one *he*: Derek McGee. She'd known him since high school. They'd dated in college. Things had even been serious just after college graduation. It hadn't worked out, and her heart was too stupid to forget him. Just thinking his name made her heart skip and jump around.

Stupid, stupid.

"He'll be there, won't he?" Beth was enjoying this too much.

"This trip is about my *mother's* man troubles."

"Man Troubles. That should be the name of your family business."

It probably should have been. Her father was to thank for that. The only good thing that man had ever done was walk out on them.

"Have fun in Cancún." What was she saying? Of course Beth and the rest of their friends would have fun. *They* weren't headed home for a family crisis intervention.

"I'll post pictures." Beth wiggled her eyebrows and grinned.

"Careful which ones," Madison warned with a laugh. "'The internet is *forever.*'"

Beth's grin grew as she tossed her things in her car. "Text me a picture of President Amazing."

"Mr. Fabulous," Madison corrected. "I'll send you a before and after shot."

"What do you plan to do to this guy?"

"Whatever it takes."

Beth gave a nod of approval. "I'll help you hide the body after I get back from Mexico."

"Perfect." It was nice to joke about the whole ridiculous situation. "See ya."

"*¡Adios!*" Beth made air castanets.

Madison sat in her car for a while after Beth pulled out of the parking lot. *I'm giving up Cancún.* She'd been looking forward to the trip for months. But someone had to save Mom from herself. And that someone was Madison. Always.

Maybe it was the fact that she'd made the trip to fix Mom's problems so many times, or maybe it was because she looked forward to spending time at home.

Either way, the following evening as she pulled off the highway at the familiar exit, the resentment that had started to take form in the bank parking lot disappeared.

Folsom Lake didn't change much. The same people. The same main street. The place was small enough to feel cozy, but large enough that even life-long residents didn't know everyone. They had their own high school, a couple of middle schools, and a smattering of elementary schools. Folsom Lake even had a multiplex, choice of grocery stores, and a branch of the same bank Madison worked at in what her grandmother called "the big city."

Madison always missed home during that first drive into town whenever she returned. By the end of her stay, though, she was always ready to leave. This time, she'd be exhausted from saving her mother from her latest romantic disaster. Watching her friends live their married lives or their I-have-a-dreamy-significant-other lives wore on her. And, though she'd managed to avoid him on her last visit, Derek McGee might get under her skin as well.

He'd smile at her the way he always had. He'd make her laugh. And for just a moment, she'd believe they could make a relationship work. She'd start dreaming again of happy-ever-afters and fairy-tale endings. But life wasn't like that.

She pulled up in front of her mom's house, bracing herself for the coming few days. At least she was taking an intervention approach this time rather than a damage-control one.

I just have to convince Mom to break it off now before the relationship implodes.

She practiced her speech by addressing the steering wheel. "Hey, Mom, I've come to visit. It's time to say goodbye to Mr. Fabulous. So, what's for dinner?"

Awkward, but doable. She'd wing it from there.

Madison pulled her little suitcase from the trunk and made her way to the door. She allowed herself only the tiniest glance down the street. Derek's parents had once lived on the corner. Coming home always made her think of him.

That's all in the past. This visit is about Mom.

She rang the bell and waited. This wouldn't be easy, but it was for the best. Preventing a mess was definitely better than trying to clean one up afterward.

Mom's squeal upon opening the door brought a smile to Madison's face.

"Why didn't you tell me you were coming?" She squeezed Madison in an almost suffocating hug, bouncing up and down.

Why didn't I tell you? So you couldn't hide Mr. Fabulous.

"Come in. Come in." Mom held the door open, her smile not slipping at all. "Look who's here," she called to someone in the next room. "Madison's come for a visit."

Who else could she be talking to but her latest: Mr. Fabulous. Mom took an all-or-nothing approach to dating. She probably spent every free minute with him. Of course he would be at the house.

I should have practiced longer with the steering wheel.

She pasted a smile on her face. No point tipping off the enemy that she had him in her sights. She followed her mom into the living room.

"Hey, Maddi."

167

She froze. Only one person had ever called her "Maddi."

"Derek."

Two

erek couldn't manage to say anything but "Hey, Maddi." He hadn't been prepared to see her again. Last summer he'd had enough warning of her visit to get out of town.

Madison Collins was the one that got away. The problem was that she kept coming back to rub it in.

She didn't look any happier to see him than he felt to see her. Maddi leaned closer to her mom and whispered something.

Mrs. Collins laughed so hard the neighbors must have heard. "Oh, Derek! She—" Laughter cut off the rest of her sentence.

"It's not that funny, Mom," Maddi muttered, shifting her weight from foot to foot.

"Not that funny?" Mrs. Collins's shoulders shook with amusement. "She thinks you and I—" More laughing.

"You and I *what*?" Derek couldn't help smiling. Mrs. Collins and her daughter had the same laugh and the same smile.

"She thinks we're *d-a-ting.*" The last word stretched into three separate syllables, divided by bursts of laughter.

Maddi's entire face turned pink. He liked that she still blushed so easily. *Careful. Madison Collins is your personal poison, and you know it.*

"What did you expect me to think, Mom? I get epistle-length texts about this new guy you're seeing, and Derek is here in your living room." Maddi managed to make the conclusion sound almost logical. "I had to at least ask."

Derek couldn't resist. He slid up right next to Mrs. Collins and put an arm around her. "We should tell her the truth, Teresa." Calling her by her first name felt strange, even though he wasn't a kid anymore. "It's time we stopped hiding."

"You're absolutely right." Mrs. Collins put an arm around him as well.

"Maddi," he said. "Your mother—" He pretended to fight his conscience. "This is difficult for me to confess."

He could see Maddi push down her amusement. He'd always liked giving her a hard time.

"You should know before you hear it from someone else. Your mother is dating . . . my Uncle Grant." He pushed out an immediate breath, pressing a fist to his forehead. "It feels good to get that off my chest."

"Shut up." But Maddi didn't actually look annoyed.

Derek gave her a side-by-side hug, feeling the awkwardness of seeing her again even more than when she first walked in the room. There'd been a time when an embrace between them would have been the least affectionate part of saying hello.

"How are you?" he asked.

She nodded, not quite looking at him. "Fine. A little tired from the drive." She stepped away, her attention back on her mom. "So, Grant McGee?"

Mrs. Collins flashed that bright, cheerful smile. Of the two Collins ladies, Mrs. Collins had always been the most optimistic. Maddi had never been a downer or a pessimist; a *realist* was probably the right word. And a worrier. He didn't know if that made her the worst person to work as a bank loan officer or the perfect one.

"Let's put your things in your room," Mrs. Collins said, ushering Maddi off. "Grant went up the street to get some ice cream. He'll be so happy to see you again. How long has it been?"

"I only think I've met him once. Long time ago," Maddi said as she walked out of the room, her voice trailing off as she disappeared.

Survived that. Barely, Derek thought.

Maddi hadn't changed much. She was stunning, her brown hair wavy like it always had been, her brown eyes sharp and breathtaking. She still had that killer smile. She wasn't as approachable as he remembered her, though. Maybe that was part of the awkwardness of being in the same room as the only woman he'd ever loved, knowing that she'd moved out of the state rather than settle down with him.

Weren't *guys* supposed to be the ones afraid of commitment?

Uncle Grant breezed in through the door the next moment. "Whose clunker is that out there?" He set the carton of fudge ripple on the kitchen counter.

Clunker? He could easily guess. "A green Altima?"

Uncle Grant nodded. "Looks like it got dragged backward through a junk yard."

A beat up green Altima. Derek shook his head. That was Maddi straight through. She could afford to replace the beater, but wouldn't spend the money as long as it was still running. "That's Maddi's. She's had it since freshman year of college."

"Madison's here?" Uncle Grant lit up like a Christmas tree, smiling beneath his bushy mustache. "Teresa's happy about that, I bet."

"Happy and surprised," Derek said.

The usual twinkle in Uncle Grant's eyes grew. "Describing Teresa's feelings about it, or yours?"

Fair enough. Every member of the McGee family knew that Derek and Maddi had dated. A few could even tell he hadn't gotten over her.

"I'm surprised, definitely." Derek wandered toward the kitchen side of the large room.

Uncle Grant pulled out some bowls for the ice cream he'd bought. He knew the kitchen well after a few months of dating Mrs. Collins. "You're surprised, but not happy?"

"Maddi has visited before," Derek said. "It never works out."

"Never say never."

Mrs. Collins and Uncle Grant were a perfect match. They were both optimists, even if it meant believing in the impossible.

Derek peeled back the lid on the ice cream carton. "Are we still going to watch this movie tonight, or what?"

That changed the subject. Even when the Collins ladies returned, things weren't as awkward as before. Derek could almost ignore the memories that hung around Maddi. He could almost pretend she was just an acquaintance sitting in on a last-minute movie night.

Almost.

Maddi settled in as if she'd never been gone. It was like the last two years had never happened, like the two of them were still together. She was the same Maddi he'd fallen hard for, just hanging out at her mom's place. She even ate ice cream the same way she used to, flipping the spoon over after each bite to have one more go at whatever she'd missed with the first pass.

He spent most of the movie watching her. Though she glanced his way once in a while, Maddi was definitely not watching him. But she wasn't paying attention to the movie either. She was watching her mom. More specifically, she was watching her mom *and Uncle Grant.*

Was that was the reason for her drive down? To check out her mom's new boyfriend?

What, did you think she came to say she was wrong to break things off? That she's changed her mind after two years? That's not gonna happen.

He knew better. He'd accepted years ago that she had cut things off totally. It still hurt.

Derek made a break for it before the closing credits were done rolling. There was a reason he'd skipped town the last time Madison Collins came home.

Three

Grant McGee had done a good job of seeming like a decent guy. Madison, though, wasn't entirely convinced. All of Mom's boyfriends had *started out* okay.

"Wear this blue one." Mom pulled a top out of Madison's closet. "You look great in blue."

"I'm not going, Mom. I came to see *you*, not my old friends." She'd also come to ward off a disaster, but that was best left unsaid.

Mom didn't argue. She simply went on as though Madison hadn't made any objections. "Definitely the blue one. What jewelry did you bring?"

Madison took the blue top from Mom and hung it up again. "We're ordering in, remember? I don't need to accessorize to throw back a carton of General Tso's from Chang's."

"*Grant and I* are having Chang's. *You* are meeting your friends for dinner." Mom pulled the blue top out again.

"They want to see you. You don't visit often. Besides, Derek will be there."

All the more reason not to go. "Derek and I broke up two years ago."

Mom shrugged. "I didn't mean it like that." If her guilty expression was anything to go by, she'd meant it exactly like that. "Only that he's a friend, like the others who will be there, and they're all expecting you tonight."

But how can I spy on you and your new boyfriend if I'm not here?

"They're counting on you," Mom said, which slammed the last nail in that coffin.

Madison had known her fair share of people who fell through when people were counting on them. She refused to be one of those people.

She managed to keep her sigh of resignation silent. "I brought my big, chunky, yellow necklace."

Mom grinned, dropping the blue top on the bed. "Perfect! What about shoes?"

Before Madison had a chance to catch her breath, she was dressed for a night out and pulling up to Romanelli's on Vine.

"I came home to save Mom from herself. How did she manage to distract me?" Madison leaned back against the headrest. "Tonight was the perfect opportunity to keep an eye on things, but here I am at Romanelli's."

And Derek is here too.

She was still wrapping her brain around having seen him the night before after not seeing him in a year. That year had been good to him. Even though spring had only begun, he was a little tan, with a touch of gold in his hair. He'd never been a jock, but he was always athletic. That clearly hadn't changed.

And those eyes. Oh, those eyes.

She hit her palm against the steering wheel. What kind

of idiot sat in her car dying over a pair of hazel eyes? Especially when those eyes belonged to someone she broke up with two years ago? At the sound of someone knocking on the driver's side window, she turned. She could have rolled her eyes.

Derek. Of course.

Madison forced a friendly smile so he'd think she was totally comfortable. She put down the window. "Hey."

He raised an eyebrow. "Still talking to your steering wheel?"

She'd been doing that for years. "Yeah, well it's a really good listener."

He leaned his arm across the top of the car, leaning over to talk through the open window. "Come on inside. Everyone's here. They're all excited to see you."

She could picture them all sitting at the big table, paired up all the way around. That was the worst part of seeing them all again: everyone had someone except for her and Derek. "We aren't going to be the only single people in the group, are we?"

"You're assuming I'm single."

He was, wasn't he? Madison's stomach fell all the way to her feet. A sick, almost panicked, feeling welled up inside her. He *was* single still, wasn't he? Mom would have texted her a saga detailing the whole thing if Derek had a girlfriend.

Except that Mom's head was full of Mr. Fabulous. She probably hadn't even noticed Derek.

"I really should be spending more time with my mom." She could be home in five minutes—two if she hit all green lights. "That's why I came home, to visit her."

"Sure. That's why." His smile tipped to the left side, just the way it always had when he teased her. "It didn't have anything to do with warning off your mom's new boyfriend?"

"I . . . That's not . . ."

He walked around the front of the car. He opened the passenger door and took a seat.

"What are you doing?"

He pulled the door closed and leaned the seat back.

"Are you settling in?"

"So you *didn't* come back to Folsom Lake to decide if my uncle Grant was good enough for your mom?"

She kept her gaze forward. If she had to look at him sitting there so comfortable in her car the way he used to, thinking about him and some phantom girlfriend, she'd start all over again with the what-ifs and if-onlys.

"I only came to visit." She almost sounded convincing.

"I know you better than that, Maddi."

She shook her head. "You always *thought* you did."

He leaned in, close enough to whisper in her ear. "I know you well enough to know you talk to your steering wheel."

Derek still wore the same cologne. The two years they'd been apart disappeared at a single whiff of that scent.

The flood of memories brought an unexpected smile to her face. "I know you're addicted to Chang's spring rolls," she said. He probably single-handedly kept Chang's in business.

"And you can't live without diet soda."

She laughed. "And you prefer w—"

She turned as she spoke and his nearness cut the words short. He was so close. They were almost touching. She could see every speck of color in his eyes.

"You prefer water." She could hardly breathe, let alone come up with a more coherent thing to say.

"Water and spring rolls and—" His next breath sounded strained. His eyes didn't leave hers.

He touched her face. Her heart jumped from her feet to her throat. Every thought fled.

Derek leaned closer. She could feel his breath on her lips. She remembered with perfectly clarity how it felt to kiss Derek McGee. No one kissed like he did. No one. The comparison had ended more than a couple potential relationships. One kiss, and she would be lost again. She would be under that spell he wove, forgetting as she melted that this wasn't what she wanted.

I can't do this again.

She took in a deep breath, finding her center again. "Everyone is waiting inside." Including his girlfriend.

What is wrong with me?

She grabbed the door handle and scrambled out. Why had she let Mom talk her into wearing these wedges? She could have slipped out with more grace in a pair of flats.

Derek's longer legs caught up with her before she'd even reached the restaurant door. "Wait, Maddi. Come on. Don't run off."

"I'm not running. I'm going in for dinner."

He stepped in front of her. "Don't go in mad."

"I'm not mad."

That crooked smile came back in a flash. "Neither am I."

"Why would you be mad? Guilty is what you should be."

His brows pulled together. "Guilty?"

"I don't think your girlfriend would appreciate knowing you were a breath away from making out with another woman in a parked car." It sounded even worse out loud.

"First of all." Derek stepped right up next to her, even closer than he'd been in the car. "If I'd been 'a breath away' from making out with you, we'd still be in the car."

She refused to look at him. He'd see in her eyes just how much the idea of being kissed by him still appealed to her even after their years apart.

"What's the second of all?" she muttered.

"Second of all, I *don't* have a girlfriend." With that, he walked into the restaurant, leaving her there to try to find her equilibrium.

Four

"You want me to plot against my own daughter?"

"Absolutely." Derek looked between Mrs. Collins and his uncle, hoping they would be the willing accomplices he'd pegged them as. "Maybe I'm a complete idiot, and maybe I'll regret this later, but there was still something there between us last night. I just want to see whether—"

"No need to convince me, hon." Mrs. Collins waved off his argument. "Madison was never happier than when the two of you were together. You plot away and give me an assignment."

He grinned. That was exactly what he wanted to hear.

"And you, Uncle Grant?"

Uncle Grant wrapped his arms around Mrs. Collins, leaning his chin on her shoulder from behind. "Whatever will make Teresa happy."

She reached up and patted his cheek. "Sweet man."

"Are you sure?" Uncle Grant asked, a troublemaker glint in his eyes again. "Madison seems to think I'm the devil himself."

Derek smiled. "Figured that out, did you?"

Mrs. Collins laughed. "Madison doesn't think much of my love-life intelligence, but I'm not stupid. I know she came home to get rid of Grant."

"And that doesn't offend you?" Derek looked at his uncle.

"Madison loves her mother. Since I do too, I can't be offended by that."

The two of them were kind of disgustingly happy. Derek envied his uncle that. The only time *he* had been out of his mind in love with someone was Maddi. He hadn't ever gotten her out of his system. Maybe he really was an idiot. He was, after all, about to try again, despite being shot down so entirely the last time.

"Both of you knowing exactly what Maddi's up to will make this work even better," he said. "I'm going to offer to help her with her sleuthing. Give her a chance to spy on you when you're . . . uh . . . supposedly oblivious."

"Fake spying?" Mrs. Collins asked.

"No. I want her to see how things really are." He knew his uncle well enough not to worry at all that Maddi would see her mother being mistreated in any way. "I don't have private-eye skills. No matter how covert I tried to be, you'll probably realize we're there."

Uncle Grant nodded slowly. "So our role in this is to pretend we don't see the two of you?"

"Exactly," Derek said. "Just be yourselves, the way you always are. And pretend you aren't being spied on."

Uncle Grant turned his gaze back to Mrs. Collins. "What do you think? Will your girl see through this?"

Mrs. Collins eyed Derek for a moment in silence. "She might have some suspicions. But if Derek is smart, she'll be too distracted in the end to care."

"I can distract her, especially if you go places Maddi will enjoy." Derek grabbed his jacket from the coat rack by the door. "Where are you two going to be tonight?"

"We were just going to stay here and watch a movie, pop popcorn or something." Mrs. Collins seemed to reconsider their plans even as she said it. "But maybe we should go out."

They were catching on fast.

"Would Madison enjoy the new movie at the Cineplex?" Uncle Grant asked.

A couple seats in the dark, back corner of the movie theater? "Let's do it."

Uncle Grant pulled the door open for him. "We'll go about seven-thirty. There has to be a showing around then."

That would work. "We'll start our stakeout around seven o'clock. I'll watch for you to pass, and we'll follow."

Mrs. Collins looked beyond excited. "We'll have to think of something *really* romantic for us to do tomorrow night. Let us know if you have any ideas."

They'd not only be covertly watching their relatives, she'd be unknowingly going on a date with him every night. Nice.

He waited until a quarter to seven before going to Maddi's house, trying to act covert and sneaky. She answered the door, and he pulled her outside, looking both ways before pulling the door closed.

She looked at him like he was completely nuts. "What are you doing?"

"I'm going to help you go all Sherlock Holmes on your mother."

"*What?*"

"Shh." He pressed his fingers to her lips. Pretending that touch didn't affect him pushed his acting skills to their limit. "Stealth, Maddi. You need stealth." He reached around her and opened her mom's front door again. "Tell her you're going out—going to someone's house or something."

"Are you bossing me around?" Her offended tone was a little overdone.

He gave her a half smile. "I wouldn't dare boss you around. You'd rip me to shreds."

"You know it." She ruined her show of arrogance by rolling her eyes like a teenager. She leaned in the doorway. "Hey, Mom?"

"Yeah?" came the answer from inside.

"I'm going out for a while, okay?"

"Okay. Have fun."

Maddi gave him a "good enough?" look. He nodded approval.

"What now, Dr. Watson?" she asked.

"I have a stakeout vehicle parked at the end of the street." He took her hand, not giving her even a minute to object, and walked quickly that direction.

"You're putting a lot of effort into spying on your own uncle."

"You took off work and drove across state lines to spy on your own mother." He winked at her.

She still blushes. It was adorable.

He kept her hand in his all the way to his car up the street. He held the door while she got in, then let himself in on the driver's side.

"Do I smell spring rolls?" she asked. It almost sounded like an accusation. "Are you still in denial? Admitting you have a problem is the first step to recovery."

"And what about your 'problem'?" He tapped the plastic lid of the takeout cup in the passenger-side cup holder.

She pressed her lips together, eyes growing wide. "Is that what I think it is?"

"Twenty ounces."

She picked up the cup. "You're terrible." She took a long pull on the straw. "Terrible."

"Yup." He reached back and grabbed the bag of Chang's takeout he'd picked up before parking. He popped open the carton of spring rolls. "Want one?"

She nodded as she sipped, reaching in and pulling out a roll.

"We're really spying on your uncle?" she asked.

He swallowed a bite. "You need to know your mom is happy. If following them around will set your mind at ease . . ." He shrugged and took another bite.

"What if we follow him around, and we find out that he's a jerk?"

Derek just smiled.

"You're that confident?"

"I know my uncle pretty well."

"We'll see." She took a bite.

"Yes, we will."

They chatted while they sat there. Nothing important came up, but it was good talking to her again. She clearly loved her work. Whether she realized it or not, she was lonely. He could tell.

Still, he stuck to light topics and kept his distance. He'd admitted to himself that he'd gone too fast the night before.

Maddi didn't trust anyone easily, especially men. Her dad had walked out on them when she was just a little girl. Then Mrs. Collins had gone through a long string of relationships. They all ended badly. He'd have to take his time.

But she wouldn't be in Folsom Lake very long, so time was one thing he didn't have a lot of. He'd let her run away two years earlier without a fight. He wasn't going to make the same mistake again.

Five

"What movie did they pick?" Madison was enjoying their stakeout despite herself. "Please tell me they aren't seeing that dad-saves-his-daughter-from-kidnappers movie? You'd think after four movies, those kidnappers would decide to take someone else."

Derek gave one of his half laughs of agreement. She'd heard those so many times while they were together. No one else made that sound. It was cute. "Kidnappers are notoriously stupid," he said. "Fortunately, for us, your mom and Grant chose the sappy, romantic flick."

"'Sappy'?"

"Did I say that? I meant, *wonderful, heartwarming* romantic flick." He obviously didn't mean that at all, but he held up two tickets, so he apparently thought the movie was worth enduring in the name of covert operations. "Do you think they've had enough time to get popcorn and all that?"

"Peek in the window," she said, motioning ahead of them.

He waved her over with him, leaning enough to glance in the tinted glass. "I kind of feel like a criminal. If anyone asks, I'm saying this was all your idea."

"Hey, we're in this together. If I go down, we both go down." She'd forgotten how much fun they used to have. Their sense of humor was the same. They both enjoyed being just a little crazy, though she didn't think either of them had ever admitted it.

"You ratted me out, see," he said with a 1920s gangster inflection. "So I'm taking you out with me, see."

She laughed. "Your twenties gangster impression needs work."

"You no-good, dirty rat." He even tried to make a Humphrey Bogart face. That hadn't improved since the night they watched *Angels with Dirty Faces* on cable because he'd been sick and didn't feel good enough to leave his apartment. He'd been doing that ridiculous impression ever since. She'd been laughing at it from day one.

"So, Bugsy," Maddi said. "Is the coast clear?"

Derek looked inside again. "We have a clear shot to the concession stand. We can get you some Junior Mints before the show starts."

"Wow. Dinner *and* dessert."

He flashed her a big, goofy grin. "That's right. I know how to show a girl a good time."

"I probably should be footing the bill for this. It's my investigation, after all."

He pushed open the door, holding it for her. "You can pay for tomorrow's itinerary."

"Tomorrow's?" She stopped halfway through the door. He was planning to spend the next night with her as well?

He looked surprised by her confusion. "Did you think you would find out everything you needed to know about my uncle in one night? I thought you'd want to be more thorough than that."

She *had* taken off a full week of work, after all. If Mr. Fabulous had been a pig from the first minute, she'd have sent him off and spent the rest of her vacation with Mom. But a more subtle jerk, she realized, would require more observation. So far, Grant McGee didn't seem like a jerk at all. Either he wasn't one—which was hard to even imagine— or he was better at hiding it than most.

"I intend to be completely thorough," she told Derek.

His nod seemed like approval. She liked that. No lecture, no treating her like an incompetent child. Not enough men were like him.

He ordered a large popcorn like he always had and got her a box of Junior Mints. She, of course, remembered his usual movie-theater snack, but it surprised her that *he* remembered hers. Her own father didn't remember her birthday half the time, let alone her favorite candy.

Derek stuck his head in the theater where their movie was showing, checking to see where Mom and his uncle were sitting. Folsom Lake didn't have the new stadium-style theaters, but the old school ones with the entrance at the very back.

"We're in luck. They're about halfway to the front. If we take a seat here in the back, they'll never spot us. Maybe in the corner where light from the door won't hit us."

Dark corner. In the back. She liked the idea, but she couldn't deny the fact that most of the appeal had nothing to do with hiding from her mom.

They slid into the back row, taking the two seats closest to the wall. Apparently Derek remembered she preferred not being next to the wall. He took that seat without having to be asked.

"A person could fall asleep here, and no one would see them for days," she whispered.

The theater was only about a quarter full. Enough people to go unnoticed, and not so many that they couldn't whisper now and then without getting shushed.

"Here's what I'm thinking," he whispered. "You keep an eye on your mom—watch for any signs of being unhappy or miserable or anything. I'll watch Uncle Grant and let you know if he does anything you might object to."

Her eyes hadn't adjusted yet; she could only just make out Derek's silhouette in the dark. How could he possibly see what his uncle was doing from clear across the room?

"What kind of things will you be watching for?" She squinted, trying to get a better look at her mom in the dark.

"Well, if he pulls the old yawn-and-stretch move, like this." Derek gave an exaggerated yawn, then held one arm out, as if getting a good stretch, and rested it along the back of her chair, effectively putting his arm around her.

"Mom won't fall for that."

"Probably not." He settled in with his arm still around her shoulders. "I'll also let you know if he leans in too close to whisper in her ear." He, of course, leaned in close to whisper the last few words—where else?—in her ear. "Or if he convinces her to sit alone with him in a dark corner of the theater."

She whipped her head around to look at him. By now, her eyes had adjusted enough to see the look of mischief in his eyes.

"I don't think we really have to worry about that last one, though," he whispered. "There aren't any corners left."

On that declaration, the previews ended and the movie began. Derek didn't show any signs of pulling away. He sat casually eating his popcorn with his arm around her, leaning in her direction.

Her box of Junior Mints sat unopened in her hand as her stomach had tied itself in knots. Derek's cologne, the warmth of him next to her, the sound of his voice and the feel of his breath on her ear. She hadn't been prepared for this.

Just as the on-screen couple had their mandatory contrived misunderstanding, Derek balanced a popcorn kernel on the top of her Junior Mints box. He set another one next to it. Then another.

"What are you doing?" she whispered.

"Uncle Grant isn't doing anything. I'm bored."

He tried to fit another kernel on the box, but it fell to the floor.

"Boring is good. It means he's behaving."

Derek leaned in close again, his breath tickling her ear. "Did you notice he whispered to her a few times?"

"*He* didn't get as close as you are right now." She turned her head enough to look at him out of the corner of her eye. Having him so close actually scared her. Not in a fear-for-her-safety kind of way, but she felt . . . worried. "You should set a better example for him. You're making me wonder if your entire family—"

Derek popped the kernels from her candy box into her mouth, cutting off her words. "You're interrupting the movie."

She chewed at the unexpected mouthful as she tore open the candy box. She pulled out a mint and tried so stick it in Derek's mouth, but he turned away. The candy almost went up his nose.

Madison laughed—she couldn't help herself.

Derek put his hands over her mouth, though she could hear him fighting back a chuckle himself. A couple people in the theater looked over their shoulders at them. They slid down in their seats in perfect unison.

"This is not very covert," Derek said. The flickering light of the movie illuminated his grinning face. "We're gonna get caught."

Madison bit her lips together. If she laughed half as hard as she thought she might, the entire theater would march over and throw them out.

The onscreen couple made up and broke up again before Madison had herself under control. She and Derek didn't even look at each other. The first hint of a glance, and they'd start all over again.

As the movie reached the big final, convenient solution to everyone's problems, Derek broke the silence between them.

"Do we try to sneak out now, before our relatives see us, or do we wait here until we know they're gone?"

"We wait," she whispered back.

"So did Uncle Grant pass this first test?"

She shrugged. "He did okay, I guess. *You*, on the other hand . . ."

That smile of his did her in. It always had. "I shared my popcorn with you. Don't I get credit for that? And"—he pointed as if emphasizing the importance of his next example—"I let you shove a Junior Mint up my nose."

She didn't hold back the laugh that time.

The theater cleared out quickly, so they were able to slip away. He tossed his almost-empty popcorn bucket in the trash on the way out. It was a typical cool spring evening. She should have brought a jacket. She'd have to remember that tomorrow.

Tomorrow. She would spend another night with Derek. There were certainly worse things in the world.

She'd thought of him many times over the last two years, but had never let her thoughts linger. That night she spent hours doing just that, and found herself walking a dangerous line. Spending so much time with Derek McGee could only lead to heartache. She'd start to remember all the reasons she loved being with him. If she wasn't very careful, she'd forget all about the pain men always brought into her life, and she would open herself up to be hurt all over again.

Six

erek managed to talk Uncle Grant and Teresa—
during the course of their conspiracy, they'd
switched to first names—into making their fifth
"fake date" a walk around Folsom Lake. The night after the
movie, they'd gone for dinner at Romanelli's. That had been
interesting to explain to the person who'd seated them:

"We want a seat in view of those people's table, but
where they can't see us."

But the ridiculousness of it had made Maddi laugh, so it
was worth every moment of embarrassment.

After Romanelli's, they'd hit the bowling alley, picking a
lane as far from Uncle Grant and Teresa as they could.

Last night he and Maddi had made up a lame excuse
about him needing banking advice for his insurance office.
They'd sat at Teresa's kitchen table, in full view of the living
room and the horrible made-for-TV movie their relatives
were staying at home to watch.

Five dates wasn't exactly rekindling their relationship,

but they were enjoying each other again. Maddi was smiling and laughing with him. It was almost as if that night two years earlier had never happened.

He could still perfectly picture the moment. She had been shoving the last of her things in the trunk of that beat-up Altima.

"I took a job," she'd said. "Out of state."

"Permanently?" There'd been no warning, no hints that she was getting ready to leave. "Were you going to tell me about this?"

"An opportunity came along, and I'm taking it." She didn't even look at him, just slammed the trunk closed.

"What happens to us, Maddi? You're packing up and taking off without even telling me? You're leaving the state."

She pulled open the driver's door. "It's just . . . it's time."

"Time to what? To move on?"

She'd kept her gaze on the inside of her car, not even glancing his way. "I'm sorry."

"You've told me you love me, Maddi. Did that change?" He remembered so clearly feeling like she'd punched him right in the gut.

"I'm sorry," she'd whispered and climbed in her car.

She'd driven away, leaving him baffled in the street. Every time she'd come home after that, and they'd run into each other, things were awkward. Whenever she was in town, he avoided her street. Last time, he'd simply left.

But she was here again. And he was here. The awkwardness was gone. Things between them were like they had been before she left.

Being with her that week had shown him something about himself that he hadn't admitted over the past two years: he still loved her. He'd never stopped loving her. And he only had two more days to find out if she felt the same way.

"Your uncle thinks like you," Maddi said as they walked up toward the path around the lake.

"What do you mean?"

"A walk around the lake." She said it as if that alone should make her meaning clear. "Where have I seen *that* date idea before?"

She remembered. Their time together must have meant something if she still thought about it.

"You realize, of course," he said, using the conspiratorial tone they'd adopted over the last few days, "that if their date ends the way ours did the last time we walked around Folsom Lake, you'll have to decide if you're going to interfere."

That brought color back to her face. Yes, she definitely remembered that walk.

"Do you plan to stand around and watch them?" He laughed at the picture forming in his head: the two of them ducking behind bushes, spying on the older couple lost in a passionate kiss.

Maddi smiled, then grinned, then finally laughed outright. "No. I'm not going to watch."

"You trust him enough, then?"

She thought about that a moment as they walked along. "I guess I do. Not entirely, but enough for that."

"Are you still going to try to break them up?"

She shrugged a little. "Your uncle seems like a nice guy."

"But you're still not sure?"

She looked exasperated, frustrated. "I am glad he didn't turn out to be a total jerk, but that doesn't mean this won't end badly. I worry about my mom, Derek. She's been through a lot. I just don't want to see her hurt. Not again."

Derek put his arm around her waist and pulled her up next to him. She laid her head on his shoulder—exactly what he hoped she'd do.

"Did I ever tell you how great it is that you love your mom so much?" That probably sounded stupid to her, or cheesy. Still, he was glad he said it. He hadn't always been good about telling her how he felt. Maybe that was partly why she'd left.

"She called me a 'helicopter mom' yesterday." Though Maddi laughed, he could hear that the comment had hurt. "I don't mean to hover over her, I just . . . Her life has fallen apart so many times. I want to save her from that. I don't want to see her hurt again."

"I know. I think she's knows too." He twisted his neck enough to kiss the top of her head. "But it has to be hard as a mom to need your daughter to come save you from your mistakes."

Maddi put her arm around him as well. Definitely promising. "It's not her fault. It's how things work for us."

For us? "Men abandoning her throughout the Western U.S.? Breaking her heart? That's 'how things work' for the both of you?"

"My dad walked out when I was a kid. No man has stuck around us since then."

He stopped in his tracks. *No man? Us?* "I didn't abandon you. I didn't walk out on you, not once."

She looked up at him. He didn't see a denial in her eyes. He also didn't see a defense of him. "Well, no, but—" She bit off whatever she was going to say.

"But *what?*" He pulled away, looking at her closely. She couldn't accuse him of walking out on her. She was the one who had walked out on *him*, without any explanation, without any warning. "I stayed by you. I never even thought of leaving."

She crossed her arms over her chest, gaze turned away. It was the same posture he'd seen that day by her car. How had this happened again so quickly?

"I didn't leave," he said again. "*You* did."

"Before you could leave me," she tossed back. "I left first. I had to."

Before I could leave? What made her think he ever would? "I didn't say I was leaving."

"You didn't have to. It's what everyone does. Everyone. And I wasn't going to let that happen, not with you, not when it would have—" She turned away, walking back in the direction they'd come.

He followed after her. "Would have what? Not when it would have *what*?"

She didn't answer. If anything, she walked faster.

"Talk to me, Maddi."

"I don't want to." She kept going, not looking at him, not slowing. "I can't talk about this, not now."

"Then when? You're leaving in two days. I know what that means—that I won't hear from you for months. That when you do come back, I'll only see you by accident."

He grabbed hold of her arm to stop her from running off. He turned her around.

"You left with no explanation. You never told me why. I have wondered for two years what went wrong." He kept his hands on her upper arms and looked her in the eye. He couldn't help the tense and unhappy tone. That moment from two years earlier was coming back hard and fast. "Don't you think I deserve an explanation? After everything we were together, I think I at least should have been told why."

"Because I had to." The words snapped out of her. "Things were getting too serious. I didn't want—I didn't want it. I didn't want *this*."

"What this? Me?"

She didn't deny it.

"But we were good together."

She dropped her eyes. "I know."

Those two words took the fight out of him. "Then why did you leave?"

"I had to," Maddi little more than whispered. She took a quick step backward. "I'm sorry." She shook her head then shook it again. "I never should have come home."

They had driven to the lake separately, so when she practically ran up the path toward her parked car, he knew she didn't have to wait for him. She would get in her Altima exactly like she had before. And she would leave.

And, once again, he couldn't stop her.

Seven

om came in while Madison was packing. "Where are you going?"

"I have to get back to work." She dropped socks in her suitcase.

"You said you were staying until Sunday."

In went a pair jeans. "I'm not worried about Grant anymore. And you seem happy, so I'm heading back."

"What about Derek?" Mom dropped onto the bed. "You two seemed to be enjoying each other the last few nights."

Had she seen them together? "I don't know what you mean."

Mom actually rolled her eyes. "The two of you are great people, but you're terrible spies."

Madison sat down next to her mother. "Did Grant see us too?"

"Of course. But don't worry; he didn't act any differently than he always does." Mom patted her hand. "He really is as fabulous as he seems."

"That's hard to believe. Our family track record isn't very promising."

Madison scooted back, sitting up next to the headboard. Mom did the same. They'd had conversations in that position many times when she was growing up.

"I haven't made many good decisions where men are concerned," Mom said. "I've gone with the cream of the loser crop."

Madison could actually laugh a little at that.

"But you have done so much better than I have."

She shook her head. "You only say that because you haven't met some of the guys I've gone out with since I moved away."

"You've mentioned a few of those dates." Mom smiled over at her. "Men can be such idiots."

Madison thought of Derek. He wasn't that way at all. He was the nicest, most sincere man she'd ever known.

"How many of those idiots did you go on more than a couple dates with?"

"None." They had fallen so far short of the bar that Derek had set, she'd never wanted to go beyond a date or two. They just didn't compare.

How pathetic is that? You haven't had a relationship since you broke it off with him because no one was as great as he was. Pathetic.

"Do you know why I started going with Grant?" Mom asked.

Madison shook her head.

"Because he reminded me of Derek."

"What?"

Mom turned enough to face her more directly. "I watched you two the whole time you and Derek were together. I saw how he treated you, how he looked at you. And I realized how happy you were together. I wanted that."

Her mother had never said that before. They'd never really discussed relationships.

"Grant treated me the same way. He was kind and thoughtful. He wasn't selfish and controlling and . . ." Mom shrugged. "He was nice. So I gave him a shot."

"Aren't you afraid he'll hurt you like all the others have?"

"A little. But not because he, personally, worries me."

Madison knew exactly what she meant. "But because everyone else has."

"I'm beginning to realize that my mistakes have made you afraid. You're afraid of being abandoned because your father left, because every guy I've dated since then has walked out on me. You're afraid of being hurt because you've seen my heart break so many times."

She shook her head. "No, Mom, don't blame—"

"It's true. I can see that it is."

Madison pulled her legs up to her chest and wrapped her arms around her legs. She *was* afraid. The only emotion that had been stronger than her heartbreak when she'd left Folsom Lake two years earlier was fear. "I love him, Mom. I love him so much that it will kill me when he leaves. It'll hurt so much, I don't know if I'll ever get over it."

"You would die a little inside." Mom spoke from obvious experience. "But living without him—how is that working out?"

Madison took a deep breath, surprised by the emotion bubbling inside. "I'm fine. I have friends and things I like doing. And I don't spend every minute worrying that someone's going to break my heart."

"So you're not really *living* without him. You're surviving."

Madison bent her neck and rested her head on her knees.

"You need to go talk to him, dear. Before you go, talk to him. Before you decide he's going to walk out on you, find out how likely it is that he'd walk out on you. You might just find out trusting him is worth the risk."

❦

Madison had seldom been so nervous in her life. She waited at Derek's apartment door, trying to decide what she would say.

He opened the door. "Maddi." Was that a good look of surprise, or a bad one?

"You were right," she said. "You deserved to know why."

He looked hesitant, unsure. "Why you left, you mean?"

Madison nodded. He motioned her inside, pulling the door open all the way. She stood in the middle of the living room, trying to gather up her courage. "You've redecorated."

"A little. My parents gave me some furniture when they downsized." He moved to stand in front of her.

She couldn't put it off any longer. "I left because I was afraid."

"Of what?"

"Of you." That hadn't come out right. "Not you as a person."

"Then what?"

The confession she'd come to make wasn't proving easy. Opening herself up more only meant that he could hurt her that much more deeply.

Derek took her hands in his. "I don't know for sure what you were afraid of—*are* afraid of. But I have some idea."

She could feel heat rushing across her face. Making personal confessions was not her favorite thing.

"Do you know how many people I've dated since you left?"

Did she know? She didn't *want* to know.

"None. I've had a date here or there, but not a relationship."

If she'd doubted before that she still had feelings for him, the relief she felt at hearing that would have told her for certain that she did.

"No one I went out with was ever what I wanted." His hands slid up her arms, her shoulders, her neck, and settled on either side of her face. "No one was ever *you*."

She closed her eyes, unsure if the tears she felt building up were happiness or confusion or fear.

"I know your dad walked out on you," he went on. "Every man your mom has ever been involved with has left too." His thumbs rubbed gently along her jaw. "I have a feeling what you were afraid of was that I would eventually do the same thing. I thought, while we were together, that you knew that wasn't me, that you got that about us. Obviously I need to be more blunt."

She felt him lightly kiss her forehead. His lips trailed past her temple to her ear.

"No one will ever be you, Maddi," he whispered. "I haven't moved on after two years, even though *you* walked out on *me*."

She rested her hands against his chest. She wanted so badly to believe him, but he was promising her the moon. She could not pin all her hopes on impossible dreams.

"You cut off everything between us, but my heart couldn't move on. There was no one who fit there like you do, no one who fit me like you do."

His arms wrapped around her, but his face stayed close to hers, his words whispered directly into her ear.

"There has been no one for me but you ever since the day you sat next to me in high-school biology. I didn't get up the nerve to ask you out until college, and only after going through agony, fearing you'd pick a school in another state, and I'd never see you again." He kissed her temple again, his arms firmly around her. "I'm not perfect. We've had our disagreements, even a fight or two. But we were good together. We always have been."

"I know." Somehow she found the voice to say what she was thinking. "But believing in a miracle only makes the disappointment worse when it doesn't happen."

He leaned his forehead against hers. "Then trust me. Look back on all we've been through together. Listen to what I'm saying now. All of those things are reasons to believe that this is real. You have to trust me that much."

"That's a lot." Trusting someone with her heart was enormous when she knew how fragile an organ it really was.

"I know," he said, repeating her earlier words. "I'm only asking you to trust me enough to try."

She opened her eyes and looked into his, so close to hers. "Sometimes a person is too broken to fix."

"You don't need to be fixed. You just need to be loved."

He shifted the tiniest bit, and their lips touched. It was a tentative moment, neither of them giving over to the sensation of being together again.

His scent. His touch. His kiss. Her heart pounded and turned. She couldn't help but steal a moment of that to keep for later.

Her hands slipped about his middle, and she returned his kiss with none of her earlier hesitation. His fingers threaded through her hair, cradling her head and pulling her to him until nothing remained between them but the air they breathed.

Madison poured two years of loneliness and regret and fear into that desperate moment, knowing she couldn't stay, knowing she didn't have the strength to put herself so

entirely on the line. He would break her heart, and she would never recover.

The first tear trickled from her eyes, running down her face before rolling onto his. She wiped at it with her thumb as she pulled back.

"I can't do this." Her voice broke. Her heart cracked a little more.

"I know." He lifted her hand to his lips and kissed it gently. "I know."

She stepped back, moving toward the door.

"Maddi?"

She looked back over her shoulder.

He gave her a tiny, tender, painful smile. "When you're ready, come back to me."

Eight

*M*adison had spent so much time during her first day back at work talking about APRs and refinances and small-business loans that she was tired of the sound of her own voice. Foot traffic slowed down in the branch midafternoon. Madison leaned back in her chair as Beth stepped inside her cubicle and dropped into the seat across from her desk.

"Cancún was amazing." Beth sighed long and dramatic. "You should have come."

"I'm sure it was great. But it was nice being back home too."

"So how was your mom's boyfriend? Total loser again?"

Madison realized with a jolt that she hadn't thought about Grant McGee much since leaving Folsom Lake. Apparently she really wasn't worried about him. Or she was too distracted. "He seems like a really nice guy, actually. And I haven't seen Mom so happy in a really long time."

You were happy with Derek. Mom's voice spoke in her thoughts, all the things she'd said about liking Grant because he was so much like his nephew.

Beth was talking about pristine beaches and snorkeling in crystal-blue water. Exactly the things that originally pulled Madison to the idea of Cancún. She should have been writhing with jealousy, or at least hanging on every descriptive word.

Instead, her thoughts were full of hair touched by hints of gold, hazel eyes full of laughter, Chang's spring rolls. She tried to shake it off and focus. Derek did that to her so easily. He was such a deeply entrenched part of her that she never could completely get him out of her system.

"The second night we were there," Beth continued. "We met these guys. They were hot. I don't mean hot like they knew it, kind of hot. They were nice-guy hot. Nice guys. And hot. At the same time. I mean, when does that happen?"

A hot, nice guy. If she'd gone to Mexico with her friends, she would have met these mystery men. But they would have turned out like every other guy she'd met in the last two years. She'd be intrigued at first, then vaguely disappointed.

No one I went out with was ever what I wanted. Derek had said that, but she could have said it herself and meant it completely.

No one was ever you. He'd said that too.

"We were all saying that we should go again next year. Or at least go *somewhere* next year." Beth shifted forward, leaning a little against the edge of Madison's desk. "But you have to come. You can't miss out again."

"I didn't really miss out." She was surprised to find she meant it. "I had a good time in Folsom Lake. I really did."

Spying in a movie. Junior Mints and popcorn. Sitting in Derek's car. She did have fun. She couldn't remember the last time she'd been so content, so easily happy.

"Wait." Beth looked more than a little suspicious. "*He* was there, wasn't he? Not just there—you saw him."

Madison let herself smile a little. "We spent a lot of time together. It was . . . nice."

"You got back with the old boyfriend? Madison. How could you go all day without telling me this?"

She had Beth's complete attention now. "It's not a big deal."

"Not a big deal?" Beth held her hands out, like the enormity of this was obvious. "You've been talking about Derek McGee for a year. And you always look all heartbroken and lonely. What happened? Did things get going between you two again?"

"No." She shrugged at that. "Maybe a little, but not really."

"Madison." Beth sounded like Mom always had when she was in trouble.

"It didn't work in the end, okay? It never does."

Beth slouched again. "You gave it an entire week. That'll tell you a lot."

"I gave it years the first time, Beth. He is the same person. I'm the same person. It'll just turn out the same way it did before."

Beth's eyes narrowed. "Is he seeing someone?" Madison reluctantly shook her head.

"Has he been serious with anyone since you dumped him two years ago?"

Dumped wasn't the word she would have used. "He hasn't."

Beth didn't let up on the interrogation. "Did he seem interested again? Interested still?"

She thought back on that farewell kiss, on all the times in the last week he'd held her hand or put his arm around her. He'd even said he still loved her. "Yeah, he is definitely still interested."

Beth's eyes widened far beyond normal. "Then why are you here? You have a hunky guy who is still so into you that he hasn't dated anyone for years, even though you dumped him. And don't tell me you don't still have feelings for him. I'm not stupid."

Madison propped her elbows on the table and leaned her head into her upturned hands. "I can't do it again, Beth. What happens when it falls apart? I'll be right back where I was before. I don't want that."

Beth came around her desk and gave her a friendly hug. "Your mom's taking a chance, and she's had far more relationship failures than you have. She found a good guy, but so have you. Go take the chance."

"I don't know."

"Missing Cancún is one kind of regret," Beth said. "But missing a chance to be with the person you have always loved who feels exactly the same way? That's a completely different thing. That's a regret most people couldn't live with."

Nine

erek could only take so much of the conversation over dinner with Teresa and Uncle Grant. He'd hoped a night with someone else for company, anyone but himself, would take his mind off the month that had passed since Maddi left. Spring was giving way to summer. Life was going on, but his heart wasn't in it.

He'd honestly thought she would come back. He'd sat facing his door all night when she'd first left. He'd set the table for two every night for a week. He still did a double-take whenever a green car drove past.

He knew he needed a distraction, but Maddi's mom was the wrong choice. She would laugh, and he would hear *her* daughter. She would smile, and he would see Maddi.

They talked about everything from the unusually mild weather to the latest Hollywood scandal to the bank getting a new manager to music they'd listened to as teenagers. Derek spent the dinner hour picking at his food and trying to think of an excuse to leave.

In the end he didn't have to. Uncle Grant gave him an understanding look and motioned to the front door with his head. Teresa nodded, her motherly expression coming a little too close to pity.

He thanked her for the meal and took the escape they offered. A drive around town didn't help. Sitting for an hour at Folsom Lake was even worse. He finally settled on a takeout order of spring rolls from Chang's. There had to be a game on. He didn't care what sport or what team. He just needed something to do other than think about what a jerk Fate was sometimes.

Derek turned in at his complex's parking lot. He parked in his space and sat in his car. He slouched in the seat, eyeing the steering wheel.

"This is ridiculous, and I know," he told his steering wheel. "I wasn't this bad when she left the first time." The steering wheel was no help. "I don't know why Maddi does this all the time."

Everything always came back to her. He shook his head. *I'm so lame.* He grabbed his takeout then pushed open his door. Two steps from his car, he stopped.

A beat-up green Altima sat parked under a streetlight right by his apartment. *Now I'm seeing things.* Hallucination or not, he stepped closer. He didn't see anyone sitting inside. It had to be Maddi. But he didn't dare let himself believe it. If it was her car, where was she? There was no one standing by his door. The parking lot was empty. "It has to be her."

If she wasn't in the parking lot . . . He looked toward his apartment door. She knew where he kept the spare key. She used to let herself in all the time.

Maddi's back. His keys fumbled around in his hand before he managed to get the right one in the lock and open his apartment door.

"Maddi?" *She has to be here.* "Maddi?"

He pushed the door shut behind him with his foot. His heart missed the next beat. There she was, standing in his living room, looking unsure of herself.

He tossed his carton of egg rolls on the coffee table as he rushed toward her. His arms were around her in an instant. He kept repeating her name, unable to think of anything else to say. She was back. He didn't know why or for how long. But she was there, and for the moment, that was enough.

He pulled back enough to look at her. "Are you here for another vacation?"

The answer had better be no.

She shook her head. "I got a new job."

He could tell he was grinning like an idiot, but he didn't care. "A job in Folsom Lake?"

"I'm the new bank manager at the branch here."

He'd never felt so much like pumping his fist in the air. "Your mom didn't say anything."

"She doesn't know yet. I wanted to tell you first."

"Why me?" He watched her closely, looking for the answer in her eyes.

"You're the one who told me to come back."

"I told you to come back *when you were ready*."

She wrapped her arms around him, leaning against him.

It was all he needed. He held her close, rubbing her back and taking in the citrusy smell that always filled her hair. "You came back to me."

"I can't promise not to freak out sometimes," she said from inside his embrace. "And I'll probably be paranoid and worried and seriously messed up. But I'll try."

"I just want you here, with me, for better or worse, through the ups and downs. It's all I've wanted for two years, Maddi. Longer than that, really. I wanted it even before you left."

She looked up at him, an aura of hope in her eyes he hadn't seen before. "You are the only one who's ever been worth the risk, Derek. The only one."

In moments like that, there's really not much to be said. He kissed her, long and deep, with all the passion he'd held back a month earlier. She held tightly to him, as if determined not to let him get away from her. He wasn't going anywhere. Not ever.

He took in the scent of her, the feel of her back in his arms and in his life for good. This was home to him. His Maddi was back, the one who got away, his lost love, his one and only. This time, he would never let her go.

Sarah M. Eden is the author of multiple historical romances, including Whitney Award finalists *Seeking Persephone*, *Courting Miss Lancaster* and *Longing for Home*. Combining her obsession with history and affinity for tender love stories, Sarah loves crafting witty characters and heartfelt romances. She holds a bachelor's degree in research and happily spends hours perusing the reference shelves of her local library. Sarah has twice served as the Master of Ceremonies for the LDStorymakers Writers Conference, acted as the Writer in Residence at the Northwest Writers Retreat, and is one-third of the team at the AppendixPodcast.com. Sarah is represented by Pam van Hylckama Vlieg at Foreword Literary Agency. Visit her website at www.sarahmeden.com

Twitter: @SarahMEden
Facebook: Sarah M. Eden

Picture Perfect

An Aliso Creek novella
Heather B. Moore

Other Works by Heather B. Moore

The Aliso Creek Novella Series

The Newport Ladies Book Club Series

Heart of the Ocean

The Fortune Café

Published under H.B. Moore

Esther the Queen

Finding Sheba

Beneath

Daughters of Jared

One

"I can't go," Arie said, the pout in her voice carrying through the phone. "If I lose this client, I'll lose my promotion."

Gemma exhaled with frustration. Arie was the second one to cancel for the weekend. Granted, her excuse was solid, but Gemma had gone through a lot to get three days off for their annual spring vacation. She stared out her condo window at the scenery that never seemed to change—green trees, blue skies—San Diego's temperatures fluctuated only about twenty degrees throughout the year. "Jess isn't coming, and now you aren't. What about Liz and Drew?"

"Liz is still going, but I don't know about Drew," Arie said. "I haven't talked to him much this year. He didn't come last time; I wonder if that means something."

Gemma talked to Drew quite a bit—well, about once a month. A text or quick phone call. They'd managed to stay in touch over the years since high school. All of them had stayed in touch—the "Five." Other friends had come and gone—heck, husbands, boyfriends, girlfriends—they'd all been a part of the group at one time or another. But currently, it was back to the original Five for this weekend. Or it was supposed to be.

Gemma could hardly believe it had been twelve years since they'd graduated from Aliso Creek High, which, of course, reminded her that she'd just turned thirty. She was the last of the group to hit that milestone—which made her the baby of the Five.

Arie was saying something else about work, and Gemma forced herself to tune back in. She already felt the despondency hit. First, turning thirty . . . next, her boyfriend, Randy, had been weird lately, but that was probably the funky phase that all relationships went through . . . then everyone was cancelling on the spring vacation plans. She'd been looking forward to the trip more than she'd realized.

"So sorry, Gem," Arie said. "We'll do lunch later this month."

"Okay," Gemma said. "Love you." When she hung up, Gemma texted Drew and Liz separately.

R u still planning on this weekend?

Liz texted back immediately. *Yep, can't wait! What time will u be there?*

Leaving @ 9 am Friday. Should be there 11 @ the latest, Gemma wrote.

Sounds good. I'll be there @ 12.

Gemma tossed the phone on the couch and went to her bedroom to start packing. It looked like it would just be the three of them, assuming Drew was coming. She slowed as she passed the hallway mirror. She'd hardly changed a thing about her appearance since high school. Throughout college, she'd sported the same straight brown hair. The only evidence of the passing years was fluctuating weight and an inch here or there on the length of her hair.

I look average. Her hair was pulled into its usual ponytail, the easiest way to wear it while working at the floral shop. She brushed the top of her black pants—another item from work. She and all of her employees—which amounted to two—wore the same thing: black pants and pale green shirts. Gemma had read a study that if the employees wore matching clothing, they looked more professional.

Perhaps it was true. Gemma's floral shop had done well, allowing her to hire a full timer and a part timer. Her parents had been disappointed that she hadn't gone into the corporate world, but they seemed more supportive now that they saw her success. In fact, about once a week, her dad stopped in to buy flowers for her mom.

It was kind of sweet.

Totally sweet, she corrected herself. Her parents had one of those magical marriages, where they were still in love and weren't afraid to show it. Gemma sighed and readjusted her ponytail. It had been at least two years since her parents had bothered her about the M word. And that was because of Randy. Yet now she didn't know what to make of him. On the one hand, she didn't want to admit to herself that the past few months had felt *off*. She couldn't quite explain it. They were great together. Besides, she was thirty now, and it was time to take things more seriously. Maybe that was it— she didn't see Randy as being equally serious.

She knew one thing: her parents definitely approved of him—a corporate tax lawyer, blond, good looking, from a great family—what's not to love?

Me. The word popped into her head, unwelcome. Randy had said he loved her. Maybe not as often as she wanted, but sometimes—like now—when she was feeling sorry for herself, she doubted.

Which is completely normal. All couples go through doubts.

Gemma walked in her room and pulled out the small suitcase from under her bed. *I just need to be more patient with Randy. Maybe it's just an off month for him.* If everyone canceled spring vacation on her, she'd go alone, and she'd love it. She'd already arranged for others to cover for her at the shop, which was easy to justify, as she hadn't been gone more than a few days since opening three years ago.

Something Randy regularly complained about. But she'd explained over and over that her vacations weren't paid, unlike the corporate-sponsored cruises and resort escapes Randy's company sent him on.

Gemma opened her closet and tugged a couple of shirts down from their hangers. Now that she thought about it, Randy hadn't been complaining about anything lately. He'd been quiet overall, often waiting a day or two before returning her calls. Tonight they'd be going out for dinner, though, so maybe she could ask what was bothering him then.

As long as it didn't turn into a fight—she didn't want to go into her vacation with an upset boyfriend back home. She looked at the two shirts she held and scowled. She'd probably worn them at the last spring vacation, and the one before that. Everything in her closet was old.

Just like I am now.

Of course, she didn't think thirty was necessarily *old*, but she hadn't thought that at thirty, she'd still be living alone, with no husband, no kids, no marriage like her parents'. Or that she'd still be hanging out with her high-school friends—not that she didn't love them.

Really, out of the five of them, the only one who could be counted as making a name for himself was Drew. Yet even he hadn't married and settled down. His photographs were now national sensations, and he'd landed gigs with some of the largest fashion magazines in the country. He'd even moved to New York for a couple of years, but now he was back, where he said his "bones didn't get cold."

Gemma smiled at the thought. Nothing about Drew was cold—even at thirty. He could still be considered hot. And, like most good-looking, successful men, he knew it. He had an arsenal of girlfriends to stroke his ego, which pretty much meant he was a gigantic tease to his "sisters" from high school.

Arie was next on the totem pole of success. She was close to making vice president of a real-estate company. And Jess, scattered Jess, was lucky to have a job at all. She ran a home business making jewelry, but that didn't bring in much income. Gemma had once mistakenly offered her a job at the shop. When Jess didn't show up for work three days in a row, Gemma reluctantly let her go.

The best way to describe Jess was a cute bag lady, who seemed to get whatever she wanted, even when she became a widow. It didn't hurt that her former husband was twenty-five years older and had left her quite a bit of money when he died. Jess seemed to have a hard time with jobs that were structured and required consistent hours. Hence her brief stint in Gemma's floral shop.

Then there was Liz—twice divorced, with a six-year-old from her first marriage. Liz had changed when she became a mom—less spontaneous—but Gemma didn't blame her. Liz was dating someone she thought was perfect, so Gemma was sure he would be the main topic of conversation for the weekend.

What will I tell her about Randy? Gemma wondered. *Still dating. Still no proposal. Still living separately. Still working crazy hours. Nothing's changed.*

Gemma pulled down another shirt then tossed it on the bed. Nothing had changed in her life. Different boyfriend, different condo, different job, but really, she was essentially the same as she had been in high school. Gemma dug through her clothes, looking for anything that looked remotely interesting, but only found more of the same.

She glanced at the clock by her bed. It was only 4:30 pm, and she didn't have to meet Randy until 7:00. She hadn't braved any clothing stores in a long time, since ordering the basics online was so much easier.

Mind made up, she grabbed her keys and purse, leaving the packing for later.

Two

Gemma turned the rearview mirror to catch her reflection and nearly gasped again. She'd done it. Once in the mall, something had snapped inside her. Maybe it was seeing all the stylish mannequins and their cropped hair, thin bodies, and glittering clothing, but whatever it was, before she knew it, she had walked into one of those trendy salons.

The result now stared back at her. Pixie-short hair, streaked with blonde and auburn, blended with her regular brown. She didn't know whether to laugh or squeeze her eyes shut. What would Randy think? She started the car, her hands trembling as she pulled out of the parking lot. She'd texted to tell him she'd meet him at The Grille. In ten minutes, she'd see him. Or more accurately, he'd see *her*.

She thought for a second that she should change into one of the new tops she'd purchased, but then decided that Randy should probably be exposed to the new Gemma in smaller doses. She'd spent nearly $400 at the mall aside from the salon, more than she'd spent on clothing in, well, ever.

When she walked into the restaurant, Randy was on the phone in the waiting area. He gave her a slight nod then did a double-take. "I'll call you back," he said and snapped the phone shut.

"Sorry I'm late," Gemma rushed to say.

"What did you do?" He eyed the top of her head.

She took a deep breath, trying to sound normal as she spoke. "Just a haircut. Wanted to try something different."

Randy frowned. *Frowned!* Was chivalry really dead? Couldn't he compliment her? Even if it was a lie?

Gaze still on her hair, Randy said, "Do you mind if we sit at the bar? Service is faster there, and I have another . . . thing to get to after dinner."

"No problem." Gemma followed him through the tables until they reached the bar in the center of the restaurant. The music was louder in that area, and at this point, Gemma wasn't sure if that was a good thing or a bad thing.

Randy's presence at the bar drew a wide smile from the female bartender. Something pinched in Gemma's heart. She should be used to it by now, and she supposed she was. Randy was a good-looking man, tanned, blond, fit, pretty much the California surfer type all grown up and serious. Other women always gave him a second look.

But what really made her heart hurt tonight was that there had been no physical contact between them when she came into the restaurant.

And Randy was an affectionate man. But he hadn't greeted her with a kiss or taken her hand. Nothing. Definitely unusual. Not that Gemma couldn't instigate any of those things, but she sensed a distance in him tonight. Gemma folded her hands in her lap, clenching them together. She'd hoped tonight might be different. He knew she'd be gone all weekend, and with him having something else after dinner, that negated asking him over to her condo.

"So . . ." His fingers tapped the bar counter. "What will you have?"

Anything alcoholic sounded divine right now, but Gemma was seriously doubtful she'd be able to stop at one. Randy's dismissal of her new look was certainly not helping her struggling psyche right now. She ordered a virgin piña colada while Randy ordered some red wine. If he was surprised at her choice, he said nothing.

A couple sat down at the bar a few stools away. As luck would have it, they were practically on top of each other, seemingly not even able to break away long enough to look at their menus. Wasn't there some law against PDA or something?

Stop it, she told herself. *You're not a prude, and just because Randy is being weird doesn't mean you have to criticize other people.*

Still, her gaze kept straying to the very happy and lusty couple. They had no wedding rings in sight. Of course. Then her attention shifted to Randy. He was texting. The female bartender delivered their drinks and flashed Randy another smile.

Out of the corner of her eye, Gemma saw him return that smile, although she wasn't sure if it was directed at the woman's face or her cleavage. For an insane moment, Gemma wanted to throw the piña colada at something—at Randy or the bartender. She wasn't picky.

"How was work?" Gemma asked when Randy took a break from his texting long enough to sip his wine.

"Busier than hell," Randy said.

Standard answer to a standard question. *How boring can we be?* Although she had the feeling that if the bartender walked over right now and asked the same question, Randy would say something else.

"Look, Gemma, I really didn't want to do this here . . ."

All thoughts of the bartender left her mind as she looked at Randy. His blue eyes were intent on her.

"Do what?" she asked. Did he want to go to a quieter restaurant? "Should we go someplace else to eat?"

"It's not that," he said, still staring right at her, until she wondered if she had something on her face. Maybe her makeup had smeared at the salon.

"It's . . ." He reached over and took her hand.

That's when her heart sank. His tone, his pleading eyes, his touch when he hadn't touched her in a while. It could only mean one thing.

"It's not you, please believe that," he said. "You're beautiful and wonderful, and I don't deserve you."

The words coming from Randy's mouth seemed like a clichéd dream. Except for the fact that they were coming from Randy—the man she'd been dating for two years, the man her parents *approved* of. The man she'd said "I love you" to.

But his mouth kept moving, and the words kept coming.

"There's no one to blame." His tone was smooth, devoid of emotion. "And you have to believe me, there's no one else. It's just . . . Sometimes when I see another woman and think about how I can never get to know her, I feel trapped, like I'm blocked into a corner. And if I wanted to get to know that woman, theoretically, I couldn't. I know I shouldn't *want* to feel that, which is what makes this is so hard." He exhaled. "I don't think either of us should feel trapped."

Gemma might have nodded. Or maybe she shook her head. She wasn't sure.

His other hand grabbed hers. "But then I think about you, and I know I feel something for you. I know I love you." He wasn't looking at her though. He was looking past her, into the crowded restaurant.

Could anyone hear what he was saying? How many strangers were witnessing this?

"I just can't see myself with you forever, you know? Not like your parents, or mine. It's not that you aren't a great girl, or we aren't a good match. My parents love you too. In fact, they'll be very upset when I tell them." He stopped, looking at her again.

"When you tell them we broke up?" she said, surprised she could even speak.

"I'm really sorry, I don't want to hurt you," Randy said.

Gemma slid her hands out from under his. She took another sip of her piña colada then stood. Her eyes stung with tears, but she refused to let them fall. "Thanks for telling me. I know you're busy, so I'll let you get to your . . . thing."

Just then the bartender arrived, a slight smile on her face. Gemma glanced at her, noticing that her nametag: Cherie.

Gemma leaned toward Randy. "I'll bet she'll give you her number."

His face flushed. Gemma thought she'd be sick at his instant reaction. Somehow, she managed to walk out of there with her head up and her back straight. Maybe it was the new haircut, or maybe it was the $400 she'd spent on the clothes waiting for her in the car. Whatever it was, the Gemma who'd left her condo that afternoon was not the same woman who had returned to it.

Three

"He said *what*?" Drew said through Gemma's Bluetooth.

"That his parents loved me too, and they'd be upset about the breakup." Gemma's hands gripped the steering wheel as she headed up the coast to Dana Point. At least they were no longer trembling.

"Ouch."

"Yeah, ouch." Gemma changed lanes. The next exit led to Dana Point Harbor.

Drew was silent for a couple of moments, and she imagined his brows drawn together as they did when he got that serious look on his face, which wasn't often. Everything in life seemed to come easy for him—the photography jobs, the awards, the women . . .

"So it will just be the three of us then?" Gemma said.

There seemed to be a brief pause before he answered, as if his mind was elsewhere. "Yep, I'll be there around 4:00. Just finishing a shoot."

"Who's this one for?"

"Oh, a little publication called *Redbook*." The laziness was back in his voice.

She scoffed. "Wow. Your head is huge."

He laughed; the sound of his laughter spread over her like a cozy blanket, and for the first time in twelve hours, she felt like things might turn out all right. Normalcy might return to her life. *Without Randy.* She had yet to tell her parents. Maybe she'd do it with Liz and Drew spoon-feeding her ice cream and massaging her feet. Although Gemma was determined that this weekend would be fun—she wouldn't bring down the party. She'd put up with Liz raving about her boyfriend, and she'd laugh over Drew's crazy stories of models who refused to eat a single cookie, yet gorged on Big Macs when they thought no one was looking.

"See you soon, sweetheart," Drew said.

They hung up, and Gemma smiled. Not even Randy called her *sweetheart,* not that it meant anything coming from Drew—that was just how he talked—but it felt good knowing that someone cared about her. The conversation with Drew had been all about her. In fact, he was the one who'd called. He hadn't replied to the text she'd sent the day before. So when her phone rang, Gemma assumed it was about the weekend, but then she blurted out what happened with Randy.

If she thought back over the years, she was sure that she and Drew had discussed every one of her breakups, and most of his. He hadn't said anything about dating anyone new, but Gemma hadn't exactly given him a chance. His last serious relationship was a couple of years back, ending about the same time she started dating Randy. Valentina was her name. Drew dated the most interesting women, with the most interesting names.

Valentina was from Puerto Rico, absolutely gorgeous in

the magazine-cover way, and, of course, she was a model. Turning onto Crown Parkway, Gemma couldn't exactly remember why Valentina and Drew broke up. For a while it seemed they were close to being engaged, but Drew had been vague about the details.

Gemma bit her lip as her eyes involuntarily watered. She'd be spending the weekend listening to Liz and Drew talk about their exciting lives, while hers was in a major dead end. She shook her head, willing the tears back. She wasn't going to feel sorry for herself; she hadn't escaped work for three days to wallow. She tried to imagine what sorts of stories Drew would have, and who he might be dating.

The Five had always been a unique combination. None of the girls had dated Drew. Why not, she wasn't sure, exactly. It was just sort of an unspoken rule. He was plenty good looking, even in high school, when he'd been as skinny as a rail. But it seemed they were all just good friends, and that was fine with everyone. It kept things from getting weird or awkward, which meant the Five were always a safe place to be themselves. A couple of years ago, Drew and Gemma had gone on a spur-of-the-moment double date. It wasn't anything official—just a lot of fun. She'd been out a few times with Randy by then and was starting to like him a lot.

So she didn't see the date with her and Drew as anything more than hanging out with a friend, and what made it entertaining was that the other couple they were with got into a huge fight. It made for a hilarious night—after the fact, of course. For months, she and Drew randomly texted each other things like *Are you mad at me?* to keep the joke going.

By the time the ocean came into view, Gemma discovered she was grinning at the memories. Grinning was good. Much better than crying over Randy. She hadn't cried as much as she thought she would, and maybe that was because she sensed the tears coming and had steeled herself against them. Yet the tears were still there, waiting.

Gemma opened the car window, letting the warm sea air in. This weekend would be a turning point. New hair, new clothes, new relationship status. She glanced at her image in the rearview mirror, and her confidence went up a notch. She loved her new look, even if Randy hated it.

"Gemma!" a woman screamed as she climbed out of her car.

Liz was early. She barreled across driveway and pulled Gemma into a death squeeze—her trademark, which went perfectly with her saucy red curls and dimpled smile.

"I. Love. It!" Liz squealed. She drew away and took in Gemma's hair.

"You do? I got it done yesterday."

"If I hadn't recognized your car, I wouldn't have known it was you," Liz said, hugging her again.

Gemma laughed then gasped for breath. "You don't think it's too much?"

"Drew is going to freak, and then he'll start taking pictures." Liz finally released her. "What does Randy think?"

"Oh." For a moment Gemma had forgotten. The familiar burn started at the back of her eyes. "He didn't say much about it. In fact, we broke up last night."

Liz's jaw dropped, and for a weird moment, Gemma admired her dental work. Her teeth were white and even, like a dental implant commercial.

"I didn't know. I'm so-o-o sorry." Liz's eyes rounded. "What happened?"

"Let's go inside," Gemma said, not wanting to have this conversation on the side of the PCH with cars whizzing by. She grabbed her suitcase from the trunk then followed Liz inside the beach house. They rented the same one every year from a nice Japanese couple who divided themselves between continents. Somehow their place was always available during spring vacation.

"You are *so* getting the master bedroom," Liz said, linking her arm through Gemma's as they walked into the living room. The place was immaculate: pale blue walls, white couches, and gorgeous Turkish rugs.

"No, that's okay," Gemma said quickly. The master bed was massive, and it would make her feel even more single if she had to sleep in it. "I'll take my usual room upstairs. It's my favorite one."

"Really, you can have the master. My boyfriend isn't coming, and I don't think Drew's bringing anyone."

Gemma hoped he wasn't bringing anyone. Then again, she'd probably be on better behavior if he did. She would definitely sulk less about her pathetic breakup.

"Come in the kitchen," Liz said. "While you spill the details, I'm making you brownies."

That was Liz. Even before she had a kid, she'd been the mom of the group, always feeding them and watching out for everyone. "You're amazing," Gemma said.

"It's just from a mix," Liz said, pulling out a box from one of the grocery bags on the counter.

Gemma perched on a stool, and as Liz prepared the batter, Gemma told her about last night. Then she summarized the past couple of months with Randy. "I guess you could say I saw it coming, but maybe I didn't want to know, so I never confronted him. And it turns out I was right. Things between us *had* changed."

Liz reached across the counter and squeezed Gemma's hand. "It sounds like with his eyes and brain wandering, his body would have been next."

Gemma propped her elbows on the counter and rested her chin on her hands. "I know. It's just that we'd dated for so long, I thought we were past all of that."

"About two years, right?"

Gemma nodded. Liz slid the pan into one of the ovens.

Gemma couldn't imagine why the owners needed more than one oven with just the two of them. Maybe they entertained a lot. Liz pulled out a bag of licorice from another grocery sack then offered it to Gemma.

"If you keep this up, I'm going to have to go to the gym tomorrow," Gemma said.

Liz laughed. "Monday. We'll all go Monday, but not a minute sooner."

"Does your daughter know what a junk-food addict you are?"

"No one knows," Liz said, her dimple showing. "So we have to eat it before Drew gets here."

Gemma snatched the bag and ripped open the top. If she couldn't have love, there was always sugar. They settled on the couch, and their conversation turned to Liz's boyfriend, Sloane. Gemma encouraged her to tell the latest, keeping a smile on her face. She didn't want Liz to know that inside, she wanted to go crawl into the bed upstairs.

When a knock sounded at the front door, Gemma glanced at the clock. They'd been talking for two hours. The time had flown. "Is that Drew already?"

Liz jumped up and ran to the door. By her squeal, Gemma knew it was him.

She stood and turned to watch him enter. He smiled when he saw her, but there was something soft behind the smile, as if he was remembering their conversation on the phone. His dark hair was shorter than last time, but it still had its spikey look.

When he crossed over to hug her, Gemma said, "Oh my gosh. Do I see some gray?" She reached up to touch his short sideburns, and he swiped her hand away with a laugh then pulled her into a hug.

If there was one thing about Drew that Gemma loved, it was that he always gave the best hugs, ones that made a person feel cared for, which made Gemma envy his girlfriends. She could only imagine what else he did well.

Her face heated. *What am I thinking?* She pulled away and reached for his hair again. This time he let her touch it, a half smile on his face. "Why do men always look great with gray hair?"

He grabbed her hand. "You should talk. Look at you."

Oh yeah.

"Don't you love it?" Liz said, all smiles. She passed them and went into the kitchen to cut brownies for Drew.

"I do love it," Drew said, his gaze on Gemma. His eyes held a bunch of questions.

She guessed what he was wondering. "I told Liz about Randy."

He nodded and seemed to relax a bit, but he was still watching her, his hazel eyes greener than usual. "How are *you* doing?"

She shrugged. "Fine. It's weird, I know, but I'm fine." She let out a big sigh.

Drew gave her another hug, and this time Gemma allowed herself to melt against him. She appreciated his height, six-foot something, versus Randy, who was only an inch taller than her 5'8". Drew seemed reluctant to let her go.

Finally Gemma said, "I'll be fine. Really."

"It's great to see you," Drew said, releasing her. "Your haircut is awesome."

Gemma touched her hair. "I think it was the final straw for Randy."

Drew quirked a brow like he didn't believe her. "What did he say?"

"It's what he *didn't* say." Gemma headed for the kitchen.

Liz had piled a bunch of brownies on a plate and was leaning against the counter, texting or emailing on her phone.

"So y'all know my relationship saga," Gemma said, settling on a stool. "What about you, Drew? Did you invite someone to join us this weekend?"

"Nope." Drew popped a whole brownie in his mouth. One bite, and it was gone.

Men get away with a lot.

Liz slid a glass of milk in his direction, where he'd sat next to Gemma. He took a long drink then reached for another brownie.

"Not so fast," Gemma said. "Who's your new lady love?"

Liz pulled the plate of brownies out of Drew's reach, joining the game. "Yeah, who is she? A *Sports Illustrated* swimsuit model?"

Drew groaned and folded his arms, shaking his head.

"One of those runway models from Milan?" Gemma asked.

Drew dipped his head and scrubbed at his hair. "I prefer women who weigh more than a hundred pounds, thank you. Give me some credit."

Liz smirked. "You get no credit with us. Not after all the women we've had to meet and play nice around. Fess up. Is she from France? Beijing?"

Drew cracked a smile.

"I knew it!" Liz said. "She's Asian!"

"No." Drew spread his hands out. "She's not Asian; she's not anything. I'm not dating anyone."

Liz laughed, and Gemma joined her. Drew not dating was as rare as a quiet Friday afternoon on a California freeway.

He half stood and snatched the plate from Liz. Before she could stop him, he'd grabbed two brownies. "You don't have to believe me, but it's the truth. I haven't dated anyone since . . . well, for a couple of years now, I guess."

"Two *years*?" Liz asked. "Since . . . Valentina?"

"After we broke up, things got really busy, and I was traveling more than anything else." He popped one of the brownies in his mouth.

Gemma couldn't believe he didn't have at least one or two women wondering where he was this weekend, and doubted Liz believed him either. But they had three days to get the truth out of him.

Four

Liz had taken off to browse a few touristy shops in search of a gift for her daughter, so Gemma decided to join Drew at the beach. He'd brought a surfboard he'd "pulled out of retirement."

Gemma didn't remember Drew surfing much in high school, but then again, every California kid surfed at some point.

With a moment to herself, she climbed the stairs to her bedroom and changed into the new swimsuit she'd bought the day before. It was yellow and white striped, two-piece, and way different than her usual black or navy suits.

But I'm a new Gemma now.

She turned in the mirror, checking the fit. She definitely wasn't a 100-pound model. She was in decent shape, but could probably be better if she were obsessive about it. Still, she pulled on a tank shirt and a sarong skirt and walked down the steps to the beach.

Gemma spotted Drew's towel spread out on the sand, but no Drew. Six or seven surfers rode the swells. Gemma couldn't pick him out, since they all wore the same type of wetsuits, but she set her bag and towel by Drew's.

She slipped out of her top and skirt, then lathered on sunscreen—a vast difference from high school, when she used nothing but tanning oil. These days, her tans were more like a rash of freckles. The ocean sounds were soothing, filling her ears with repetitive calm. Gulls screeched, but even their cries were no match for the volume of the incoming waves.

Gemma hugged her knees to her chest and closed her eyes, relishing the warm, salty breeze and relaxing with the knowledge that she had no place to be today or tomorrow or the next day. She blew out a breath then inhaled. Her body relaxed. If only she could get her mind to do the same.

On impulse, she dug her phone out of her bag and dialed her mom's number. Maybe if she got over this one hurdle, she could really relax. She'd already blubbered to Drew and Liz—why not to her parents? Get it done with all in the same day.

When her mom picked up, answering in a cheery voice, Gemma almost changed her mind. But then she decided to plow through and gave her mom the rundown of the Randy breakup.

Her mom was quiet for several moments on the other end of the line. "It seems so sudden, especially after two years together."

Gemma explained that she'd known something was off for at least a month. Then her dad got on the phone, and Gemma repeated most of the story. Her dad wasn't quite as understanding as her mom, and used a few choice words to describe Randy.

"It's better this way," Gemma said when her dad was done ranting. "I'd rather know now than later, like when we're engaged or married."

A dozen yards in front of her, Drew emerged from the water, carrying a surfboard.

Gemma reiterated to her parents that she was spending the weekend on the beach and would see them sometime Monday. She hung up just as Drew spotted her. She waved; he smiled and continued in her direction. Gemma realized she was staring at Drew as he walked toward her in his fitted wetsuit. She forced herself to look away.

When he reached her, he peeled off the wetsuit until he was only in his board shorts, then he dropped down beside her. He was dripping wet and out of breath. "Wow," he said. "I almost died out there." He flopped back and stared at the sky, breathing heavily.

"Out of shape?" Gemma asked. He looked far from that. Proof of another man thing: eating a plate of brownies, never working out more than shooting a few pictures, yet enjoying defined abs. She looked away, suddenly aware she was staring too much.

"I can't feel my feet. They're numb." He closed his eyes as if he had completely run out of all energy.

Gemma moved and touched his feet. "They're still there."

Drew laughed. "I'll take your word for it." His eyes stayed closed, and his breathing started to slow.

She settled back on her towel, but her eyes strayed to Drew's lengthened body. Was she really checking him out?

What's wrong with me? Drew is one of my best friends.

With determination, she closed her eyes and let the sun bathe her face, completely ignoring the man next to her.

The April sun was warm, not too hot, just perfect. And maybe it was because Gemma had told her parents about the breakup, or because she was spending a lazy afternoon with a friend, but she surprised herself by falling asleep.

Something soft and warm trickled on her stomach. It took Gemma a moment to realize where she was. She opened her eyes to see Drew lying on his side, facing her, his hand suspended above her torso as he dribbled sand onto her.

"Excuse me?" She lifted up on her elbows and watched the sand slide off on either side. "I don't exactly enjoy sand in the crevices of my body."

Drew's mouth twisted with amusement. "You were way too clean. No one should be so clean at the beach. It doesn't even count. You might as well stay at home."

"Ha ha." Gemma's stomach flinched as Drew scooped another handful of sand and poured it on. "What? Are you ten?"

"Sometimes I wish I still were."

Gemma laughed. "Don't we all. Moms tucking us in bed at night. Dads calling us princess."

"Speak for yourself." Drew scooped another handful of sand.

Gemma watched the grains slide from his fingers like a miniature waterfall, then pool on her stomach, only to slide off onto the towel. She made no move to stop him. The falling sand was mesmerizing, like watching the flames of a campfire.

The sand stopped, and she blinked. "Your dad didn't call you princess?" she said.

"Nope. But I seem to remember being called some other names, ones I can't say in front of a lady."

"I'm sure it wasn't that bad. You were like a straight A student."

His brow lifted. "You remember that?"

"We all thought you'd be a doctor or a scientist or something."

Drew scooped more sand. "Life has a funny way of changing plans, doesn't it?"

Gemma nodded, but then stopped, captured by his gaze. It was so intent, so serious, so *not* Drew. She looked away first and started brushing the sand from her stomach.

"Oh, sorry," Drew said, his smile back. "I'll do it." He ran his fingers along her stomach, clearing off the sand granules.

His touch sent goose bumps along her arms and stomach, and she inhaled. It was strange having Drew this close, his hand on her bare stomach. But this was just Drew, she reminded herself. Her friend. And he was only teasing her, as usual.

"I was wondering about something," he said, his low voice drawing her out of her thoughts. He moved away, no longer touching her.

I don't want him to move away. The thought slammed into her, and she blushed. *What am I thinking?* Thankfully, he wasn't looking directly at her.

"Why do you think you and I never dated?" And then his gaze slid to hers. His hazel eyes seemed to flash gold.

If she'd swallowed a cupful of sand, her throat couldn't have been any drier.

"I mean," he said, rolling onto his back and propped his hands behind his head, looking up at the sky. "We've always had fun together."

"Yeah," she said in a slow voice, having no idea what else to say—having no idea where he was going with this. "But we did go out once."

He turned his head toward her. "Are you mad at me?"

Gemma laughed, remembering the joke from a few years ago. "Are you mad at me?"

He grinned. "Never. And that wasn't really a date."

"No?"

"No."

"You took pictures. Doesn't that prove we were on a date together?" Gemma said.

He moved to his elbow again, facing her. She tried not to let her gaze slide along his torso. His tanned skin and the warm sun playing off his muscled shoulders wasn't helping her concentration. There was a reason he always had a dozen women after him at a time.

"I think I still have those pictures," he said. "Wouldn't it be funny if I found them?"

"That was like three years ago."

"Two. It was just before you got serious with Randy."

Two . . . Drew sure had a good memory. And Gemma realized she hadn't thought about Randy for several minutes until Drew brought him up.

He pulled out a camera from his bag and snapped a picture of her.

"Hey. I didn't sign a release form for my picture to be taken," she said.

A smile touched his mouth. "Close your eyes. With the cloud overhead, the light is perfect on your face."

She obeyed, and the camera clicked several times. Drew had been taking pictures of everyone forever, but now that he earned big bucks to do it, it was strange to be the focus.

Gemma opened her eyes to find him staring at her. To thwart a blush she said, "Aren't you worried about getting sand in your camera?"

He glanced at the camera in his hands. "This isn't one of my better ones. And it's pretty hardy."

She sat up. "Can I see it?"

He handed it over then leaned in and showed her the basic settings. She snapped a couple of pictures of him before he could protest. Then she started to scroll through the pictures he'd taken. A bunch of scenic shots, followed by close-ups of plants and rocks. Some of the plants were unique, and quite a few she didn't recognize. "Where's this?"

"The South Coast Botanical Gardens. We should go there sometime."

Gemma ignored the increase in her pulse at his suggestion. "It's beautiful." She felt his eyes on her. She continued through the pictures stopping at a picture of a dark-haired woman laughing, sunglasses perched on her head.

For some reason, her heart dropped. Maybe this was the woman he wasn't telling them about. "Who's this?"

"Avery. An editor for *Redbook*."

"She's really pretty," Gemma said, scrolling through more pictures of Avery.

"I guess. She wanted me to take some pictures of her to send to her husband."

So he isn't dating this one. Another woman popped up on the screen. A skinny blonde at a café, holding a cup of coffee. Her painted lips smirked at the camera. Gemma's throat tightened. Surely there was something behind her look that had to do with Drew.

"One of your models?" she asked.

"Luisa. She nearly passed out at a shoot, and I forced her to eat a bagel and drink some coffee. I haven't stopped teasing her since."

She nodded. "So is Luisa the mystery girlfriend you aren't telling us about?"

"Gemma," he started. "There's no mystery girlfriend." He reached over, his arm brushing hers, and deleted the picture.

"I didn't mean for you to delete it," Gemma said, feeling terrible. "I was just kidding."

"I know." He nudged her shoulder.

She hoped she hadn't annoyed him. She didn't want to go through any more pictures, and she handed the camera back, only to find his eyes intent on her.

"I was serious when I said I haven't been dating anyone for two years."

Two years. Why does that keep coming up? He broke up

with Valentina two years ago. Two years ago, they'd went on that crazy double date with the couple from hell. Two years ago, Gemma started dating Randy.

Before she could reply, Drew said, "Gem, I want to ask you something."

"There you guys are!" Liz called.

Gemma turned to see Liz coming toward them, a couple of shopping bags in her hands. She was all smiles as she settled on Gemma's towel and opened her bags.

Liz focused on Gemma. "Cute swimsuit."

"I agree," Drew said, snapping another picture.

"Hey," Gemma said, reaching for her tank top and pulling it on.

Drew smiled and took another picture. "You can't hide from a camera."

Liz looked between Drew and Gemma, her brows arched. "Okay, you guys sound like you had fun. But I had more fun. Look at this adorable sarong I bought."

Gemma gave the proper oohs and ahhs over Liz's stuff. Within seconds, Drew was on his feet. "Well, ladies, I'm encrusted with salt, so I'm going to go shower. Anyone up for grabbing something to eat after?"

"I'm starving," Liz pronounced.

"Me, too," Gemma added.

"We'll meet you in a few," Liz said. As Drew walked away, she said, "That's one fine man." She laughed. "Not that I'm looking. Sloane is a fine man too."

Gemma smiled. "Missing Sloane already?"

A sly smile came onto Liz's face. "Just a little. But, holy crap, Drew was totally checking you out."

Gemma tried not to let her mouth drop open. "He was *not*. I'm like dog breath compared to the women he knows. Plus, he's *Drew*. Like-a-*brother* Drew."

"Drew is *not* your brother," Liz said, narrowing her

eyes. "And just because he's one of our best friends doesn't mean—"

Gemma covered her ears with her hands. "Don't say it. The Five are the best thing that ever happened to me in high school."

Liz pursed her lips together as she gathered up her stuff. "Did you find out about his girlfriend?"

"I looked through some of his pictures, but he insisted he doesn't have one."

Liz met Gemma's gaze, her eyes gleaming. "You know what I think?"

Gemma said nothing; she didn't want to know what Liz was cooking up.

"He hasn't dated since breaking up with Valentina because he's been waiting for *you*, Gem." Liz stood, her bags in hand.

Gemma scrambled to her feet, facing Liz. "Don't say that. It's not true." Her heart thundered, and she felt breathless, but that was because Liz was talking crazy. There was no way Drew would ever be interested in her like that. Sure, they were awesome friends, and she loved him—like a brother, of course—but Drew would never . . .

Liz was trudging back to the beach house. Gemma grabbed her towel, sarong, and bag, hurrying after her.

As soon as she reached the house, she'd take a cold shower.

Five

They ended up at a charming Mexican restaurant with yellow-painted walls and red shelves holding multi-colored pottery. Gemma couldn't help but be on high alert around Drew now, and she cursed Liz for putting her there. Gemma focused on keeping the conversation on Liz and the other girls in the Five who weren't there, talking about updates in everyone else's lives but hers.

For once, Gemma wished the restaurant music was louder and the place more crowded. Then talking would have taken more of an effort. But as luck would have it, the restaurant wasn't busy tonight, and Gemma had plenty of opportunities to steal glances in Drew's direction. He was his regular self though, laughing, teasing, joking, and sharing bizarre stories about some of his shoots.

Gemma tried to read more into his stories with various models, but there was nothing she could pinpoint that would show that he was in a relationship. The only thing left was the fact that he really was single, available, and not serious with any other women.

But why? And had it really been for two years? Despite Liz's theory, Gemma decided that things with Valentina had messed with his head more than Drew himself probably realized.

Yes. That was it—he was still hung up on Valentina. Gemma could breathe easier now, relax, and not worry. This weekend would be fun catching up on old times, and then she'd go back to normal life. Still, she stuck with nonalcoholic drinks.

"What are you guys up for tonight?" Liz asked, on her second glass of wine. "Clubbing?"

Gemma was surprised that Liz would want to go clubbing, with the whole mom-thing, but then, Liz always surprised her.

Drew shrugged, his hazel eyes landing on Gemma. "I'll go if Gemma wants to."

She ignored the significant look that Liz threw her. "I didn't sleep much last night," Gemma said. "So maybe we should just watch a movie at the house."

A smile played on Drew's lips. "Sounds perfect. I've got a bunch of new releases on my laptop." It was hard to ignore Drew's smile. He was a bit of a movie-expert and always seemed to have new releases in advance of their actual release date.

Liz let out a yawn. "Yeah, I guess you guys are right. I forget that I'm on a kid schedule."

Back at the beach house, Drew hooked his laptop to the big screen in the living room. Liz started popping a bunch of popcorn, while Gemma grabbed a blanket and sat in the middle of the couch. She curled up in the blanket and pulled one of the throw pillows onto her lap. Cozy. Perfect.

"What movie is this?" Gemma asked Drew as he fiddled with the television.

"*The Bourne Legacy*. Did you see the earlier films?" he asked then turned off the overhead light.

"At least one of them," Gemma said. "Is this even on DVD yet?"

"Nope."

The screen glowed with the opening credits, and Drew sat by her. As in, right next to her. He'd taken off his jacket, so his bare arm was right next to hers, save for the blanket.

Gemma was grateful that the blanket covered her goose bumps.

Liz came in with two bowls of hot popcorn and handed one to Drew. She kept the second one and settled on the other side of Gemma.

"I don't get my own bowl?" Gemma asked.

"You and Drew can share," Liz said with a laugh. "I never get anything to myself, so tonight I'm indulging."

"So, catch me up," Gemma said to Drew. That was a mistake, because Drew obeyed and leaned closer, practically whispering in her ear.

The goose bumps were back in full force. Gemma was suddenly grateful for the dimness of the room. Liz seemed oblivious, eating her popcorn, focused on the screen. Gemma took a couple of handfuls of popcorn then stopped eating. She was still full from dinner.

About thirty minutes into the movie, Liz started snoring.

Drew snickered, reaching over Gemma and moving Liz's bowl to the floor. He stood and found another blanket, which he draped over Liz. Gemma watched his gentlemanly actions and silently agreed with Liz that Drew was a fine man.

Fine, but unattainable. Besides, Gemma valued their friendship way more than anything else.

Drew left the room and came back with two chilled water bottles. He handed her one. He turned down the volume a little on the television before sitting by Gemma. "Care to share your blanket?"

Gemma's heart went into overdrive. *Settle down,* she ordered herself. She moved the blanket over to include him. Now their arms and their legs were touching.

What's wrong with me? Talk about rebounding.

She couldn't concentrate on the movie, but the last thing she was going to do was ask Drew what was happening on screen. She didn't know if she could handle him talking so close to her ear.

Liz's snores continued, so Gemma decided she had been inducted into the twilight zone. She hoped the movie wasn't one of those three-hour ones. Sitting this close to Drew for that long wouldn't be good, not when her brain was a mess.

"Hey," Drew said in her ear, nearly causing her to jump. "You still watching?"

"Um . . . sort of."

He laughed quietly. "I have a better idea." He stood and turned off the movie. After unhooking his laptop, he brought it over to the couch. It was darker in the room now, the only light coming from the kitchen behind them and the laptop.

Liz shifted, letting out a huge yawn. "Did I fall asleep?"

"Yeah," Drew said, his voice sounding like he was trying not to laugh.

"Is the movie over already?" Liz asked in a voice thick with sleep. "I can't believe I fell asleep." She rose from the couch and crossed the room with a slight sway to her steps. "I'm going to bed. See you guys in the morning." She disappeared into the master bedroom, shutting the door behind her.

"Good night," Gemma said.

"Happy snoring," Drew called after her, but not loud enough that Liz would hear.

Gemma nudged him. "What if I start snoring? Will you make fun of me?"

His eyes flickered to her, capturing her gaze in the dimness. "Are you admitting that you snore?"

"I'm not admitting anything."

He laughed, and his arm slid across her shoulders. "I don't think I'd mind your snoring."

The warmth of Drew's body so close caught Gemma by surprise.

He's teasing, she told herself. *Nothing more.* Sure enough, he removed his arm and fiddled with his laptop, pulling up various files.

"This might be it," he said, clicking on one of the files. "Yep."

Gemma stared at a shot of her at the Japanese restaurant they'd gone to with that crazy couple. The memories of that night came flooding back. "That was right before they started arguing."

Drew clicked to the next picture.

Gemma gasped. "You didn't!"

"Had the flash off," he said. "So they never knew."

Drew had taken pictures of the couple arguing. "Amazing the emotion that can come through a camera."

"No kidding." Gemma gazed at the animated faces. The next picture showed Gemma, wide eyed, staring at the fighting couple. "Wow, that was an insane night."

"Completely insane." Drew closed the file. The wallpaper of an aquarium stared back at them. "That's why we need a redo."

"A what?"

He shifted so that he was facing her. Part of Drew's face was lit up by the screen, his eyes nearly black as they focused on Gemma. She suddenly felt breathless as Liz's words floated through her mind.

He hasn't been dating for two years because he's been waiting for you, Gem.

But that was impossible.

"You know, another date," he said. "This time without that couple."

"As if they're still together," Gemma said in a joking tone, while everything inside her was on high alert. What was Drew saying? What did he mean?

Drew shrugged. "Who knows? Maybe they just fight a lot—maybe it works for them."

Gemma didn't know what to say.

"So what do you think?" he asked.

She didn't know what to think, or what Drew was really asking. "I don't know." Why did he want to go out on a date anyway? He had a million women to choose from—most of them supermodels.

His voice went quiet. "What don't you know, Gemma? Is it . . . because of Randy?"

The mention of Randy was like turning on a blinding spotlight. This couldn't be happening. Drew couldn't really be interested in her like *this*. She clutched the pillow in her lap.

"To be honest . . ." She took a deep breath. "I'm not really sure what you're saying. You and I have been friends forever. I just . . . Sorry, my brain is slow right now. You have to tell me what you mean."

Drew was silent for a moment. He closed the laptop and set it on the floor. The only light came from the kitchen now. He turned toward her and moved his hand to her shoulder. Gemma's heart fluttered at his touch. When his fingers brushed her neck, she thought she might ignite.

"What I mean is that I want to take you on a date." His fingers moved behind her neck, touching her hair. "A date that's between two people, in which the guy likes the woman, and the woman might like the guy. *Hopefully* she likes him. Hopefully it will be fun, and maybe there will be another date after that." His eyes burned into her.

Gemma wasn't sure if she was breathing; she could barely think when he was touching her like that, but she managed to move her mouth and say, "Oh."

His voice lowered to almost a whisper. "Is that a yes? Will you go on a date with me?"

This isn't really happening. It was impossible. This was Drew—*her* Drew—her friend and the man who was pretty much the most gorgeous person she knew. No one would believe that Drew was interested in her. But the way he looked at her right now almost convinced her that Liz had been right.

"Okay," she whispered back.

His mouth moved into a half smile, and his eyebrow rose. "Okay?"

She nodded, not trusting her voice.

"Then can I ask you another question?"

Gemma nodded, her mind reeling. Every perception she'd had of Drew had changed in an instant.

"Can I kiss you?"

Gemma couldn't believe the words coming from his mouth, but as he said them, she realized she wanted him to kiss her—more than anything she could ever remember wanting. Even though one part of her shouted that she probably shouldn't kiss Drew for a million and one reasons, the other part of her wasn't listening—the part that was burning beneath Drew's touch.

She stared at him for a moment then moved her hands to his shoulders and pressed her mouth against his. If he was surprised, he got over it quickly. His lips parted, and soon she was lost in his warmth and heat. He pulled her onto his lap, and his kisses became more demanding as he drew her closer.

Gemma couldn't believe she was kissing Drew, that he was kissing her back as if he'd been waiting for it a long time.

It was as if his patience had finally cracked, and every moment of waiting was now poured into his kiss. The more she kissed him, the more she realized she'd been waiting too—she just hadn't realized it.

She moved her hands along his chest, then to his stomach. He tugged off his shirt, and the heat from his body made her want to melt.

"Gemma," he said. "You're so beautiful."

His words caused her throat to hitch. Drew thought she was beautiful. Coming from him, that was amazing.

"You're the one who's beautiful," she whispered against his mouth.

He laughed and rotated her until we were both lying on the couch, their legs intertwined. "I can't believe I waited so long to kiss you." His lips pressed against her neck, then moved up to her jaw. When his mouth met hers again, his kisses were slower, more patient.

Gemma nestled against him, fitting her curves against his body. She'd always thought he was pretty much perfect, but she hadn't realized how amazing it would feel to be pressed against him. His hand moved to her waist, touching bare skin where her shirt had ridden up.

Gemma inhaled, furious heat pulsing through her, and Drew lifted his head, his eyes on her. Things were moving fast, really fast, and her heart pounded even harder when she realized she wanted them to keep going.

Drew brushed his lips against hers then sighed. "I think I need to take a cold shower before you slap me."

"I'm not going to slap you," Gemma said, breathless. She ran her hands along his arm, then to his chest. He was right. This was new. And this was moving extremely fast.

Drew pulled her into a hug, and Gemma clung to him for a moment, feeling their hearts beating together. When he released her, she didn't stop him from climbing off the couch. She stood, smoothing her clothing and running a hand through her hair. Before she knew it, she was in his arms again.

This time he didn't kiss her, just held her. When he stepped back, he stroked her cheek and said, "Good night, Gemma."

"Good night," she whispered, her throat too thick to speak aloud.

She stood there, listening to him go up the stairs. When she heard the shower running, she smiled, sinking onto the couch. Pulling the blanket around her, she lay down and clutched a pillow to her chest. She and Drew had broken every rule of the Five, but she didn't care. She had quite possibly had the best night of her life.

Six

She sound of sizzling woke Gemma, not to mention the overpowering smell of bacon. Gemma's stomach growled in response, and she opened her eyes. *Why am I on the couch?* Then she remembered. *Drew.*

Heat shot through her as she thought about the night before. She sat up, madly combing her fingers through her messy hair and wondering how she'd let herself fall asleep on the couch. Drew had probably walked by a dozen times, viewing her in her sleeping state.

She was afraid to check whether he was in the kitchen. No voices came from there. Maybe Liz was still asleep, or maybe *she* was cooking breakfast, and Drew was still asleep. Hoping that was the case, Gemma crept up the stairs. Drew's room was across from hers, and the door stood open. From the top of the stairs, Gemma could see his bed already made. So Drew was the bacon cooker.

Gemma went into the bathroom, and took a quick shower, then changed into fresh clothing. She headed downstairs to the kitchen, bracing herself. Would seeing Drew be awkward? Sweet? Gemma didn't feel ready to face him, but putting it off would only make the knot in her stomach tighter.

She entered the kitchen with a ready smile, only to see that it wasn't Drew cooking the bacon. "Liz?"

"Good morning. Thought this would wake you up." Liz slid a couple of pancakes onto a plate. "The bacon's almost done."

"Thanks," Gemma said, the brightness of her voice sounded false. "So where's Drew?"

"He had to take off. Something about a photo shoot that went wrong with his competition, so when they called him, he couldn't turn it down. Said he'd be back tonight, or maybe tomorrow morning at the latest." Liz poured orange juice into a glass. "I told him we needed girl time anyway."

"Oh, yeah," Gemma said. Her stomach felt like a rock. He hadn't even said good-bye. "What time did he leave?"

"I don't know, about an hour ago? Maybe 8:00?" Liz turned toward the fridge then whipped back around. "What happened between you two?"

Gemma cursed the heat spreading to her neck. "Nothing. Why?"

Liz narrowed her eyes. "Because he told me to make sure to tell you he was sorry. Which I didn't think anything of, until now." She folded her arms. "Out with it."

Gemma sat at the counter and dropped her head into her hands.

"You . . . didn't," Liz said.

Gemma lifted her head. "We didn't, but we might have kissed a little. Or a lot."

Covering her mouth with her hand, Liz stared at Gemma. "Oh. My. Gosh." She rushed around the counter and threw her arms around Gemma with a squeal.

Gemma felt like she was being crushed. Why did she tell Liz? Now everyone in the Five would find out. Mortification pounded through her. It was all weird, and new, and maybe it wasn't real. Maybe that's why Drew left.

When Liz relaxed her vice grip, she said, "Tell me all of it. Every minute." Her eyebrows pulled together. "Was it after I went to bed?"

Gemma nodded, then closed her eyes and blew out a breath. "Maybe it was just the moment. I was so tired and not in my right mind. One minute Randy breaks up with me, and twenty-four hours later . . ." She couldn't finish. Letting out a moan she stood up. "I don't know what to think."

"I'm so happy for you guys," Liz gushed. "I always thought you'd be great together." She sashayed around the corner and turned off the element beneath the frying pan. She used tongs to remove the bacon then set the pieces on a pile of paper towels.

Gemma swallowed against her tight throat. She wasn't hungry anymore. "How long have you thought that? Does everyone else think so too?"

Liz shrugged. "Maybe we talked about it a time or two, but I guess we figured that if you guys were smart, you'd see the light."

Gemma ran her hand through her still-damp hair. "So everyone was in on this but me?"

A grin spread on Liz's face.

Looking at her hands, Gemma thought about last night. Did Drew truly care for her that much? Had he been waiting for her to break up with Randy? Images of all of the girlfriends she'd met flashed through her mind. Last night's memories pushed them out of the way.

"Look at you," Liz said. "You're blushing."

Gemma touched her warm cheeks. "I'm confused."

Liz put a couple of pieces of bacon on Gemma's plate. "That will clear up. Maybe around the time Drew gets back." She laughed. "Seriously, Gem, this is awesome."

Gemma's phone rang, coming from the direction of the living room. She scrambled to find it, thinking it might be Drew. By the time she grabbed her phone, it was on its last ring.

The caller ID told her it was Randy. Her stomach twisted. Why was he calling her?

She sat on the couch, staring at the screen. The voicemail icon popped up. She didn't want to listen, didn't want to hear what kind of message he left, but she retrieved it anyway.

"Gemma . . . we need to talk. I'm really sorry about the other night. Call me as soon as you get this . . . Love ya."

Love ya?

Gemma's pulse went into hyper-drive. This was unbelievable. A myriad of questions collided together. *Why is he apologizing? Does he want to get back together?* She leaned over and, with a groan, put her head on her knees.

If she'd thought she was confused before, it was now worse. She'd completely written Randy off, but now what was she supposed to think . . .

"So, you up for the spa?" Liz's voice came from behind her.

Gemma looked up. Liz had walked into the living room. She tilted her head. "Are you all right?"

"Yeah," Gemma said, standing and slipping her phone in her pocket. She didn't want to say anything about Randy's call. What if Liz told Drew? Gemma didn't know what she wanted Drew to know . . .

※

Gemma and Liz spent the morning at Tranquility Spa, getting facials and pedicures. Gemma tried to relax, but she was constantly thinking about either Randy or Drew, and not exactly in the same way. The more she thought of Drew, the less she wanted to reconcile with Randy. Once she returned to the dressing room, she checked her phone. Nothing from Drew. But a text message from Randy: *Call me, babe.*

Babe? The word rocked through Gemma. She knew without a doubt that Randy wanted to get back together. Her thumbs hovered over her phone as she wondered if she should reply.

No, don't reply. He broke up with you. He said he wanted to be available to get to know other women.

Why hadn't Drew texted her? Even if he was working, was he at least thinking about her? Or was he happy to be gone? When he woke up this morning, did he regret what happened last night?

Did I imagine everything with Drew? How it felt to be in his arms?

Maybe I was just a night of fun for him.

Another woman to add to his trophy case.

Gemma put away her phone then dressed. A few minutes later she met Liz in the lobby.

"Let's eat," Liz said, her face pinked from the facial.

Gemma let Liz drag her shopping after lunch. Gemma tried to immerse herself in trinkets and clothing and home décor, but her mind was always someplace else. Still no contact with Drew, and nothing else came in from Randy.

It was nearly dark when they walked back to the beach house, hands full of shopping bags. Gemma wasn't even sure what she'd bought, but she did know she'd spent way too much. She hoped the floral shop had a great prom season.

Gemma munched on chips and salsa while Liz heated water for the pasta she'd brought. "At least let me make the salad," Gemma said. "You don't have to cook for everyone all the time."

"It's nice to fix food that will actually be eaten." Liz flashed a dimpled smile. "My daughter is so picky."

Gemma reached for the cutting board and started

chopping carrots, then moved on to slicing tomatoes. A knock sounded at the door, sending Gemma's heart racing.

"Did Drew forget his key?" Liz asked.

Gemma shrugged, although inside, she was a knot of nerves.

Liz passed her, and Gemma listened for a greeting at the door. The voice that spoke to Liz was definitely a man. Drew? Then why wasn't he coming into the kitchen? Finally Gemma turned around. Liz came into view. Behind her, was Randy.

Gemma thought her heart might stop.

Randy grinned, holding a huge bouquet of flowers. He walked right up to her and bent to kiss her cheek. "Hi, babe. Sorry for barging in on your weekend, but I couldn't wait to see you." He looked around the kitchen. "Where's all your friends?"

Gemma stood frozen in place.

Liz filled him in on everyone's whereabouts, but Randy didn't seem to be paying much attention. He took a seat next to Gemma as if he were the honored guest, and there was nothing weird about him showing up and giving her roses after breaking up with her so cruelly.

Gemma's hand went to her cheek where he'd kissed her. What had just happened?

"Mmm. Pasta for dinner?" Randy said.

"Yep. You're . . . uh, welcome to stay," Liz said, her voice sounding a bit hesitant. Both Randy and Liz looked at Gemma. She blinked, the lights in the kitchen suddenly too hot and the room too warm.

"What are you doing here, Randy?" Gemma asked.

An uncomfortable smile crossed his face. "Sorry, babe, I know it was kind of out of the blue." His eyes flicked to Liz, who turned down the element then made herself scarce.

Don't leave me with him, Gemma wanted to say. But she knew she had to face this—as unwelcome as it was.

Randy reached for her hand. Gemma started to pull away, but he wrapped her hand in his. "Did you get my message?"

Gemma nodded. Her pulse was pounding like crazy. Not because he was trying to get her back, but because he *thought* he could get her back with some sweet words and flowers. Anger shot through her. "What do you want?" she asked, keeping her voice even. It had only been two days since their breakup, but sitting next to him now made her realize that she didn't want him back.

His fingers caressed hers. "I just want to talk. I don't like how things ended the other night."

She swallowed back the revulsion that his touch gave her. "You don't like how you broke up with me?"

He leaned toward her, his expression contrite. "I was an idiot." He lifted his hand and touched her cheek. "I wasn't thinking clearly. Maybe it took having that fight to realize how much I care about you."

It wasn't a fight, Gemma wanted to yell. *You told me you didn't want to be trapped. And even now, when you want to get back together, you say* care, *not love.*

She closed her eyes and blew out a breath. She had no choice but to tell him she didn't want to get back together, ever. But before she could open her eyes and speak, she felt his lips on hers. Gemma pulled away with a gasp.

"Oh," Liz said, entering the kitchen.

Drew was right behind her.

Gemma wanted to die, but she didn't know how much until Drew turned and left. Not a word to her, not a word to Randy. No explanation to Liz either. Drew didn't give her a chance to explain that what he saw was far from what had really happened. The sound of a door shutting was almost as awful as hearing his car peel out onto the street.

"Wow, what's up with him?" Randy said in the dead silence.

Gemma felt like she was in a horrible dream, or more accurately, a nightmare. She'd give anything to wake up someplace with all of this as some hazy memory. She stood and hurried out of the kitchen. She took the stairs two at a time to her bedroom, then shut the door and locked it. With trembling hands, she pulled her phone out of her pocket and called Drew's number.

Tears burned her eyes. If Drew answered, she'd sound like a crying mess. But she didn't care. She had to talk to him—had to explain. Later, she'd also have to apologize for leaving Liz alone with Randy—what would she tell him?

Four rings, and the call went into Drew's voicemail. Her heart ached as she listened to his voice. She hung up before it clicked over and dialed again. Two rings, and then it stopped. He'd cancelled the call.

Gemma sank onto her bed, her arms wrapped around her torso. She felt sick, but it still couldn't be as bad as Drew must feel. Just seeing the pained look on his face before he stormed out told her more than anything Drew had said last night, and more than the way he'd kissed and held her.

Last night was real for Drew, Gemma realized. *I wasn't a one-time distraction.*

She sent him a text, hoping he hadn't blocked her number. *Please call me. I didn't know Randy was coming over or that he wanted to get back together. He kissed me by surprise.*

She waited a few minutes. No reply. Gemma fell onto her bed, tears soaking her face. She heard the downstairs door shut, and then a few moments later, Liz speaking on the other side of her door.

"You okay, Gem?" She knocked softly. "Randy left."

Randy is gone, Gemma texted. *Please come back.*

"Gemma?" Liz said.

"I'll be out in a minute." Gemma's voice felt scratchy and shaky. She took a deep breath and texted Drew again.

When I woke up and you were gone, I didn't know what you thought about last night. Maybe I was insecure, so I didn't text or call you all day, wondering if you regretted it.

Minutes passed with no answer.

I'm so sorry. Please know that Randy showing up was as horrible for me as it was for you.

No reply. Gemma pulled a pillow over her head and screamed into it.

Drew, you're way more important to me than Randy is— than Randy ever was.

There, she'd made her feelings clear. Drew could either reply or not. Gemma couldn't do anything more if he refused to talk to her. Now she had lost both Drew and Randy. She curled up on her bed, clutching the pillow to her chest, praying that the phone would ring or a text message would come in. But everything remained silent.

Liz came back. "I brought you some tea," she said through the door.

Gemma got up, her head feeling like it might split in half. She opened the door and let Liz in. She had her hair pulled back into a tight ponytail and had washed her makeup off. They sat together on the floor, leaning against the bed.

"If you didn't look so miserable, this would be really funny," Liz said.

"I don't think it will ever be funny." The tea scalded Gemma's throat as she took a sip, but she didn't care.

After a few moments of sitting in silence, Liz said, "So it looks like Randy wanted to get back together."

"Apparently . . . and in front of everyone too," Gemma mumbled.

Liz patted Gemma's leg. "A man who likes to stake his claim."

Gemma shook her head. "Talk about the worst timing ever. I could kill Randy."

"So you don't want to get back together with him?"

"No," Gemma retorted. "How can you ask that?"

Liz pursed her lips. "Just wanted to be sure. I think that will make Drew very happy."

"Ha," Gemma said. "He won't even answer my calls or texts."

"You called him?"

"Twice," Gemma whispered. She slumped against the bed; she was exhausted. From everything and everyone. And none of it was her fault. Randy had broken up with *her*, Randy had showed up with flowers, and Drew happened to walk in at the worst possible moment. He wouldn't even let her explain before he took off. If anything, the *men* were to blame for this mess.

"Randy wasn't too happy when you ran upstairs," Liz said. "But I think he got the hint. He shoved the roses in the kitchen garbage."

"Really?" Gemma asked, her voice gaining strength. It sounded like she wouldn't have to have another breakup conversation with him.

Liz put her arm around Gemma and squeezed. "Drew will be back."

But Gemma wasn't so sure. "Something always seems to come between us."

"Yeah, *you*," Liz said.

Gemma looked at Liz. "What are you talking about?"

"What if . . . what if you went to find him?" Liz raised a brow. "Tell him how you feel."

How I feel? "I don't even know where he lives—he moved over the summer."

"Hmm. I didn't know that," Liz said. "Maybe he'll answer if *I* text him."

"No, don't," Gemma said, grabbing Liz's arm. "You're right. I have to do something. I'll figure it out."

Seven

*M*orning took forever to arrive, but even when it did, Gemma still didn't know how to repair things with Drew. Maybe she couldn't, but her heart's rapid beating told her that she needed to at least try.

She started by getting on the computer in the beach house office. Thankfully the internet service was active. She searched for Drew's photography website, but that didn't give her any leads. Was he still working on that last-minute assignment? Or maybe he'd finished it, and he was home or somewhere else.

Gemma checked her phone again, even though it was fully charged and the volume was all the way up. Still no reply from Drew. Randy had been silent too, which was a good thing.

She rubbed her forehead and exhaled. About the only thing left to do was to try tracking him down through his sister or his parents. She felt like an idiot contacting them like this, but if Gemma didn't act now, it might be too late to talk to Drew.

When she found his parents' number online, she recognized it right away. It was the same number he'd had in high school. She checked the time and hoped that 9:00 on a Sunday morning wasn't too early.

A woman's voice answered—Drew's mom. "Mrs. Chandler? This is Gemma Staheli . . ." The next few moments were spent with pleasantries. Then Gemma asked Drew's mom if she knew where he might be working today, or if he was at his new place. Gemma claimed to have lost his number.

"I thought he was with all you high-school friends this weekend," Mrs. Chandler said. "He's not at his new place— there was a pipe break last week, so he's been staying here. But I haven't seen him since he left for the reunion."

Where did he stay last night? "He was called on a last-minute job and had to leave suddenly." Sort of true. "We wanted to swing by and say good-bye, and, of course, get his number again." None of that was true.

"I'm not exactly sure where he'd be, dear, especially if it was last minute."

Gemma tried not to sigh aloud.

"But you know those photographers—they have their favorite haunts. You might try the Dana Point Marine Cove or Ruby Park in Laguna Beach—he made us do our family photos there last year. Other than that, he could be anywhere. Drew doesn't always have a say with magazines, you know."

Gemma scrambled for a pen to write down the locations on a Post-it. Two places to check were better than none. She thanked Drew's mom and hung up. Gemma doubted he'd be as close as the Marina; they could practically walk there from the beach house. She finished getting ready, pulling on one of her new sundresses she'd bought—it was a little cold to wear in the morning, but Gemma decided she'd be warm enough from nerves.

She left a note for Liz then slipped out of the beach house. First she drove to the marina. No cars were in the parking lot except a van with the Dana Point Marina logo on it. So she turned around and headed north up the PCH. Traffic was minimal on a Sunday morning, and Gemma drove slowly, looking for the turn off to Ruby Park. About half a dozen cars were parked in front, but they could be there for anything—joggers, dog walkers; she'd even seen morning weddings on the beach. Although a wedding would mean a lot more cars.

When she saw Drew's black SUV, she braked. Gemma parked a few slots down and climbed out of her car. She walked slowly over to the SUV, just to be sure. The corner of the window had a Killer Dana Surf Shop sticker. Gemma's heart pounded. Drew was either in the park or on the coast right next to it. Judging by the number of cars, he was probably working, which meant they wouldn't be alone.

Hesitating, Gemma tried to talk herself out of approaching Drew. Maybe she could watch from afar, and if he happened to see her and acknowledge her, then they could talk. At least she could apologize if nothing else.

Her phone buzzed, and she checked the text message. Her breath caught. It was from Drew.

Are you going back to Randy?

Gemma waited a heartbeat before replying. *No.* Should she say something else? Finally, she pressed send.

She stared at the screen, waiting for his reply.

K.

K? That was it? K . . . what? But at least he'd texted her; he'd responded. That was a big deal. Gemma started breathing again. *Maybe I should go back to the beach house and wait. See if he shows up later.* But waiting without knowing would practically kill her.

She walked around the SUV and headed toward the

sound of waves. At the end of the path, she stopped where she could see down the coast. A couple was walking with a dog along the surf. Farther down, a lone man sat in the sand, a camera in his hands.

Gemma's heart stilled. Drew. He wasn't working on a shoot. *And he just texted me, which means he's thinking about me.*

She shivered and folded her bare arms then started walking toward him. She wasn't sure exactly when he saw her, but one moment he was staring out at the ocean, and the next he was standing, facing her, his camera slung over his shoulder, his hands in his pockets.

He didn't move as she approached, as if he was waiting for her to make the journey. For *her* to walk to *him*. Which should be the case, Gemma realized, her breathing growing erratic. It was her turn to choose him.

When she was close enough to see the hazel of his eyes, she unfolded her arms and stopped a couple of feet away from him. Neither of them spoke. Gemma gazed at him, remembering every moment of the night before, and the way he'd kissed her.

His gaze soaked her in, and fresh goose bumps broke out on her skin. The side of his mouth twitched, and she took the final two steps and threw her arms around his neck. Drew pulled her tightly against him and lifted her off her heels. He slowly spun her in a circle. She closed her eyes, feeling the solid strength of his arms holding her up and the warm bareness of his neck against her face.

When he set her down, his hands remained at her hips. "How did you find me?"

"I called your mom." Gemma tried to keep her voice normal, even though she felt like his touch would melt her.

His eyebrows lifted. "My mom?"

"She told me a couple of places to look."

Drew laughed.

Gemma smiled, watching him, her heart pounding. She did not expect his easy acceptance of her return, but then again, maybe she should have. This was what made him Drew. And she loved him for it.

I love him.

"I am so sorry," she said.

Drew's smile faded, and his eyes searched hers. "I'm sorry you had to deal with him again." He touched her shoulder, and then his fingers trailed along her neck.

She slid her hands over his chest, stopping at his heart. Its beat seemed to pulse through her skin, then along her arm until it connected her heart to his. "I was scared you wouldn't ever talk to me again."

Drew lowered his chin and closed his eyes. "I needed to separate myself from what I saw—to think about things—about us." He opened his eyes. "I had to decide if I was going to fight for you or let you go again."

Again? "What do you mean?"

He searched her eyes, hesitating. "You were why we broke up."

"*Me?*" Gemma said. "How?"

"Valentina guessed how I felt about you, even before I was willing to admit it." He was quiet for a moment. The intensity of his gaze made her sundress feel like a wool coat. "Valentina knew that I was in love with you."

Gemma stared at him.

His hands cradled her face, and he lowered his head to hers then kissed her slowly as if he had all the time in the world. Her body melted against his, held up only by the strength of his arms.

When he broke away to breathe, he said, "I've been in love with you for ten years, Gemma, maybe longer."

She opened her mouth to respond, but he started kissing her again. How could she not have known? How could she not have seen it? Her eyes filled with tears as she thought of how blind she'd been, of how much time they'd wasted.

She pulled away from him, catching her breath. "Why didn't you tell me?"

His smile was sad. "We were such great friends. I didn't think I could have it both ways. But when you kissed me last night, it gave me hope."

She ran her fingers along his jawline. "I don't know who's more dense—me or you." She lifted herself on her toes and kissed him softly. "Because I have a confession to make. I'm in love with you too."

His hands tightened around her back as he pulled her close. "So will you go out with me then? Or are you mad at me?"

She laughed. "You won't be able to get rid of me, no matter who's mad at who."

"I can't imagine anything better," he whispered against her ear. He kissed her earlobe then moved down her neck. "I think our first real date should begin now. Let's go get breakfast."

"All right," Gemma said, reluctantly releasing her hold on him.

He grabbed her hand, threading their fingers together. He held up his camera and snapped a picture of their intertwined hands. "That's what I call picture perfect."

And it was. Gemma couldn't imagine anything better than walking with Drew, hand in hand on the beach, at the beginning of a beautiful day.

Other Aliso Creek Novellas

Third Time's the Charm

Lost then Found

One Chance

The Daisy Chain

Heather B. Moore is a *USA Today* bestselling author. She has ten historical thrillers written under the pen name H.B. Moore, her latest is *Finding Sheba*. Under Heather B. Moore she writes romance and women's fiction. She's the co-author of The Newport Ladies Book Club series. Other women's novels include *Heart of the Ocean, The Fortune Café,* the Aliso Creek Series and A Timeless Romance Anthology Series.

Author website: www.hbmoore.com
Blog: http://mywriterslair.blogspot.com
Twitter: @HeatherBMoore
Facebook: *Fans of H.B. Moore* or *Heather Brown Moore*

The Science of Sentiment

Aubrey Mace

Other Works by Aubrey Mace

Spare Change

Santa Maybe

My Fairy Grandmother

One

*I*t was the perfect kiss—tentative, but passionate at the same time. It was tender, yet somehow insistent. As I felt heat creeping from my neck to my hairline, I knew that something about this kiss was different. It was sweet and breathless and exciting and scary, all at the same time. The kiss by which all other kisses would be judged and found wanting.

As pleasant as it was to dwell on the past, the fact that I'd since broken up with the aforementioned kisser kind of soured the memory for me. The idea that I'd dated multiple guys since without a fraction of the spark made it even more bitter. I sighed and forced myself to focus on the view instead. The snow-capped mountains were beautiful, but I couldn't help being a little disappointed.

When I'd come up with the idea of driving to my grandfather's cabin for spring break, I had a different picture in mind. I'd been there many times, and all the memories were happy ones. They were also warmer ones, from summer or fall, when the world was verdant green or even orange or red or bright yellow—not the omnipresent white and gray surrounding me now. My brain had been anticipating one thing, but the reality was quite another. To me, "spring break" implied some *spring* involved, but apparently Park City hadn't gotten the memo.

For someone who was rational to a fault, I'd been incredibly irrational about taking this last-minute trip. I hadn't even brought a coat. Shivers rippled through me while I waited for my gas tank to fill, so I bought some hot chocolate at the gas station. It seemed more appropriate than the tub of Country Time lemonade in my backseat. Unfortunately, 7-11 didn't sell outerwear, and although the sky was blue, it only *looked* warm outside. I was fairly certain that the first strong breeze would send me ducking for cover under the thickest quilt I could find.

I turned off the main road, onto the gravel one that would lead me to the cabin. Even if the weather wasn't exactly what I'd hoped for, this weekend would be just what I needed. I was tired. Life had been wearing me down lately, and I couldn't wait to have some time alone to relax and try to recover my normally optimistic outlook. I had my sketchbook and pencils, and all I wanted was to draw and go for long walks so I could tune out for a while.

Everything looked so different from what I remembered. If I looked closely, I could spot familiar trees I knew and loved even with the stark branches they'd disguised themselves with. On my way up the mountain, some of the trees had the greenish tinge that comes with the first of the warmer weather, and at their bases, some even had waxy new green leaves. But at this altitude, the trees were still bare and dead looking.

When I reached the gravel driveway, I was startled to see a shiny blue truck parked in front of the cabin. It wasn't a vehicle I recognized, but Gramps was famous for opening the cabin to anyone who wanted to stay there. I had my own key, but I was sure I wasn't the only one. Now I wanted to kick myself for not checking with him to see if the place was already occupied this weekend.

I parked and left my stuff in the car. Might as well check it out first—no use hauling it all in if I wouldn't be staying, not that there was much to haul. The gravel crunching under my feet was louder than I remembered, and the mountain air, albeit chilly, smelled deliciously of pine. I had the key in my pocket, but I didn't want to alarm whoever was already in there, so I knocked politely. I waited.

No answer.

I knocked again, a bit louder than before. It was freezing. The air up here made the temperature at 7-11 seem almost tropical. I hopped from one foot to the other with my arms wrapped around me, trying to get blood flowing through my veins. I felt even sillier as I tried to reconcile my plans for lengthy strolling with my wardrobe of t-shirts and jeans. Normally, I had everything planned to the last detail, so I blamed this lapse in judgment on how stressed out I'd been lately. My fingers were starting to feel numb, so I knocked again while I still could.

Still no answer. Maybe whoever was here had brought realistic clothing and was outside somewhere, taking advantage of the beautiful but frigid day. I was about to try my key when the door opened abruptly, and I couldn't help the sudden intake of sharp, cold air that stuck in my throat. The person standing on the other side just grinned.

"Kevin," I said finally.

"Well, hey, Rosie." His voice was as steady and unsurprised as if I were the pizza delivery guy.

Kevin was, of course, the aforementioned best kiss of my life.

Two

"You know I don't like it when you call me that," I said, and after all the misery he'd put me through, it seemed an odd choice of first words. *Why did you turn out to be such a jerk?* or *Why haven't you died a slow agonizing death in a lonely ditch somewhere yet?* Either seemed infinitely more appropriate.

"You never used to mind." Still smiling that same lazy smile, cockier than ever.

Ugh. Why hadn't I called Gramps first? "What are you doing here?"

"I was invited."

I snorted, a noise that sounded appalling, like it came from some large form of wildlife. "Really? By who?"

"Gramps, of course."

I gritted my teeth to hold back the obscenity waiting to fall out. If I was irritated by Kevin's use of my nickname, I was livid about the casual use of my grandfather's. "He's *my* Gramps, not yours. And he certainly wouldn't let you stay here now—not after the way you treated me."

"From what I remember, *I* wasn't the only one who behaved badly."

"Then your memory is as faulty as the rest of you."

"At least I didn't throw things."

My face was set to perma-glare. "Do you really want to compare sins? Because I can assure you, I was not the guiltier party."

Kevin raised his hands in surrender. "You're right. Let's leave the past in the past."

"Which is where you should be. I can't believe Gramps would ask you to come here after all this time."

He shrugged. "Go on, call him. See for yourself."

I pulled my cell phone out of my pocket. "That's exactly what I'm going to do. And then you're going to leave."

He stepped aside. "Would you like to come in?"

"Thanks, but I think I'll stay out here."

"Suit yourself." He walked away but quickly returned with a heavy jacket that looked temptingly warm. He held it out to me. "At least put this on."

"I'm fine." I fiddled with my phone to keep my hands busy so they wouldn't snatch the jacket from him without my permission.

"Really? Because you look kinda cold to me."

"I said I'm fine."

He shook his head and draped the jacket around my shoulders. "Still as stubborn as ever, I see."

The jacket smelled like Kevin. It took a superhuman effort to fight the urge to tuck my face into the collar and stay there indefinitely. But I'd never let him know I still missed him—not for anything. "And you still think you know what I need better than I do?"

"Go on, make your call. I'll be inside when you're ready to talk."

"You'd better start packing your truck, because you're not staying."

"We'll see."

⊰⊱

I jumped into the car and turned the key. At least it was still warm, which was about the only thing I had going for me at the moment.

"What do you mean, you asked him?" I said, trying not to shout into the phone. I didn't want Gramps to think I was angry, even if I was. After all, it was his cabin, and he could invite anyone he wanted to stay at it. Even if that person was the one guy who had captured my heart more completely than anyone I'd ever met—then proceeded to trash it beyond repair. I'll say that much for Kevin; he was thorough. He approached everything he did with the same one-hundred percent mentality . . . even breaking my heart.

"How much snow is up there, Rosie? Is everything okay? Did the gas turn on all right?"

Everything was pretty much the complete opposite of okay. "I didn't have to mess with the gas because *someone* had already turned it on. Why did you tell Kevin it was okay for him to stay here?"

"I like Kevin."

"Yeah, I used to like him too. But we broke up a year ago, remember?"

"Sweetie," Gramps said. "I'm going to tell you something important, and I want you to listen, okay?"

"Okay," I said. I snuggled down into the coat so that Kevin couldn't see me if he was spying at the window.

"Have you ever seen salmon spawn?"

"Pardon?"

"You know, salmon swimming upstream to spawn. Have you seen it?"

"Yeah, on a nature program or something." Where was this going? I was sitting in the car with the heat turned up full blast and I was in no hurry to go back inside and face Kevin. I could afford to be indulgent.

"Salmon go through so much," Gramps went on. "They're so focused on their task that they forget to eat so they get smashed into rocks and eaten by bears. They use every last bit of their energy jumping and swimming against the current and the other fish. But the ones who keep pushing themselves get the reward. And you know what happens?"

"Tell me." I could picture Gramps on the other end and I wished we were having this conversation in person so I could see the sparkle in his eyes.

"They make it to the spawning grounds, where they can finally lay their eggs and rest and be happy."

I frowned. "I think I remember hearing that once they spawn, most of them die."

"Bah, never mind that. Animals are smart. Lots of them mate for life—did you know that? Like swans . . . and termites."

His metaphors were all over the place, but I think I finally understood his end game. "They stay together like you and Grandma, right?"

"Exactly! You know how when you look at some people, you just know they belong together?"

I blinked away the tears that were suddenly forming. The last thing I needed was to go back inside and face Kevin with puffy eyes. "Yes, you and Grandma were the perfect couple."

"I was talking about you and Kevin. You kids were made for each other. You need to give it another chance."

"Kevin broke up with me, Gramps. It wasn't my choice."

"Maybe not entirely. But it takes two to tango, you know."

"Unfortunately we're not all as lucky as you two. Not everyone rides off into the sunset together."

"It takes hard work, but it's worth it. Besides, it's only one weekend. What have you got to lose?"

No one could say my stubborn streak wasn't genetic. "You're impossible. How did you know I was coming up this weekend?"

"I didn't. Last time I saw Kevin, I told him he was welcome to come stay whenever he wanted to. And now you're there too. You know what they call that?"

"What?" I massaged my temples with my fingers.

"Fate."

Three

I hung up and closed my eyes. The Kevin smell on the jacket wasn't going away; if anything, it seemed to have intensified since putting it on, and the effect on my emotions was unnerving. The scent made me think of winter outings together in happier times.

The jacket should have come with a warning label stating that it may cause confusion or mental fogginess or, in the worse cases, temporary insanity, which was what I had to be experiencing if I had any fond memories of Kevin left in the old brain depository. But then, that's what you get when you rely on your nose to make important decisions.

Good thing my brain was still semi-functioning. I couldn't sit out here in the car with the heater running forever. It was time to quickly consider my options.

The generous thing to do would be to go home and let Kevin stay. He got here first, and all his stuff was already inside.

But I wasn't feeling particularly generous. This was my grandfather's cabin—*mine*. I had been planning this weekend of relaxation, and I needed it. Kevin had absolutely no right to be here. He should go.

Unless . . .

I shook my head, trying to dislodge the ridiculous idea that was sprouting before it managed to take root. Gramps was crazy. This wasn't a chick flick, complete with cheesy music that rose when the couple stood perilously near each other. This was real life, and Kevin didn't want to spend the weekend with me any more than I wanted to hang out with him.

Unless . . .

Why would he come here if he didn't want to see you? He must have known there was a chance you'd be here.

No. Double triple no. I had been down this dangerous road before, and nothing good could come by revisiting it. One of us would stay and one would go—it was that simple.

❧

I took a deep breath and went back inside the cabin, prepared to be the bigger person and leave. Kevin didn't hear me come in; his back was to me. I tried to ignore the taut muscles that told me he obviously hadn't been mourning our lost relationship on the couch with bag of potato chips. I watched as he put some things in the refrigerator—milk, bacon, eggs, bread, butter. Real food. Aside from hot chocolate and lemonade, I realized I had brought nothing to eat. I think there was a squashed protein bar in my purse somewhere. My lack of planning was really pathetic. I should go and let Kevin stay—at least he wouldn't starve. But the way he was stocking the fridge made me angry, like he didn't even plan on offering to be the one who went home, when the cabin was much more mine than it was his.

"What did Gramps have to say?" he said, and I jumped. He didn't turn around, but somehow he knew I was there.

"You already know what he said."

"He told me I might be surprised by how much I enjoyed it up here. 'You see some surprising things in the country,' he said. I thought maybe he meant a moose or something." He shut the refrigerator and finally turned around, the smile on his face fading when he saw how annoyed I was. "I had no idea you'd be here. I wouldn't spoil your weekend on purpose."

The look he gave me said that he was telling the truth, and for a split second, I imagined that maybe I wasn't the only one who'd been miserable for the last year. But as he was the one who'd broken my heart, he wasn't entitled to be unhappy, so I wouldn't pity him. Still, it was a nice thing to hear him say, and knowing that he actually meant it helped.

"I believe you. Well, I hope you have a nice weekend." I forced myself to turn and start walking to the door before I changed my mind.

"Wait, where are you going?"

"Home. I can relax and hide there as easily as I can here."

He looked curious. "Who are you hiding from?"

"Everyone. I need time to regroup." *Stop talking, Rose. He doesn't care anymore.*

"That doesn't sound like the world breaker I remember."

I shrugged, unwilling to pursue the topic.

"If anyone is going, it should be me. Give me a few minutes to gather up my stuff, and I'll get out of your way."

Now that he'd actually said what I'd been thinking, I felt guilty. "It's okay—you were here first. I'll go."

A small smile touched the corners of his mouth. "You know, there are two bedrooms . . ."

Oh, that mouth. I had the sudden image of us running into each other's arms and kissing for the rest of the weekend. Maybe there was a reason I hadn't brought any food. Who needs bacon and eggs when there was all that lost lip time to make up for?

Rose! Focus! Do not let your powers of reasoning be overtaken by a pretty face.

I noticed that Kevin's smile had widened considerably. I could tell he was pleased to see that he still had the same power to reduce me to speechlessness. Well, I wasn't about to give him the satisfaction of knowing that he made me weak in the knees, even if he did. I pursed my lips.

"I think that's a terrible idea. In fact, as really bad ideas go, that has to be at the top of the . . . Really Bad Idea list."

"I'd forgotten how you ramble when you were nervous. It's cute."

Crap. This wasn't going the way I intended. I wanted to come off as the Ice Queen, but instead I was spouting nonsense. It was probably best to leave now, before I said anything really embarrassing. "I'll go."

"I can be an adult if you can." He was still sporting that smug grin. Perhaps I could do something about that.

"So you've developed a new skill since we parted ways?"

He winced. "Ouch. You know what? You're right. It's a bad idea. I'm sure arguing with me wasn't your idea of a relaxing weekend. I'll go get my stuff."

"No, you're right," I said. "There's plenty of room for two *adults* here. If we play our cards right, we'll never even see each other." Determined to have the last word, I walked into the bedroom I usually stayed in, only to be confronted by Kevin's duffle bag, fishing rods, and tackle sitting on the bed. His stuff in my room was so incongruous with the picture in my head that my brain disconnected for a minute. When I finally composed myself, I turned around to leave and ran straight into Kevin, who was suddenly installed in the doorway, roadblock style. When I realized a collision was imminent, I put my hands in front of me to keep myself from running him down, but that had the unintended side effect of physical contact. It took me longer than it should have to remove my hands from his chest, and by then he was all smiles again.

"This must be your room," he said, in the buttery tone that made my head all foggy.

"It's not my cabin. I don't have a room."

"I'll take the other one. I don't mind."

"You're already in here. It's fine. I'll go get my stuff out of the car."

Kevin moved to let me pass, but I went the same direction he did, so we spent the next three minutes trying to negotiate a path. It was probably only fifteen seconds, but it seemed like an eternity. Finally I had the sense to stand still until he picked a direction. I hurried past, eager to put some distance between us.

"Let me help you bring your bags in."

I tried not to laugh as I pictured my purse and small travel bag with room for little more than a toothbrush, which were waiting for me in the car. "No, I got it. I travel light."

"Since when? I seem to remember you made Girl Scouts look unorganized."

I gave him my sweetest smile over my shoulder. "I'm evolving."

He returned my smile. I tried to ignore the way my heart instantly picked up its pace. "Just trying to be a gentleman."

If he tried any harder, I'd fall for him all over again, and that simply wouldn't do. I couldn't let him know I was even a tiny bit interested. "Good for you. *Trying* is a definite improvement, and I should know. Looks like you're evolving too."

As I walked to the car, I prided myself on recovering the upper hand while attempting to ignore the little voice saying that just because you can have the last word doesn't necessarily mean you should.

Four

hen I came back inside, Kevin was nowhere in sight, for which I was grateful. The door to his bedroom was closed. He was probably in there pouting. I went to the unoccupied bedroom and put my meager luggage on the bed before flopping down next to it. This was a disaster.

I really should have left before things got any worse. The momentary high from outwitting Kevin had already faded into something that felt remarkably like guilt. What I said earlier was true—when we were dating, he had the annoying habit of always thinking he knew what was best for me. But he'd never been anything but a gentleman, and I felt bad for implying otherwise.

Still, no matter how guilty I felt, I couldn't go to him and say I was sorry. Because then he'd give me that easy smile of his and say he'd never been bothered by it in the first place, and I'd end up flustered and lose any semblance of control I now felt over the situation. No, I had to cling tightly to the slight advantage I'd gained; better to be the Ice Queen than end up feeling like an idiot. The irony that I was acting more childish than Kevin wasn't lost on me.

I let myself sink back into the mattress, curling up on my side and pulling my feet under me. The quilt smelled a little musty, but it was pleasant. The scent reminded me of the time I came to stay here as a little girl and the cabin had been shut up for too long without fresh air or people in it. This was a much less confusing smell than that of Kevin's jacket, which I'd abandoned on the couch when I came back inside. Confusing or not, I still found myself wishing I was still wearing the jacket. Now that I was alone, drowning in the memories associated with the cologne didn't seem like such a bad way to spend an afternoon . . .

A knock on the bedroom door shook me out of my daydream. I sat up quickly. "Yeah?"

Kevin's head poked through the door. "I'm going fishing. Want to go?"

"Nah, I think I'll stay here and hang out."

"Come on, you love fishing!" He walked into the kitchen, and I followed him. He knew if he walked away, I would follow. I'd follow him anywhere; I always had—until the last time, when he had walked away for good. Even then I had a feeling he wanted me to go after him, but he hadn't seemed surprised when I let him go. We'd both had enough.

What to do now? I did love fishing, but I could think of multiple reasons why this excursion wouldn't be smart. For one thing, it was really cold outside, and it was only going to get colder as the afternoon wore on. When Kevin realized this t-shirt was the warmest clothing I brought, he would tease me mercilessly. I didn't need anyone to tell me it was silly—I mean, I could see the snow on the mountains with my own eyes. But my associations with the cabin were sunscreen and swimsuits. I couldn't help that my dominant logical side had been momentarily overridden by nostalgia. I think I'd expected to arrive to find my corner of the woods stuck in perpetual July.

Then there was the idea of having to make small talk for hours on end. It was one thing managing to dredge up a few words when I passed Kevin in the hall, but standing next to each other fishing with nothing to say for a whole afternoon was quite another. No, as much fun as fishing would be, staying in the cabin would be much safer.

"I wish I could go, but I can't."

"Why?" He looked genuinely puzzled.

"Because my shoulder is screwed up." *A health issue—that's brilliant, Rose! Can't argue with that.*

"Really?"

"Yes, really. I can't lift anything or make any repetitive motions."

True confession time: I am a really good liar. It's a gift. I don't like to make a habit of it, but when necessary I can look anyone in the eye and instantly come up with a story that would pass a lie detector with flying colors.

There was one exception to this rule, and unfortunately, he happened to be standing in front of me. However, now that we weren't a couple anymore—without all those messy emotions tied into it—I was confident I'd be able to pull this one off.

"Says who?" He raised one eyebrow, but I was determined not to let that old trick rattle me.

"I have a note from my doctor."

"You brought it with you?" he said, and I could tell he was trying not to laugh. "Who were you planning on showing it to? The squirrels?"

Okay, so maybe there was still one emotion I was going to have to get around: annoyance. I gave him the frostiest look I could manage. "I didn't *bring* it with me. It just happens to be in my purse."

He folded his arms across his chest. "All right, let's see it."

"What?"

"Let's see your doctor's note."

Was he seriously calling my bluff? Anyone else would have bought the story. When people claim to have health problems, who demands proof? "I'm not going to show you my doctor's note," I huffed.

"Why not?"

"Because it's silly."

"You don't have one, do you? You made it up."

"Of course I have it. Why would anyone make up something like that?"

"Because you needed an excuse not to spend time with me. What if I had suggested that we play cards? Would you also have a doctor's note saying you've developed a rare gambling allergy?" Although he was having way too much fun with this, his eyes looked sad.

"Whatever. I really am hurt, okay?"

"Then get your note. I want to see it."

"You want to see the note? Fine. I'll get the note." I stomped off in the direction of my bedroom with a sick feeling in my stomach. Great. Now what was I supposed to do? I felt like an airplane going down with both engines on fire and no parachutes. I said a silent prayer that somehow there would be a doctor with a prescription pad waiting in my room.

There wasn't.

I briefly considered climbing out the window and heading for someplace where no one knew me and my penchant for making up stories, someplace I could start over.

Maybe Prague . . .

Probably not. No, there was nothing to be done but face the music. Unless I could come up with a better story . . .

I took my purse into the living room and started rifling through it, trying to buy myself time while I concocted Plan B. Kevin stood with his back against the wall, waiting, arms folded, smirking like a guy in an underwear ad who knows exactly how charming and good looking he is.

The worst part is he knows you know it.

I made a big show of going through all the pockets, searching my wallet, flipping through my appointment book, all the while knowing that what I was looking for didn't exist. And Plan B wasn't happening; I couldn't concentrate. My heart pounded in my ears, and I could feel my face getting hot. It appeared that lying to Kevin was still out of my depth, relationship or not. I felt like a lunatic, but I'd taken this whole charade way too far to back out now. I was going to have to go through the motions until the bitter end, which, by my calculations, was right about . . . now.

I snuck a look at Kevin, only to discover that his smirk had gotten . . . smirkier. I dropped my purse on the couch. "I can't find it."

"Hmmm. Could that be because it never existed in the first place?"

"It must have fallen out of my purse when I stopped for gas on my way up here. Now I'll have to take a day off work and go to the doctor to get a new one."

"Oh, Rosie. Please."

"What?"

"Why can't you admit that you made it up?"

"Because I didn't."

"I think you're lying."

Nothing makes a good liar angrier than getting caught. "Go on then, make your case. You can't just accuse me of lying without the proof to back it up."

"You're proving it for me. Look how flustered you are."

I put my hands in my pockets and willed them to stop shaking. *Act casual.* "The symptoms of frustration can be remarkably similar to deception. Try again."

"Everything is science with you, isn't it? Cause and effect, deduction and analysis."

"I like science. I can conduct the same experiment a hundred times and always get the same result. People aren't dependable like that."

Kevin was smiling, but there was no joy in it. He shook his head. "Okay, how did you hurt your shoulder?"

"How did I hurt my shoulder?"

"I may not be dependable, but if you're injured, I'm concerned. How did it happen?"

"I strained my rotator cuff climbing a tree."

Kevin laughed.

I glared at him. "What? You don't think I could climb a tree?"

"Obviously not very well, since you're wounded. So why were you climbing a tree in the first place?"

"What is this, twenty questions?"

"You have to admit it's a little bizarre. I'm wondering why you did it."

By now I had come to terms with the certainty that there was no way I was going to come out on top of this story, so I said the first thing that came into my head. "To pick apples."

He paused for a minute and looked straight into my eyes. It was hard not to squirm, but I forced myself to meet his gaze.

"Red or green?"

I was focusing all my attention on winning our staring contest and the question threw me. "What?"

"Were the apples red or green?"

I threw my arms in the air. "What difference does it make?"

"I'm curious."

"Green. The apples were green, okay? Satisfied?" I could feel the pulse hammering in my neck, and I wondered how long it would take for an ambulance to reach the cabin if my blood pressure continued to spike and I had a stroke.

Kevin walked over until he was directly in front of me, so close that I could see the flecks of green in his brown eyes. I was having a hard time reconciling my conflicting emotions. I was so angry at him for backing me into this corner, but heaven help me, at the same time, I wanted him to grab me and kiss me with those magic lips of his until I couldn't breathe. He leaned in and for one terrible, blissful moment I thought he had read my mind.

"Now I know you're lying," he whispered into my ear.

I pulled back. That arrogant . . . I couldn't believe I'd been so close to surrendering only a second ago. "And what scientific finding has led you to that conclusion?"

"You hate green apples."

I made a noise that was a cross between a scream and a growl. "Not as much as I hate you right now!" I picked up my purse and pushed past him, putting one foot in front of the other on autopilot until I got to my bedroom, where I slammed the door so hard I thought the hinges might break.

Five

lone in my room after our argument, I pulled out my sketch book and pencils and began to draw—a sort of frenzied marathon of pages at the beginning when I was still angry that eased into careful, sure strokes once I'd had a chance to calm down. I heard the front door open and close as Kevin went off in search of his fish and felt myself relax even further, my shoulders deflating as the tension drained away.

Drawing always was therapy for me. Pencils were one of the few constants in my life, something I could control. I'd never be a great artist, but I knew I had some talent, and it pleased me to start with a clean, blank page and create something. Back in school, when I'd first fallen under the spell of a box of newly sharpened colored pencils, I had notebooks full of sketches, mostly nature—leaves, flowers, fish, birds and other animals. In college I had books crammed with clippings and drawings, bits of plants and feathers pressed in. Parts were beginning to crumble now, but I still thumb through them occasionally to remember my rambling walks and my battered copy of *Walden*, from the days I thought anything was possible.

I was a middle school science teacher. Well, science and art. I loved the research with the why's and eventual explanations, the detailed notes of the successes and failures. But for someone who prides herself on being a rational scientist, I was certainly behaving foolishly. It had to be because of Kevin. He always brought out the petulant six-year-old in me.

I sketched pages of apples—green *and* red—whole and sliced open with all the secrets spilling out. I drew seeds and stems and leaves, but I found that it was impossible to capture the fruit inside. No matter how I tried, the texture of the creamy middle was somehow lost on the page. Still, to any average observer, it would appear a perfectly serviceable apple. Only I could see the flaws.

My stomach grumbled, reminding me how long it had been since I'd actually eaten anything, but I wasn't desperate enough to track down the flattened protein bar yet. As I stubbornly continued in my relentless pursuit to create an apple that would leap off the page, I let my mind wander to the day that I met Kevin and the kiss that would irrevocably change my life.

The school I taught at had an annual neighborhood Fall Carnival as a fundraiser, and I had been recruited to work one of the booths. In the planning meeting, one of the younger men on staff requested a kissing booth, but the principal tactfully explained that a kissing booth was no longer politically correct. This was followed by a rebuttal from the teacher, who suggested that anyone who wanted to purchase a kiss could sign a waiver, thus relieving the school of any liability. We all laughed until, slowly, everyone realized he wasn't joking. The subject was dismissed, and we quickly moved on to other assignments before he could propose anything else.

So as the art teacher, I agreed to work in a stand that sold sketches for a dollar, which was sort of like a kissing booth minus the sexual harassment-suit potential. The sign over my head even said "kissing booth," but *kissing* had been crossed out and replaced with my more respectable offering. Either the sign maker had a sense of humor, or the same teacher was still trying to get what he wanted.

The weather that night was perfect—not too cold, but with just enough chill in the air to send people flocking to the hot chocolate and cider. Inhaling the occasional whiff of buttery popcorn, I couldn't help feeling festive in my fingerless gloves, which kept my hands warm but still enabled me to draw. Between customers, I sketched items I saw around me: pumpkins for sale, the big harvest moon, fall leaves. I was frustrated that my pencils couldn't do the vibrant leaves justice. That year they were particularly lovely, in shocking shades of red and orange and yellow hovering between reality and fantasy.

As I concentrated on trying to make the leaves on my page equal to their living counterparts, I realized I had a patron. I raised my head and was greeted by a pair of smiling brown eyes so open and inviting that it was impossible not to return the smile.

"How can I help you?" I asked.

"I'd like to purchase a kiss." He put a dollar bill on the table in front of me.

"Uh, this is a *sketching* booth," I said, pointing to the sign. "Sorry. But I can draw you a picture of whatever you'd like."

"I see you have some nice ones," he said, his eyes scanning the hastily drawn pictures in front of me.

Now I was self-conscious. "They're not my best, but what do you like for a dollar?"

I was rewarded with another smile, which seemed to make my mind go blank. "I was being serious. They're great . . ."

"But?" I said, completing his unfinished sentence.

"I'm afraid I don't see what I'm looking for."

"Well, you're in luck. I can sketch anything. What exactly are you looking for?"

"You."

I wondered if he noticed how red my face suddenly had to be. It was dark out, but there was a light in my little booth. Even if he couldn't see it, I imagined he could probably feel the heat from my blush. I was in unfamiliar territory, but hadn't yet decided whether I enjoyed being pursued by this handsome stranger. I needed to maintain at least the illusion of being in control of the situation.

"I'm not in the habit of drawing self-portraits, Mr. . . ."

"Kevin."

"Mr. Kevin."

He smiled again. "It's just Kevin. And you are?"

Sometimes when I meet new people, I have a hard time maintaining eye contact, but this was exactly the opposite. I couldn't stop looking. It was like being introduced to a particularly addictive drug. I'd only met this guy two minutes ago, and already I knew I'd have to have more of that smile, or I'd be subject to withdrawal symptoms. I pointed to my sticky name tag. "Miss Marsh."

"I told you my name."

"I know, but first I have to decide if you're a serial kissing-booth stalker."

He laughed. The smile was good, but the laugh was even better. "What can I do to prove my innocence?"

I pushed my sketchbook across the table to him. "Choose a pencil and write a sentence in cursive."

"I never write in cursive anymore."

"Just do it."

His face was puzzled. "What should I write?"

"Anything," I said. "I only need one sentence."

He grabbed a blue pencil and quickly scribbled something then passed it back to me. I read it.

Miss Marsh is very beautiful. I wish she would tell me her first name.

"That's actually two sentences," I said.

He shrugged. "I'm an overachiever."

"You might be, actually. The large loops on your H, B, and L mean you have big ambitions. See here, the way you crossed your T's near the top? That tells me you have good self-esteem. Same with your large capital letters."

"Really?"

I was pleased he seemed genuinely interested. "Really. Did you notice that your handwriting slants upward a little? That means you're optimistic. You also chose to write in blue, which means you're friendly and outgoing."

"Fascinating. So, Miss Marsh, you're a teacher, an artist, *and* a fortune teller?"

"I'm a scientist," I corrected. "Graphology is very scientific."

"Graphology?"

"Handwriting analysis."

"Right. So, I'm not a stalker?"

I smiled. "Well, it's not foolproof, but I think you're relatively safe."

"So now you can tell me your name."

"I'm afraid not."

His expression fell.

"But I will give you a clue." I took a red pencil from the box and started to draw. I kept my eyes on the page, concentrating on shaping velvety petals. I could feel him watching me. When the picture was finished, I handed it to him, suddenly feeling shy for some reason. As he took the paper, his warm fingers brushed against mine. Despite the gloves, my hands were cold. I told myself that the only reason I was possessed with the sudden desire to hold his hand was for the warmth.

"Your name is Rose!" It was a semi-ridiculous statement, given that the clue was completely obvious. But at the same time, his words kind of melted my heart. His voice was utterly triumphant, like a child who had finally gotten the hang of riding a bicycle without training wheels.

"Correct."

"I don't usually have to try this hard to get a girl's name."

"And there's the big ego I mentioned earlier."

"You didn't say big ego—you said *high self-esteem*."

I grinned. "Like I said, it isn't an exact science."

"So, Rose." The way he said my name was as if he was turning it over on his tongue, sampling it like the rare vintage of some fine wine. "Rosie."

"Just Rose," I corrected.

"Rose, I would very much like to kiss you now."

"I told you, this isn't a kissing booth." I was baffled. I wasn't the kind of girl who kissed on the first date, and I was certainly not the kind who kissed random guys I'd just met, no matter how charming. Yet I found myself considering what those lips would feel like, if they were as warm as his hands.

"If I analyzed your handwriting," he said. "I bet it would tell me that you are a very literal person. This has nothing to do with the booth. Forget the booth. I just want to kiss you."

"But—I barely know you," I stammered.

"Of course you do. You just outlined my whole personality."

"That doesn't count. I don't even know your last name."

He held up one finger, indicating that I should wait. He took my pencils and drew a crude picture of a barn with the letters *ES* next to it.

I couldn't help the laugh that bubbled out. "Barnes? Kevin Barnes?"

"See? You're not the only Monet around here."

I put my hand over my mouth to hide the giggle, but it was too late. No matter how hard I tried, I couldn't stop laughing.

"What?" he said.

"It's nothing. I was just thinking that obviously one of your big ambitions isn't art school."

He opened his mouth in shock. "Rosie Marsh, you are so mean!"

"Don't call me Rosie."

He leaned a little closer across the booth; I could smell the faded scent of his aftershave from that morning. Although it was faint, my head swam in it. "But I like Rosie," he said. "It's a nice name."

"Only my closest friends call me that."

He was near enough now that I could see how gorgeous his eyes were. I'm certain other people were standing around, but I couldn't see anything but this man who'd managed to so completely capture my interest.

"You mean the friends who get to kiss you?" he said, in a voice so quiet that I wasn't entirely sure I heard him. He leaned closer, his eyes fixed on my lips. At the last second, I had the sense to close my eyes so he didn't open his to find me staring at him like a bewildered lemur.

I felt the lightest brush of lips against mine, and then he paused momentarily. I thought he was being courteous, giving me the chance to bail if I wasn't interested, but I wondered if he wasn't more nervous than he let on. Maybe he wasn't being gentlemanly as much as trying to summon the courage to continue. Either way, he needn't have worried—I was way past interested at that point. The only thing keeping me from grabbing the front of his jacket and pulling him across the booth was the desire to not appear too desperate.

Now, stretched out on the bed in the cabin, pencils forgotten, I waited in anticipation. When I hadn't pushed him away at the booth, he renewed his kiss with increased interest. I replayed this scene over and over again in my head until it was practically choreographed down to each shaky breath. I knew what happened next as if it were yesterday.

There was a knock on the door. I opened my eyes.

That was definitely not what usually happened next.

Six

"Rosie?" Kevin's voice was muffled through the door. I wanted to ignore him and close my eyes again, inserting myself back into that starry, magical fall night. But it was like waking up at the best part of the dream then trying desperately to fall asleep again at precisely the moment where you woke up. It doesn't work.

I wasn't sure how much time had passed, as there was no window in my room, but if Kevin was already back, I must have gotten more involved in sketching than I'd thought. Or maybe reliving the memory in such detail had drifted me into the realm of dreams at some point. The door opened a crack.

"Are you in there?" he asked.

"Where else would I be?"

"Can I come in?"

"I suppose."

Kevin came through the door, and his eyes went immediately to the drawings spread across the bed. To his credit, he didn't laugh at the plethora of apples. "I see you're still sketching."

Since the only reply I could think of was *I see you're still stating the obvious,* I didn't say anything. My mother raised me to bite my tongue when I couldn't say something nice, but my sarcasm still got the better of me on a regular basis. I found it amazing how I felt irritated with him one minute and the next I was noticing the scruff on his face and wanting to run my fingers over it.

This was bad. Instead of being in a place where I could at least rationalize to myself that I was over him, I was right back where I started. It was like having a break in a bone that hadn't healed correctly. The doctor tells you that it has to be re-broken so it can finally be fixed. You know that the doctor is doing what's best for you. You know he means well, but that doesn't change the pain of the process. It still hurts like crazy, whether the end result is therapeutic or not, and all you can think about is how unfair it is that you have to suffer twice.

"You always could work miracles with those pencils. But some day you're going to have to realize that you can't find everything you need in that box."

I stared at him but couldn't think of a reply that didn't involve multiple swear words. Just because we had spent a portion of our lives together, what made him think he knew me? What made him think he was qualified to dispense advice and expect me to follow it?

"Why don't you come out here for a while so we can talk?" he said.

"I don't know if talking is such a great idea."

"Just come out and see my peace offering."

My eyes narrowed. "What peace offering?"

"Dinner."

I found myself considering it. Dinner would be fish. There was nothing better than fresh pan-fried fish, coated in herbs and cornmeal and sizzling with butter. Since I hadn't bothered to pack food, I might have to surrender to some conversation to avoid starvation. "I can never say no to fish," I admitted.

"I know."

I got up and followed him into the tiny kitchen. There were two plates on the table. Kevin pulled out my chair, and I sat down. He began filling the plates with scrambled eggs, toast and bacon.

"This isn't fish."

"I know."

"You tricked me. You said it was fish just to get me in here."

"I did not."

"Did too!"

"You said you couldn't resist fish, and I said I know. I never said dinner was fish."

"But from what I said, and what you said, it was obvious that I thought it was fish."

"I'm sorry that you assumed wrong."

I was so hungry at this point that I couldn't have cared less what was on the plate. It smelled delicious, and I couldn't believe I was arguing about the fish/not fish status of dinner. But it was the principle of the thing, and I had my pride to consider. Kevin was still doing what he always had— twisting his words to suit his purposes, saying what he knew I wanted to hear.

"Thanks, but I have plans already."

He smiled. "There's nothing of yours in the fridge. Have you given up food since we last met?"

I scowled at him. "I was planning on going into town for dinner." Which wasn't entirely true, but the more I thought about this new plan, the better I liked it. There were lots of fabulous restaurants in Park City. I could get out for the evening, have a delicious dinner, and not have to worry about arguing with Kevin. Tomorrow morning I would get up, make my excuses, and go home, where I could hopefully salvage what was left of the weekend.

Kevin was shoveling in forkfuls of eggs into his mouth. The sudden memory that he hated cold eggs filled me with something almost akin to tenderness.

"I don't think you really want leave," he said between bites.

The tenderness was gone as fast as it came, replaced with something bitter. "Because you always know what I need better than I do, right?"

He wiped his mouth with a napkin and swallowed. "No, because it's snowing."

I ran to the window and peered out, dismayed to see fluffy white flakes the size of walnuts drifting down to cover the ground. This was not good. If it kept up like this, not only would I not be going to dinner, but I'd have to stay here all weekend until the roads were clear. Feeling stupid for accusing Kevin, I went back to the table and sat down. I took a bite of eggs. They tasted like the best thing I'd eaten in days.

"These are good," I admitted grudgingly.

Kevin smiled. "Well, they're not fish, but they're better than nothing."

Now I knew what was happening here. He must have known that I'd be hungry and trapped. He knew how much I loved fish; he was doing this to torture me. He'd hoard the fish until I begged. "I suppose we can eat the fish for breakfast instead," I said, aiming for an airiness that said I didn't care one way or the other.

He took a few gulps of milk. "If you catch some, that would be great."

My mouth dropped open. "You didn't catch any fish?"

Kevin occupied himself with buttering his toast.

"Mr. I'm–not–coming–in–until–I–catch–something–be–

cause-I-am-The-Fish-Whisperer-Barnes came home empty handed?" This was too priceless.

"Hey, we're eating, aren't we? I provided this meal."

"Tell me, what kind of bait did you use to catch this bacon?"

"Look at the weather out there. I can't help it if the fish are still asleep."

"A little snow never stopped you before."

"Go on, then. You go catch something."

"Maybe I will."

He hooted. "If I didn't catch anything, you sure as heck won't."

I gave him what I hoped was a mysterious smile. "We'll see."

"You're enjoying this, aren't you? A more evolved woman wouldn't tease me about something about an obviously a painful subject."

"I hope I never get *that* evolved."

❧

It was almost eleven by the time we finished dinner. I couldn't believe it was so late. Kevin must have been out there trying to get a fish way past dark. Stubborn man.

"You look tired," he said.

"No more tired than you."

"I guess it's time for bed. Did you bring extra blankets? Because I'd be willing to loan you one of mine."

I didn't bring a jacket, and the man was asking if I'd thought to bring extra blankets? "There's a quilt on the bed. I don't need any extra blankets."

"Are you sure? I can start a fire if you want."

A fire sounded lovely, but I was just as capable of starting one as Kevin. I'm sure he was thinking that if he hadn't been there to feed me and keep me warm, I'd be dead by now. But despite my lack of preparation, I knew how to take care of myself.

"I said I'll be fine!"

"Calm down. I was just asking. I guess I'll see you in the morning."

Kevin headed off in the direction of his bedroom, with a stack of blankets large enough to hibernate under through the winter. I went into my own room and surveyed the bed. I hadn't noticed earlier, but the bedding in this room was much less . . . plentiful. Since Gramps slept with the window open even in January, I guessed this was his bed. I was cold already, and the idea of getting under the thin quilt and trying to generate enough heat to stay warm wasn't exactly enticing.

But there was no use postponing the inevitable. I took my jeans off and put on both pairs of sweat pants and pulled on both of shirts I'd brought on over the one I was wearing. I probably looked homeless, but at least I was a little warmer . . . until I got brave and crawled under the quilt.

I bet there were igloos toastier than that bed. My feet were like ice. The cold was an unwelcome visitor I couldn't escape. I hovered, semi-conscious, in a state between sleep and waking, where time seemed to extend indefinitely. All I knew for certain was that I would never be warm again. On the bright side, I knew what to get Gramps for his birthday— a memory foam mattress topper. I could feel every spring poking and jabbing my body. It was like trying to sleep on a porcupine. I tried to stay as still as possible for two reasons: attempting to keep what little body heat I had concentrated in the smallest radius, and avoiding getting stabbed with new springs coiled and ready to strike whenever I shifted.

Eventually I rolled over to check the time on my cell phone, wondering if it was too early to get up. 12:58. This was ridiculous. There was no reason to lie there suffering if I wasn't going to sleep. I might as well get up and build a fire. At least I'd be warm. I rolled out of the miserable bed and hobbled down the hall on my icy stump feet, using my cell phone for light. I didn't want to turn the lights on and risk waking Kevin, who was surely snoring like a happy bear in his nest of extra blankets. As much as misery loves company, the last thing I wanted right now was an I-told-you-so lecture.

I took a quick peek out of the window. It was still snowing, flakes drifting silently to the ground. Ugh. At least there was plenty of wood and newspaper, so I busied myself stacking them as quietly as possible in the fireplace with my cold, fumbling fingers. I felt frozen all the way through to my bones. Once I was satisfied with my pre-fire arrangements, I reached into the little pocket on the side of the wood bin for the matches.

They weren't there.

This was the last straw. I imagined the headlines on the news tomorrow—"Girl Found Frozen to Death in Cabin; Ex-boyfriend Slept Blissfully Unaware Through Her Final Hours Two Doors Down, Under a Mountain of Blankets." I giggled at the idea, glad Kevin was asleep, because I probably sounded unhinged.

Moving into the kitchen, I accidentally hooked one foot around a chair and almost fell. I tried to curse quietly, but my big toe was throbbing so much, I wondered if it was still attached. The idea of Kevin finding my bloody big toe resting on the linoleum in the morning made me start laughing again. When I could walk, I started going through the kitchen drawers with my cell-phone flashlight, searching for matches. If Jane Austen had written this story, it would be called *Pride and (un)Preparedness*. The thought made me laugh even harder; I covered my mouth trying to muffle the laughter I couldn't seem to stop.

"What are you doing out here, stumbling around in the dark, laughing?" Kevin's sleepy voice killed the merriment in a hurry.

"Looking for matches."

"You're making enough noise to wake the dead. Is the power out?" He answered his own question by flipping the switch closest to him, flooding the room with light.

I squinted. "I think I liked it better before."

He switched the light off again. It was dark, but there was enough light from the snowy white sky coming through the window to see his bewildered face. "Why are you looking for matches at one in the morning?"

"I wanted a cigarette," I deadpanned. "Why do you think I'm looking for matches? I was going to start a fire. It's freezing in here!"

"I offered to start one earlier."

Trust him to bring that up. "I wasn't cold earlier; I'm cold now. But I can't find the matches anywhere. I know they were here before, but now they're gone. It's like they got up and walked away."

"They're in my backpack. I took them with me when I went fishing." He disappeared into his room and returned with the prodigal matches.

I was furious. "I can't believe you had them the whole time. Why would you take matches fishing?"

"You know—in case I needed a cigarette," he said, grinning.

I tried to grab them out of his hand, but he held them over his head where I couldn't reach.

"I can do it," Kevin said.

"I think you've done enough already."

"Come on. I drove you to the edge of insanity looking for these. The least I can do is get the fire going."

"I can do it myself." It was ridiculous that I was standing here freezing, while we argued about who would start the fire. But I wasn't about to let Kevin sweep in and save the day when it was his fault I was cold in the first place.

"I bet I could start a fire with two sticks faster than you could with these matches," he said.

"Oh, please. I did the hard part already. The fire would have been roaring by now if *someone* hadn't hidden the matches."

"Care to make it interesting?" he said.

Good old Mr. Competitive. "What did you have in mind?"

"If I get the fire started first, you have to make hot chocolate and stay up with me the rest of the night."

"And if *I* get the fire started first, you have to pack up your stuff and leave in the morning."

His smile wavered. "You really want me to go?"

Part of me wanted to yell at him, but I was wavering a bit myself. I didn't really want him to go, but the Self-Preservation Fairy told me that it wasn't a stellar idea for him to stay, either. There were things that I quite liked about Kevin, but there was an equal amount of the infuriating.

At the beginning of our relationship, I used to think that he was 51% charming, 49% aggravating. We fought a lot, but mostly over stupid things, and the making-up part always outweighed the rest. But as time went on, the numbers started to shift in the other direction. One day I realized they had traded places—51% aggravating, 49% charming, may not seem like much, but it was enough to make me question whether there was any future for us. The difference between me and Kevin was that I only considered leaving him, but he actually left.

When I thought about the pain of the last year, my answer to the question about our future was a whole lot easier.

"Those are my terms." My voice came out much stronger than it felt. Maybe this weekend would turn out to be a good thing, seeing him again like this. Maybe it would be what I needed to banish the demon known as Kevin from my life for good.

He shrugged. "Fair enough." He tossed me the matches, and I caught them.

I should have known he would never make a bet he couldn't win.

"Hey, these matches are wet! I can't start a fire with these."

His smile lit up the darkened room. "Yeah, I know."

I threw the box at his head, but he ducked. "You cheated!"

"I wasn't about to come back without fish, but it was really cold, so I was going to start a fire and stay out later, but I accidentally dropped the matches in the stream. I was hoping they'd dry out before you noticed . . . but this turned out okay too."

"Great work. Now we're going to die of hypothermia."

"I already told you—I can make a fire with sticks."

"If you can make a fire with sticks, why did you take the matches with you?"

He was still grinning like an idiot. "Matches are easier."

I briefly considered throwing something larger at him, but I suddenly felt tired, and it didn't seem worth the effort to break something I'd have to clean up later.

Kevin knelt in front of the fireplace. When he noticed that I hadn't moved, he made a dismissive motion with one hand. "Go make the hot chocolate, wench. You're mine for the rest of the night."

I hated myself for being the tiniest bit pleased. I dismissed the little voice in my head that wondered what it said about us that his reward for winning involved spending time with me, while mine would have dictated that he vacate the premises as soon as possible.

Seven

I sipped at my hot chocolate, warming my hands on the mug and my toes by the fire. Every now and then, I glanced warily from my spot on the couch to where Kevin was sitting on the chair, only to find him staring at me, so I'd quickly fix my eyes on something else. He wasn't saying much, and this was about as far from a comfortable silence as you could get. Finally I couldn't take it anymore.

"Are you really going to make me sit out here with you all night?"

"Yes."

"You're so quiet; I swear I can hear the snowflakes falling. It's making me twitchy."

He laughed. "You're funny, Rosie. You always did make me laugh."

"This isn't funny—it's bizarre. And I can't sit here with you, staring into the fire until the sun comes up."

"We could talk instead."

This wasn't the first time he'd suggested that, but the idea of a serious conversation with Kevin was almost worse than the silence. What on earth did he think we'd talk about? Still, it was slightly better than the alternative. "Okay, sure. You start."

He considered for a moment. "On second thought, I think we should play a game instead."

"I didn't even bring food, Kevin. Do you think I have Monopoly in my trunk?"

"Not that kind of game. I want to play Truth or Dare."

Either the hot chocolate was too sweet, or I was coming down with the flu, because my stomach was suddenly churning. I was a champion liar, so surely the idea of a little game of Truth or Dare couldn't be upsetting me.

On the other hand, he did bust me quite easily earlier . . .

"Maybe I should go back to bed instead. My stomach doesn't feel that great."

"Let me guess—you have a note from your doctor saying that you have anxiety-induced ulcers and shouldn't be upset under any circumstances."

"Ha ha. Believe me, I'm way past the point where anything you say or do could upset me."

"Then you have nothing to worry about."

"Fine, you're on." I noticed that I was twirling a finger through my strawberry-blonde hair, the way I did when I was nervous. I forced myself to stop. It wouldn't do to have Mr. Barnes knowing he was unnerving me.

"I'll go first," he said. "Truth or dare?"

No way I was going to give him the opportunity to ask me anything I might have to lie about. If I stuck with the dares, everything would be okay. "Dare."

"I dare you to go outside and stand in the snow for two minutes . . ."

"Piece of cake."

"... in your underwear."

"Kevin!"

"What?"

"That's not fair."

"It isn't supposed to be. Haven't you ever played this game before?"

"Not with a sadist."

"You can get even with me when it's your turn. I'll have to do whatever you want."

The idea of coming up with something humiliating for Kevin to do was tempting, but not enough to strip down to my skivvies and parade around outside. "Pass."

He barked out a laugh. "You can't pass!"

"Sure I can. Show me in the rules where it says I can't pass."

"Strangely enough, I don't happen to have a sheet of rules in my pocket."

I folded my arms across my chest. "I rest my case."

"Rosie, there's a reason the game isn't called Truth, Dare or Pass. Pick one."

I was going to have to hope for the best. "Truth."

"How many guys have you dated since we broke up?"

"You mean since you dumped me?"

"Just answer the question."

"No."

"Come on, this is an easy one."

"No!" I insisted.

"Why?"

"Because it's a pointless question."

He shrugged. "Okay, if you don't want to answer my question, I guess you'll be going outside. . ."

I ticked them off in my head. *Andrew, Connor, Steve, John, Ethan, and Rob.* "Six," I said.

"See? That wasn't so hard. And you aren't in a relationship now, correct?"

"That's two questions. Your turn." I grinned wickedly. "Truth or dare?"

"Truth."

"What? Really?"

"Of course. You didn't think I was really going to give you the chance to make me do something ridiculous, did you?"

I was momentarily disappointed, but it didn't take me long to realize what a golden opportunity this was. Closure was so close, I could almost taste it. "Why did you break up with me?"

Maybe it was a trick of the flames dancing across his face, but I swear Kevin went pale.

"I think I want a dare instead."

"I already asked the question."

"Hey, I gave you a choice."

I cocked my head. "That's where you're wrong. I never had a choice."

The breath whooshed out of him. "Maybe this was a bad idea."

"Yeah, you think?" I never should have stayed here. From the moment I saw Kevin standing in the doorway, I should have listened to my instincts. I should have run to my car and never looked back. I didn't know who I was more disgusted with—me or him. I stood up. "I'm going back to bed."

"No, wait. I'll answer your question."

"You know what? It doesn't matter now."

"It matters to me."

I was starting to get angry and my legs were a little shaky, so I sat down again. "Why are you doing this?"

"Doing what?"

"Playing this game and pretending to be civil, like we're old friends who ran into each other at the supermarket. Like it isn't your fault we aren't together anymore."

His voice was quiet and low. "It isn't a game to me."

He looked penitent enough, but I'd finally reached my breaking point. "This whole weekend has been a game, and I've had it! Why are you *really* here? And don't say it's because you hoped you might see a moose."

"I'm here because you're here," he said simply.

"That doesn't make any sense. I'm not buying Gramps' whole fate theory. As far as I'm concerned, fate and luck fall into the same category as the Easter Bunny; they don't exist. How did you know I was going to be here?"

"I didn't."

I shook my head. "I don't believe you."

"Kiss me."

That was the last thing I expected him to say. It was beyond late, and I was tired. My brain couldn't even process his words. "What?"

"I dare you to kiss me."

For almost a year I'd longed to hear those very words. I'd dreamed about kissing Kevin again, but not as a stupid dare. "No."

"Why? Are you afraid?"

I forced a laugh. "Afraid of you? Not a chance."

"I think you're afraid you'll like it."

I held my head up as proud as I could. "There might have been a time when I was afraid you'd hurt me again. But I'm over all of that now."

"We were happy, do you remember?"

"Why are you doing this?" It was so late, and my reasoning was getting fuzzy. All I wanted was to melt into his arms, and it was getting harder and harder to remember why that wasn't a great idea.

"I've never been that happy with anyone before or since. I never will be."

I put my head in my hands. "Stop. Please."

"You know how to make me stop."

"I'm not going to kiss you."

Kevin stood from his chair, walked slowly to where I was on the couch, and sat next to me. "But if you don't have feelings for me anymore, I can kiss you, and it wouldn't mean a thing, right?"

If you kiss him now, it's all over, my brain warned. "Exactly," I said. Apparently my lips had greater faith in my abilities.

"So humor me—one last kiss for old time's sake."

His eyes were so earnest, and I knew he'd never be satisfied until I proved him wrong. I could kiss him and remain detached, and then he'd see that I didn't need him and more importantly *I'd* see that I didn't need him, and I could finally move on with my life without the ghost of this failed relationship haunting my future.

He leaned in. I braced myself, but instead of going straight for my mouth I felt his lips rest briefly against my cheek before moving to my ear. "Nothing?" he whispered.

His breath on my neck made me want to shiver, but I couldn't let him know that. "Nothing at all." My voice was a little shaky, but otherwise I was handling this admirably.

His lips brushed across my neck. "How about now?"

My response time had slowed significantly. Before I had the opportunity to come up with an answer to show how seemingly unimpressed I was, he was kissing me. Not gently, I might add. His hands were on my face, in my hair, and his lips worked the same magic they always had. But this time, something was different. This was the kiss of a man who knew he had exactly one chance to get it right. There were always plenty of sparks between us, but deep down I had the sneaking suspicion that Kevin knew how skilled he was, and thus never made much of an effort. This kiss was desperate and focused and *frantic*. Where he had merely distracted me before, this was nothing short of a revelation. This kiss made that first one I had replayed again and again in my mind look hollow somehow.

When he finally pulled away, my lungs were screaming for oxygen, but the rest of me would have happily continued kissing him until I slipped into unconsciousness. I noted smugly that Kevin was as affected as I was.

"Anything?" he said, his breathing shallow.

"There might have been . . . something," I conceded. "But it's not that simple."

"Why not?"

"For one thing, everything has gone wrong since I got here. All I wanted was a nice relaxing weekend in the sunshine. Instead I get you and snow and no fish and . . . you."

"I'm sorry you were disappointed to find me here. I felt quite the opposite."

"I wasn't disappointed, exactly. It's just . . . it took me a really long time to get over you, and suddenly here you were, and everything came flooding back, and now I'll . . ." I trailed off. Did I really want to get this personal?

Who are you kidding, Rose? You're in this up to your neck already. What do you have to lose?

I plunged ahead. "I'll have to lose you all over again."

"Maybe not." His face looked almost cheerful, but even after the kiss we'd shared, I didn't dare hope.

"Don't say it if you don't mean it."

He stared at me until I was almost positive he'd changed his mind. "And what if I mean it?"

I closed my eyes and tried to stop the world from spinning around me. "What makes you think this time will be any different?"

"Hey, I'm not saying it will be easy. But I'm willing to give it a shot if you are."

Was I? This was all happening so fast.

"You want to know why I was lucky enough to find you here, Rosie? I've been here every weekend for the last month, and I would have been here every weekend until you showed up. Luck had nothing to do with it."

I could feel tears forming, and I didn't even try to stop them. "I guess that explains how you knew to bring extra blankets."

He chuckled. "You have no idea how miserable I was that first weekend."

"I think I have a pretty good idea. But why *now*? It's been a year."

"Because I'm a fool. I'm blind. I'm an idiot. Feel free to stop me any time."

I laughed, which must have looked strange with the tears rolling down my cheeks at the same time. "Go on. I'll let you know when you can stop."

"I knew you were the one, and I was stupid enough to let you go. Mostly that was my fault, but there was something else. As good as we were together, I always felt like there was this part of you I couldn't reach. Sometimes we were so close, and other times it was like I barely knew you at all. I couldn't live like that."

"I think I did a pretty good job opening up to you, especially when I knew that everything I gave you was only more ammunition to be used against me."

Kevin looked confused. "Ammunition?"

"You already think I'm weak, and you don't know half of my issues."

"I don't think you're weak."

"But you're always babying me. It's like you think I can't do anything for myself."

"I'm not babying you—I'm trying to take care of you. That's what people do when they care for someone."

"But it doesn't feel like that," I argued. "It's like you're doing it because you think I'm incapable."

He laughed. "You're the most capable person I know. I just wish you'd let me step in and do something for you every now and then. It doesn't make you weak when you accept help, Rosie; it makes you human."

"And I wish you'd realize that there are some things I have to do by myself."

"I think maybe I could seem be a little less condescending if you could be a little more open . . ." He tried to hide a yawn, but I could see how sleepy he was.

I stood and walked to the window. The snow had stopped, and the trees were perfectly frosted in white. The brightness of the sky made it seem much later in the morning than it really was. The view was so beautiful that I was afraid I might ruin the moment by speaking. The way Kevin left the sentence open-ended like that—did he really want to try again? Did I want to? Trying again would be a huge risk for me. I didn't know if I could survive another botched attempt at love with Kevin, but what he said earlier was true of me, too; I was happier with him than I ever was without him, even with all his aggravating bits.

I should have been tired, but I knew I'd never sleep now, not with this spiky feeling of anticipation racing through my veins. I had to take a chance and say something. I took a deep breath.

"You know, I think that could be arranged." I turned to face him, smiling hesitantly. I wanted nothing more than to kiss those lips again, but unfortunately, I would have to wait. Kevin was asleep.

I covered him with a blanket and gathered a few things. I put on Gramps' boots and grabbed his flashlight and Kevin's jacket, delighted that maybe I had some claim on that scent now, no matter how tenuous. I took one last look at him before slipping out the door into the last of the frosty night. There was something I needed to do.

"Rosie? Is that you?"

"Guilty."

I was puttering around in the kitchen, heating water for hot chocolate. I had a happy, tingly sort of feeling in my limbs which was probably part euphoria, part exposure to the elements, and part exhaustion. Kevin padded into the kitchen, yawning. I tensed a little, afraid it was going to be awkward between us after being so honest with each other last night.

"Sorry, I must have fallen asleep." He put his arms around my waist from behind and kissed the top of my head. To my immense relief, it didn't feel strange at all. "You're freezing! Have you been outside?"

"Yup."

"I could have gotten more firewood, you know. You should have woken me."

I turned around in his arms and gave him a pointed look.

"But I'm sure you can fetch wood too," he said quickly. "I mean, you have arms, right?"

I gave him a quick kiss on the lips. "Better. And yes, my arms are fully functional. But I wasn't fetching wood."

"Then what were you doing outside?"

"That is a secret. Now, where were we?" I leaned in to kiss him again, but he backed away. I pushed my lower lip into a pout.

"There's plenty of time for that later. Right now I thought maybe we could continue our earlier conversation. I seem to remember that you never answered my question."

"Oh, I did. *You* didn't manage to stay awake long enough to hear it."

He groaned. "I'm sorry. I couldn't keep my eyes open."

"It's okay. I mean, it's understandable that you might be a bit sleepy at three in the morning."

"Yeah, but I don't want you to get the wrong idea. I was very, *very* interested in what you had to say. I still am." When he tried to steal a kiss, I tried to mimic his earlier evasive move to teach him a lesson, but he was too quick. He held me tight and pressed his lips against mine repeatedly. "Your. Lips. Are. Cold," he said between kisses.

"I was about to warm them with some hot chocolate, but I like your method much better."

"We'll revisit that topic . . . after breakfast. I believe it's your turn to cook, and I'm looking forward to that. Even if I do make better eggs."

I gave him an innocent look. "I'm not making eggs."

I could see the wheels turning as his brain connected the dots, and the look on his face was a mix of disbelief and admiration. "You didn't."

I opened the front door and retrieved my prize.

Two shiny trout.

About Aubrey Mace

Aubrey Mace lives in Sandy, Utah. She attended LDS Business College and Utah State University. Aubrey has three published novels: *Spare Change,* which won a Whitney Award for Best Romance, *My Fairy Grandmother,* and *Santa Maybe,* which was nominated for a Whitney Award for Best Romance. She has a romantic comedy scheduled to be released with Covenant Communication in early 2014.

When she isn't at her day job or writing, Aubrey enjoys cooking, gardening, traveling, and spending time with her family. She likes dark chocolate, birds, and British comedy; the order of preference changes, depending on the day.

Author website: www.aubreymace.com

Twitter: @AubreyMace

Facebook: Aubrey Mace

More Timeless Romance Anthologies: